Charles Santley

Student and singer; the reminiscences of Charles Santley

Third Edition

Charles Santley

Student and singer; the reminiscences of Charles Santley
Third Edition

ISBN/EAN: 9783337214999

Printed in Europe, USA, Canada, Australia, Japan

Cover: Foto ©Raphael Reischuk / pixelio.de

More available books at **www.hansebooks.com**

STUDENT AND SINGER

THE REMINISCENCES

OF

CHARLES SANTLEY

'Les premières impressions de l'adolescence ne s'effacent pas ; elles aiden
comprendre les volontés, les paroles, les actes de l'âge mûr.'—PÈRE DIDON.

THIRD EDITION

LONDON
EDWARD ARNOLD
37 BEDFORD STREET, STRAND, W.C.
Publisher to the India Office
1892

TO

THOSE WHO HAVE TAKEN AN INTEREST IN MY PROFESSIONAL CAREER,

I Dedicate these Pages

THIS BEING

THE ONLY RETURN I CAN MAKE TO THEM, AS A BODY,

For the invariable Kindness and Courtesy

They have shown me.

PREFACE.

I NEVER had any intention of submitting my reminiscences to the public; it is only at the solicitation of numerous acquaintances I do so now. So far was I from harbouring such a notion that I have preserved hardly any notes, programmes, or data to aid me; with few exceptions, I have written them from memory.

I have no pretension to sufficient literary qualification for book-writing; I have an antipathy to autobiographies, with one exception, that of Benvenuto Cellini.* His style is not polished, at times uncouth; he records his merits and his failings. I have heard him called egotistic; but surely, a man possessing talents of such a rare order as he did, is not entitled to the appellation, if he states unmistakable facts concerning his artistic skill, adventures, and exploits. Some of his failings he might have suppressed with advantage to his memory, but no doubt, in recording

* I speak of Cellini's own work, not any translation.

them, he has shown his intention to give an honest account of himself.

I have endeavoured to follow Cellini's plan of jotting down any reminiscences and reflections plainly, to the best of my ability, and I shall be quite satisfied if those to whom I have dedicated them find them sufficiently interesting to wade through.

C. S.

October, 1892.

CONTENTS.

CHAPTER I.

CHAPTER II.

CHAPTER III.

Carl Formes' Influence upon me—My Ignorance of Registers—The Mistakes of Singing Masters: Jean de Reszke, Mario, and Sims Reeves—A Plague of Doctors—Officious Friends predict my approaching Decease—The Monotony of Business—A Momentous Decision—My Farewell Concert—Sims Reeves' Encouragement—Start for Italy, October, 1855—The Tyranny of Fashion—The Art of Smoking—Mario's Fondness for Tobacco - - - - - - -

CHAPTER IV.

Farewell to Liverpool—Lack of Appreciation in my Native Town—Experiences on my Journey—A Breakfast at Havre—I witness a Performance at the Paris Opéra Comique—Cruvelli at the Italian Opera—Journey to Basle—Passage of the St. Gothard—Arrival at Milan—Scene at the Railway-station—The Milanese Dialect—An Attack of Home-sickness—Travellers, Old and New Style - - - - - - -

CHAPTER V.

My Lodgings—Milan under Austrian Rule: Vexatious Restrictions—A Humorous Episode: Pollini, Capponi and Galli—A Trying Interview with the Police—A Lucky Letter—My Interview with Lamperti—Introduction to Nava—Nava's Antecedents—His Wide Culture, Kindly Nature, and Honest Advice—Singing v. Gabbling—Duets with Ronconi and Belletti—Nava's Views on Progress—His Kindly Interference—Halcyon Days—My Lessons with Nava: Conversation as well as Singing—His Family—The Dialects of Lombardy—Locomotion as an Aid to Study—My Daily Walk—Milanese Soldiery—Performances at the Cannobiana—Giuglini as a Singer and Actor—Marini and Delle Sedie—The Scala Orchestra—Ristori - -

CHAPTER VI.

Vocalizzi and *Solfeggi*—Italian Vowel Sounds—Is Italian easy to sing?—My First Piece—The Value of Concerted Vocal Music—'Donna Pacifica'—My Fellow-pupils: Luigia Perelli and Luigia Pessina—My Friends the Maranis—'Il Signor Inglese'—The Scala Programme, 1855-56—I become a Subscriber to the Pit—Subsidies and Government Supervision—Gardoni's Experiences—A Short Way with Nervous Baritones—The

CHAPTER XIII.

CHAPTER XIV.

CHAPTER XV.

CHAPTER XVI.

CHAPTER XVII.

CHAPTER XVIII.

CHAPTER XIX.

CHAPTER XX.

CHAPTER XXI.

CHAPTER XXII.

CHAPTER XXIII.

ILLUSTRATIONS.

STUDENT AND SINGER:

THE REMINISCENCES OF

CHARLES SANTLEY.

—◦—

CHAPTER I.

The Sea : its Charms and Drawbacks—An Old Salt's Opinion—Birth
and Early Resolve to be a Sailor—Voyage to the Isle of Man—Later
Voyages and their Discomforts — Early Surroundings and Antecedents—My Father's Contemporaries—Hatton and Sivori—Hatton
at the 'Little Liver'—A Double Inheritance : Music and Nervousness — My first Song — The Tortures of School Recitation — A
Quakeress's Practical Joke and its Results—Stage-struck at Five Years
Old—Dramatic Aspirations—Dislike for Music only Superficial—
First Public Appearance in the Choir of the Baptist Chapel—Pro-
found Effect of an Orchestra in Church—My Awakening to the
Power of Music—My Debt to Haydn—A Clumsy Conductor.

'I'm on the sea ! I'm on the sea !' Though there I
would not ever be, spite of its wonderful attractions,
so graphically depicted by Barry Cornwall. What a
powerful imagination he must have possessed, for he
was one of the sickest of sailors, and detested the sea!
I had it from Mrs. Proctor, who told me she used to
tease him, humming a strain of his jovial sea-song as
he lay, a very log, huddled in shawls and a tarpaulin,
crossing the Channel, with barely sufficient animation
left to utter, ' For God's sake, my dear, don't !'

I am on the sea, on the way from Auckland to

Wellington, New Zealand. Since my arrival in the Colonies I have travelled a great deal on the sea. I always had an affection for it, and love it—to be on it (not at a seaside resort, but with the blue above, and the blue below, and sunshine wheresoe'er I go!). Though I am never troubled with sea-sickness, I am not one of those enthusiastic mariners who are always longing for a storm. I feel bored in rough weather; I cannot take any exercise; I cannot repose, even in my berth, propped in with pillows and other devices; I cannot settle myself to read much, and writing is out of the question—consequently time hangs somewhat heavily. I have many times resolved never to put my foot on shipboard again unless compelled, and as often, after a long spell of railway travelling north, south, east, and west, I am attacked by a longing to be again on the sea, which I am bound to satisfy.

During the time I was engaged at Her Majesty's Theatre, an old salt named Thomas Downes used to be a frequent visitor behind the scenes. He had been a boatswain in the navy, and afterwards became a petty officer in one of the Irish mail-boats, where I first made his acquaintance, and where he was very attentive to Mapleson and our company when we happened to cross to or from Dublin in his packet, and so he obtained the run of the house in the Haymarket. He was one of my ardent admirers, always loud in my praises whenever we met, but he invariably ended his eulogy with, ' But, Charlie, you're a good sailor spoiled! You ought to be ordering your men on board ship, instead of bawling and squalling your voice away in that stuffy theatre!'

I was born in Liverpool on February 28, 1834. At an
early age my greatest pleasure consisted in reading the
adventures of great travellers (I do not suppose I was
at all singular, for most boys delight in adventures),
such as Bruce's 'Travels in Abyssinia,' Captain Cook's
'Voyages,' Franklin's 'Expedition to the North Pole,'
and Ross's in search of him. At school—the Mechanics'
Institution, Mount Street—there was a large sprinkling
of sons of seafaring men and of men whose business
was connected with shipping ; ship-store dealers, ship-
chandlers, ropers, ship-carpenters, ship-bread bakers,
etc., who could all relate 'tales of the sea.' For some
time I was determined to be a sailor, but I never
divulged my determination. Strolling about amongst
the shipping, I discovered many unpleasant vicissitudes
attendant on a seaman's life, which entirely obliterated
the poetical conception I had formed of it. Yet,
although my illusion with regard to the life of a
sailor vanished, I still preserve a great attachment to
the sailor. I like those loose, baggy trousers, the wide
open collar and loose neckerchief ; besides, I think sea
life (on a sailing-ship, not on a steamer) has a tendency to
make men more open-hearted. As a rule, sailors are
frank and good-natured, and in my experience I have
seldom found one sullen or unwilling to do a good
turn. Even the passengers on board ship become
imbued with the spirit of freedom, and many who on
land would scarcely deign to notice a stranger, on the
sea dispense with ceremony, and make themselves
most agreeable and attentive companions.

I made my first voyage when I was seven years of
age. I had gained a prize at school, and as a reward

I was allowed to accompany my grandmother to the Isle of Man. The steamer was an old tub called the *Mona's Isle*. We must have had a rough time of it, as, to the best of my recollection, we were nine or ten hours crossing from Liverpool. We were steerage passengers, and I was very sick ; and as I lay half-dazed in a bunk below, a sailor came down and brought out a cold sole and some potatoes, which he devoured. I thought he must be a hard-hearted wretch to commit such a barbarous action with a lot of sick people lying about ; but I changed my opinion when, at my grand-mother's request, he carried me in his arms on deck to pay a necessary visit, and behaved as tenderly to me as though he had been my nurse. We had to land in a small boat. No sooner was I seated therein than the sickness left me, and I was seized with such an appetite that I could have demolished the sailor, with the sole and potatoes for seasoning.

I do not profess to be a great traveller. In these days, when you may meet shopkeepers from provincial towns ' doing ' the Pyramids of Egypt, the mosques and bazaars of Cairo, the catacombs of Rome, the wonders of Jerusalem, and the ruins of Baalbec, I can scarcely lay claim to be more than a Margate excursionist. I may say that all my travelling by sea has been for pleasure ; the voyage was my chief inducement to accept engagements in America and the Colonies. As I have before said, I have at times a longing to be on the sea ; but I should like, if time permitted, to try the real thing in a sailing-ship ; for on board a steamer I do not find the perfect repose I expected. True, there is no post, no telegraph, but there is hurry, scurry, and bustle of one sort or another night and day ; the least annoying of the noises which disturb the rest being that of the machinery, which, after a day or two, is only noticeable when it stops. In the night belated roisterers bawl to each other along the corridors, throw their boots out, slam the doors, or leave them un-fastened, so that every roll of the ship causes them to clatter. In the early morning stewards indulge in un-timely hilarity over boot-cleaning, or rush about in answer to emphatic appeals for tea and coffee. During the day meals are rushed through as though every-body had to catch an express train! Importunate agitators, who have no taste for quiet themselves, insist upon everybody joining in ridiculous uninterest-ing games. It is difficult to take exercise, for no sooner do one or two persons start for a walk than everyone else seems to be seized with the same impulse, so that between the crowd of people, the crowd of chairs—which take up half the deck—and children pushing about go-carts, there is nothing for it but to submit to be hustled and jostled about, or relinquish all idea of exercise. There is an attempt at a band, which I, for one, would willingly pay extra fare to be rid of. To pass the evenings, dramatic entertainments, recitals, and concerts are instituted, and, of course, I was pestered to take part in them. I excused myself on the ground that I required rest after a very fatiguing season ; however, I sang twice during my voyage to Australia, as a small return for the kindness and attention I received from our captain, a perfect gentleman, pro-fessionally and privately. On my passage returning from Townsville to Rockhampton, Queensland, I was pressed to sing, and declined. I had then the satisfaction of hearing several of the songs I had been singing during my tour murdered by audacious amateurs.

At the time I was born my father was a journeyman bookbinder employed in his father's workshop; shortly after he obtained a clerkship in the municipal offices, and subsequently became a collector of rates. He was always a very persevering man; he had a great love for music, and any spare time he could command he devoted to studying the piano, without the aid of a master, until by exercising strict economy he saved enough to enable him to pay for lessons. He then became a pupil of Michael Maybrick, an uncle of the singer and composer of that name, known in the latter capacity as Stephen Adams. One of his fellow-pupils was John Liptrot Hatton, the composer of 'To Anthea.' Hatton was a merry wag; he and Sivori, the violinist, were one Sunday at St. Peter's Catholic Church, Seal Street; Sivori, who was one of the shortest of men, was standing on tip-toe looking through the curtain which hid the singers from view in the organ-gallery, when Hatton, spying a good opportunity for a practical joke, seized him by the heels and jerked him three parts over the reading-desk and back again breathless, before he knew where he was. When 'Jack Sheppard' was first produced in London with the inimitable Mrs. Keeley, Paul Bedford, etc., it made such a sensation that the manager of the 'Little Liver' in Church Street* determined upon producing it with his own company rather than

* A pet name for the Liver Theatre; it was very small, and a great favourite with the Liverpudlians.

wait until the London company visited the provinces. There was only one difficulty about casting the parts. The company included some very good actors ; but they had nobody who could play Blueskin and sing the song, and Blueskin without ' Jolly Nose ' would never do. Hatton was always about the theatre. I think he played in the orchestra, and went on the stage occasionally among the crowd. He had a fairly sonorous voice, plenty of humour, and his capabilities were well-known to all connected with the theatres, so in their dilemma he was applied to to play Joe Blueskin ; his diffidence, which was not armour-plated, was soon disposed of, and he consented. The drama had a run of several weeks, and was received with uproarious applause, Hatton having to sing the song three times every night. When the London company came down to Liverpool and played it at the Theatre Royal it fell flat, spite of the ' only Jack.' It had been performed ever so many times better at the ' Liver.' As to Paul Bedford, he was nowhere, after Jack Hatton !

My mother possessed, as did several members of her family, a peculiarly sympathetic voice, so I presume I inherited from my parents a musical nature. Both were of very nervous temperament, which I inherited also. The first song I ever learned was ' When I was a little boy scarce thirty years ago,' which I was often called on to sing for the amusement of visitors. I was so nervous that I would have run miles away to escape the dreadful ordeal ; but my nervousness was set down to obstinacy and ill-will, and many a bitter moment I endured in consequence.

I could not have been more than eight when my

father commenced teaching my elder sister and me our notes. I loved music, but my dread of singing before anyone held me back, and I was constantly reprimanded for obstinacy and indifference when no such feelings influenced me ; so that what otherwise might have been a source of amusement and delight became an intolerably irksome task. I began to loathe the sound of the piano, and tried by every means in my power to escape music in any form.

At school, at times, I was accused of idleness and lack of zeal, when in reality nervousness prevented me from putting myself forward. At examinations I never could do myself justice. An hour each week was devoted to recitations ; my first was Bishop Heber's hymn, ' From Greenland's icy mountains.' Each week, after it had been given me to learn, I sat shuddering, cold as the ' icy mountains,' my heart beating so loudly that I fancied my neighbour could hear it, such was my dread of being called on to recite before the boys. I avoided the master's eye in the hope of escaping his notice, but at length the fatal moment arrived, and I had to go to execution. I tottered on to the platform, my teeth chattering and the nerves of my mouth twitching as though I had been seized with St. Vitus's dance. I knew the piece perfectly, but I had barely uttered the first line when I broke out into a violent fit of sobbing. The professor, though a strict disciplinarian, was very kind-hearted, and evidently comprehending the cause of my distress, allowed me to return to my place. When the class was dismissed he called me to him and spoke so kindly and encouragingly that I determined to do my best to over-

come my weakness. To a great extent I succeeded.
I gained sufficient command over myself to be able to
repeat the words, but rarely with the force and expression I felt.

At the breaking-up for the Midsummer vacation the
recitations were given in the lecture hall of the institution, in the presence of the pupils and their parents
and friends. On one occasion I had to take the part
of Miss Lucretia Mac Tabb in a scene from 'The
Poor Gentleman.' I performed it very badly, for
besides my nervousness I felt I was an object of
ridicule to my schoolfellows in my attempt to portray
the vagaries of an ancient coquette. The summer I
left school I took the part of Hamlet in the scene with
the Gravedigger. I believe I did that fairly well, but
I was in great trepidation lest the skull should roll out
of my hand whilst I was delivering the lines, ' Alas!
poor Yorick,' so violently did I tremble.

My natural nervousness was increased by a fright I
had when about ten years of age. I was out one
evening playing with my companions on some waste
ground near our house, when the maid came out and
informed me that my father wished to see me immediately. I was loath to leave my play, but I knew I
must obey, so ran off in great haste, and knocked at the
door, which was opened by an awful-looking figure. I
uttered a fearful shriek and dropped almost insensible
on the steps. When I recovered I crawled back to
join my playfellows, but all my spirit was gone. I
remained out of doors until very late, and not until I
had been positively assured there was nothing to fear
would I venture home. A young Quakeress, a friend

of my sister's, had coloured her face with Spanish juice and clothed herself in some outlandish garments, intending to create a bit of fun at my expense. For some time I never entered the house without a shudder. A year after, when the effect of the shock had nearly worn off, the joke was repeated, with a similar result, a hideous mask being substituted for the paint.

Although nervousness at times has prevented my doing all I wished and felt I was capable of doing, I could always command myself to such an extent that it was only apparent to those intimately acquainted with me. I suffered from it when I took part with others. The first few times I played in an orchestra I could scarcely keep the bow steady on the strings of my fiddle, and when I began to sing in the chorus I had difficulty in keeping my breath and my voice under control.

The intimate desire of my heart was to be an actor, but of this I never breathed a word to anyone. My family had been brought up with the Puritanical notion that all stage-players, singers, and such-like were no better than they ought to be, and in general much worse. I seldom saw the inside of a theatre before I was seventeen or eighteen ; on rare occasions I was taken, and more rarely still allowed to accompany a friend to see a play. When I was about four or five my aunt took my sister and me to see Ducrow's circus. The first part of the performance was the drama of ' St. George and the Dragon,' and I suppose I was stage-struck. In spite of the nervousness I suffered from when called upon to recite at school, I tried all in my power to obtain permission to have a whole play acted by the boys as part of the entertainment at the breaking-up, but without success. I read Shakespeare's plays, of which ' Macbeth ' was my favourite, constantly ; two or three of them I knew by heart. My father had some volumes of miscellaneous plays, among them ' Cato,' ' Venice Preserved,' ' Tamerlane,' ' The Hypocrite,' ' The Jew,' with the original casts and descriptions of costumes, which I read and re-read. I used to study all the playbills, and picture to myself, when quiet at home in the evening, the scenes which I longed to see represented.

I have said before that music became irksome to me, and that I tried to escape from it in any form. This was the result of making it a task instead of a pleasure, an error which I imagine many parents fall into through misunderstanding the child's nature. I was called stubborn, whereas I was nervous and diffident, and very much averse to being shown off. I had plenty of work to do at school, and tasks to prepare at home, and I deemed it unjust that the little time I had for recreation should be employed in a study which, with my parents' ideas of professional life, could lead to nothing.

My dislike, however, must have been superficial ; the spirit of music lay dormant in my heart, only awaiting the proper touch to waken it into a passion— and thus it happened. My father was organist at the old Catholic church of St. Mary, Edmund Street, for some years before it was demolished to make room for a more convenient structure ; he then removed to the Baptist Chapel, Myrtle Street, which had just been opened. When the new St. Mary's was completed, he was invited to return to his old post ; but having a good organ at his disposal, and finding himself in all other respects at his ease, he preferred remaining at the new one. It was here I first joined in public musical performances. I sang alto, and I was so small that a platform was made for me to stand on, in order that I might be on a level with the other members of the choir. On the occasion of an important Catholic festival they arranged to perform Haydn's First Mass, with full orchestral accompaniment, at St. Mary's. The organist, having to conduct, invited my father to preside at the organ ; he found a substitute to take his own place, and accepted the invitation. I accompanied him, curious to hear an orchestra in church. The effect on me was profound ; the chord was struck, and from that time I lived on and for music.

It may be interesting to note how many of my first experiences at the commencement of my career were furnished by Haydn's works. My first awakening to the charm and power of music was in the performance of Haydn's First Mass, as I have related above. My first attempt as a bass soloist was in Haydn's Second Mass, and my first paid engagement was to sing in Haydn's Third Mass at St. John's Cathedral, Salford. The first time I assisted in the chorus at a public performance was in the ' Creation,' when Jenny Lind sang at the Collegiate Institution, Liverpool, in 1849. The first oratorio I heard in London was the ' Creation,' at Exeter Hall, in 1851. I made my first appearance in London at St. Martin's Hall, November 16, 1857, and my first appearance at Exeter Hall in 1858, in the same oratorio. I had an experience of another kind in the same work at Southampton in 1869. Twice I received a blow on my crown, enough to stun me, from the *bâton* of a clumsy individual who was trying to conduct for the first time.

CHAPTER II.

THE chord was struck!—how, I know not. Though
I remember every sensation the music roused in me, I
cannot describe one. Disillusion and disappointment
have long since warped the pure, innocent feeling of
delight, and the aspirations it gave rise to, which filled
my boy's heart. Indeed, it would not be difficult to
indulge in sarcastic comments on the innocent belief
which I then cherished in the omnipotence of artistic
merit. I had not then learned that talent, unaccom-
panied by the blast of trumpets, has a weary, toilsome
road to trace in order to obtain, if ever it does obtain,
due recognition. I did not then know (as now I do
know) that it was necessary for an artist himself to tell
the world he was great, and wherein his greatness lay,

in order that the world might recognise his great qualities. I did not know that pinchbeck was frequently preferred to gold, impudent sham to modest reality ; and I had not read ' Sartor Resartus,' nor meditated on the *fact* that ' man is not only a gullible animal, but that he prefers to be gulled.' I have learned all this in the course of my career, as much greater men than I have done. I have seen that monstrous incompetency, aided by ' backsheesh ' of one kind or another, is more than a match for titanic genius, and that a pat on the back from a royal hand is of more avail than consummate talent. And I have learned that fuss and talk about Art, Poetry, Painting, Architecture, Music, is mostly cant and hypocrisy.

I never read one of Hazlitt's essays, but I came across this quotation in a little book called ' Noon,' by Sidney Lear :

' I think that, though there is very little downright hypocrisy in the world, there is a great deal of cant. Cant is the voluntary overcharging or prolongation of a real sentiment ; hypocrisy is the setting up of a pretension to a feeling you never had and have no wish for.

' Though very few people have the face to set up for the very thing they in their hearts despise, we almost all want to be thought better than we are, and affect a greater admiration or abhorrence of certain things than we really feel. There are people who are made up of cant—that is, of mawkish affectation—but who have not sincerity enough to be hypocrites—that is, have not hearty dislike or contempt enough for anything to give the lie to their puling professions of admiration and esteem for it.'

Of all cants I believe that most in vogue is the cant about Art. It displays itself in various ways; very commonly in the way of patronage—patronage bestowed on the deference paid to the patron, rather than on the merits of the patronized ; patronage, the destruction of many young people who might have been usefully and profitably employed in trade and commerce, but who, carried away by the flattery of ignorant would-be patrons of Art, have dared to pass in at the door of her temple, only to be shouldered out and left to starve by the roadside.

There is the cant about educating the masses from their childhood, and teaching them to appreciate Art, which, as far as music is concerned, costs the British nation a large sum of money—money which, instead of being thrown in the gutter, as it is, might be employed in the endowment of establishments where those who by hard work have made themselves worthy to be called artists could find sure employment for their talents.

And there is the worst cant of all, about a National Opera, which, as every schoolboy knows (to use a well-known and favourite *cant* phrase), will never exist unless the British nation agrees to subsidize theatres and pension singers as in Germany and France. But even then the patrons of Art must be prepared to support the undertaking by constant attendance, not merely by putting in an appearance to hear a favourite singer.

The greatest disappointment I have met with through life has been the lack of earnestness I have experienced in the major part of my fellow-workers, whether in my commercial or professional career. I can understand men who, having no particular bent, are doomed to pass their lives as clerks, with nothing to look forward to but uninteresting work poorly paid, finding the monotonous drudgery of an office not by any means conducive to exertion beyond that which is necessary to earn their pay ; but I cannot understand a man professing to be an artist being contented to remain at the bottom of the ladder, when he knows that, in defiance of all obstacles, he must rise if he wishes so to do. He may not rise to the top, for all men are not endowed with the necessary means ; to some are given five talents, to some three, and to some only one, and from each of them only a proportionate result is expected. But what a number of instances I could cite where that expectation, far from being fulfilled, has not even been approached! At the same time, I must say I have known instances where limited natural resources have been turned to so good an account by hard work and perseverance, that they have outstripped and eclipsed gifts which ought to have carried their possessors to the top of the ladder. Discontent with their humble means prevents some from striving ; vanity and laziness many whose brilliant natural endowments ought, with conscientious work, to place them in the front rank. Man is naturally vain and lazy, and I think a singer, to become a real artist, has to make a harder struggle against these natural defects than the followers of any other art, and for this reason. The essential natural qualification for a singer is a sonorous voice of sympathetic quality ; the unintellectual public is satisfied with the sound which pleases its ear, and bestows its applause irrespective of artistic merit. Vanity and laziness step in and say, 'The public is content, the money rolls in ; why study more?' Conscience is thrust aside. How many promising young artists have come to an untimely end in consequence! Yet I have known some who, when the voice has begun to lose its charm, roused by the voice of conscience, with determined efforts have succeeded in making Art a more than efficient substitute for the magic of a fresh voice.

The singer has a difficulty to contend with which does not affect any other artist, except, in a less degree, the actor. The singer's work is a picture painted on air. No sooner is it depicted than it is gone ; while the poet's, painter's, sculptor's and architect's works remain, and can be examined and analyzed at leisure. Delicacy of treatment is the quality which is slowest to make an impression on the public eye or ear. The delicacy of a poem, a picture, a statue, or an edifice, though it may not strike at a first reading or view, will gradually impress itself on further acquaintance. The aerial picture of the singer, on the other hand, vanishes, and there remains nothing more than a dim shadow, insufficient to recall any real impression of its merit. Hence, almost unconsciously, in order to produce an immediate impression, the singer lays on strong, glaring colour and deep shadows where his artistic sense would suggest more delicate treatment.

On Christmas Day, 1848, I sang my first solo in public at the Unitarian Chapel, Toxteth Park, where my sister and I had been engaged some months. My voice was steadily growing uncertain, which increased my trepidation, but I got through it without breaking down, and felt very thankful. In a few months my alto voice had gone completely, and was succeeded by what one of my relations described as an 'ugly noise.' Except in the solitude of my own chamber, I did not exercise the noise for some time. I thought (perhaps the wish was father to the thought) my register lay in the baritone or bass clef; my father thought otherwise, and as soon as my voice became somewhat settled, I adopted the tenor clef. I do not think I troubled myself much about the matter at that time, so anxious was I to take part in the chorus in a performance of ' Elijah,' in which Jenny Lind was to sing, and to gain my object I would have tried to sing any part. I was disappointed, however ; I was shelved on account of my youth, and so missed a rare treat and a fine lesson.

The first result of my wakening up to the charms of music was the development of an ardent desire to learn the violin, not with any idea of becoming a soloist, but simply to enable me to play in an orchestra. As a child my sympathy was with the brass instruments, especially the trumpet ; to the wood instruments in general I had a decided antipathy. I remember Charles Horn giving a series of entertainments—they may have been lectures—in the Lecture Hall of the Mechanics' Institution ; the illustrations were performed by a small band of ten or twelve instruments, assisted by the piano. Among them there was a piccolo, who, to judge by the vigour he displayed, earned his money ' by the sweat of his brow '; the shrill noise he produced acted so acutely on my nerves, that I felt perfectly terrified, and entreated to be taken home.

I begged to be allowed to learn the violin, but my father, thinking it was only a whim, insisted on my turning my attention to the piano or organ, the instruments to which he himself was attached, though I had no love for either. The organ I disliked, probably on account of the many weary hours I had passed blowing the bellows whilst my father practised. I tried to learn the piano, but failed to make anything of it. A friend of ours, an amateur of music, and also of cabinet-making, had constructed a violin of a novel shape; he induced my father to allow him to lend it to me, and gave me some preparatory lessons in order to test whether I was in earnest. My progress was sufficiently satisfactory, and in a short time I possessed a violin of my own, and had some lessons from a professor. I never was a violinist, but in about eighteen months I was able to join the 'Società Armonica,' an amateur orchestral society, as a second violin, with which I was quite content.

In a biographical sketch which appeared shortly after I came to London, it was stated that, besides being a vocalist of merit, I was an accomplished violinist, which kindly-intentioned announcement placed me on one occasion in a ludicrous dilemma. I was invited to assist at a musical *soirée* at Ernst Pauer's one evening. The first item in the programme was a string quartette in which Joachim was to play first violin, and as the gentleman who had promised to play second had not arrived some time after the time fixed for commencing, to my dismay I was asked to take

his place, being an 'accomplished violinist.' I respectfully declined, and felt very much ashamed of having
sailed under false colours, although I had nothing
to do with the statement, whose author I do not
know, nor do I know whence he received his information.

My school-days were drawing to a close. At midsummer, 1849, I was to make my entry into the commercial world, or as soon after as I could procure a
situation. I did not look forward with unalloyed
pleasure to office-work, but as I saw it was my inevitable fate, I resigned myself with as good a grace as I
could. On my fifteenth birthday I passed my examination, and was elected a performing member of
the Philharmonic Society. The new hall was to be
opened in the following August, and I must confess I
sincerely hoped my fate would not dispose of me
before that time, and so prevent my taking part in the
inaugural performances. My father and sister were
also elected members, but without any trial, as their
capacity was already known. Soon after my election
I sang in the chorus in the performance of the
'Creation' I have noticed at the end of the previous
chapter, and in the summer I was one of a picked
chorus who sang in the 'Messiah' at the Eisteddfod
held in Rhuddlan Castle. Misses Lucombe (afterwards Mrs. Sims Reeves), Camilla Chipp, and
Charlotte Dolby, and Messrs. Sims Reeves and
Machin were the soloists. The orchestra was not large,
but fortunately very choice, or the worthy man who
tried to conduct would have led us all to destruction.

It is unwise in a man who has not had the chance

of gaining experience to undertake to conduct an orchestra on an important occasion. The attractions of the 'stick,' however, seem to be irresistible. I have suffered from it to no small extent during my career.

As soon as the crush-room of the new hall could be made ready, and sufficient of an organ erected to accompany, we proceeded to rehearse the music to be performed at the festival—at first once, later on twice and three times a week. As the rehearsals became frequent I found singing in too high a register strained my voice, and occasionally when I could escape observation I took a rest—much against my will, as I was very earnest in the work. To force myself to keep silence I distracted my attention, noting what was going on about me, for which my elevated position—near the back row of the orchestra—furnished me with ample opportunity. Of those in my immediate vicinity, I could not avoid remarking some to whom even a simple psalm-tune without accompaniment must have been a hard nut to crack. Down below, in front of me, the conductor (the treasurer and sub-conductor of the society) proved an attractive distraction ; had his ability been proportionate to his gymnastic vigour we might have mastered all our work for the festival in a third of the time we spent over it. He must have cost the society a small fortune in sticks : the pieces flew about at times like a shower of hail. But the most amusing distraction of all I found in watching some half-dozen amateur violinists, performing members, who volunteered their services to assist at the rehearsals. In the *fortes* it seemed as though no cords manufactured from silkworms' or even cats' intestines could resist the terrific sweep of their bows ; but in the *pianos*, where Best (our organist) left them free scope to shine out, I noticed—the result probably of the vigorous bowing aforesaid—strings required mending or bows had to be cleared of loose hairs. The flies and other noxious insects sent to torment the wicked Israelites apparently renounced all idea of a concerted plan of attack and flew about wildly in all directions ; the fire caused the hail to evaporate before it could reach the ground, and Elijah's prayers were responded to by the feeble dribblings of a leaky watering-pot.

Occasionally a bandmaster named Gribbin attended these rehearsals to lead the amateurs to the attack. He was a rough, energetic fiddler, and a practical joker ; when opportunity offered he would make a feint of attacking vigorously, inducing his unwary followers to rush on to their destruction, and exposing them to the ire of the conductor and the derisive cheers of the choristers.

Fortune favoured me : I was free to assist at the festival, and I looked forward with unbounded delight to the great musical feast I was about to enjoy. The chorus, numbering about three hundred, was in a highly efficient state ; by dint of going over the same ground so often even the most obtuse had succeeded in absorbing their music ; the sub-conductor abdicated, and the amateur fiddlers were relegated to the auditorium. The full rehearsals commenced with the ' Elijah.' I was so excited I had the utmost difficulty in keeping my attention fixed on my own work ; do what I would, I could not avoid listening to the orchestra, which, except a few of the strings, consisted of the leading members of the London orchestras, then in their prime—Sainton, Blagrove, Hill, Lucas, Piatti, Howell, Bottesini, Barrett, Nicholson, Lazarus, Maycock, Baumann, Platt, Harper, Cioffi, Prospere, and Chipp.

The 'Elijah,' being comparatively a new work, was rehearsed in its entirety, so I had an opportunity of hearing the solo parts as well as the choruses, with the orchestral accompaniment. I was too young and inexperienced to grasp all its beauties (after all these years I find new ones each time I take part in it), but what I did seize sufficed to impress me with the reality of the genius of its immortal composer. As the fine dramatic scenes succeeded each other my excitement increased, until the rush of the deluge of tropical rain utterly overwhelmed me. I dropped into my seat powerless; it seemed as though the heavens had opened in reality and poured down their waters in a cataract on my devoted head. The whole week was one of intense excitement ; I ate, drank, and dreamed music. At the rehearsal of Rossini's 'Stabat Mater,' in my eagerness, I did not notice the bar's rest before the 'Amen,' and performed a solo, which called forth some witty remark from Benedict about the future career of the singer who made the 'domino,' and some merriment at my expense from the orchestra.

For the sake of uniformity the committee requested the gentlemen of the chorus to appear at the morning performances in black frock-coats and dark waistcoats and trousers, at the evening concerts in black dress-

coats and trousers and white waistcoats. I still wore
an Eton jacket, so had no difficulty about the coat;
but I did not possess a white waistcoat, nor had I
money to invest in one. I accepted the loan of one,
several sizes too large, from an uncle, which had to be
pinned up to fit my then slender frame. I was perfectly satisfied, but I must have cut a comical figure,
as I was made the object of an extensive display of
wit, against which my courage was not proof, so after
the first evening I wore my Sunday vest of blue
cashmere.

I have no notes or programmes of the performances ;
I cannot therefore give any detailed account of them.
Of the singers the one who impressed me most was
Madame Viardot Garcia, signally in the scene of
Queen Jezebel in the ' Elijah'; the song, ' If guiltless
blood,' from ' Susannah'; and the great air, ' Leise,
leise, Fromme weise,' from ' Der Freischütz.' No
woman in my day has ever approached Madame
Viardot as a dramatic singer ; she was perfect, as far as
it is possible to attain perfection, both as singer and
actress. The only man who was worthy to rank with
her was Giorgio Ronconi ; he was not engaged at the
festival, but I cannot help introducing his name here
whilst speaking of Madame Viardot. I had the good
fortune to hear them together as Papageno and Papagena, in the ' Magic Flute,' at Covent Garden, in
1851 ; the duet in the last act was a fine piece of low
comedy. Ronconi was a perfect imp at playing tricks,
but he never played the fool, however farcical the
scene in which he was engaged. Many frequenters of
the Royal Italian Opera must still remember his won-

derful by-play whilst Adelina Patti was singing 'Batti, batti' and 'Vedrai carino' in 'Don Giovanni'; how he added to the effect of her singing without distracting the attention of the audience from herself. I have seen Madame Viardot play Donna Anna in 'Don Giovanni,' Desdemona in Rossini's 'Otello,' and Fides in 'Il Profeta,' three fine specimens of tragedy; Rosina in the 'Barbiere di Siviglia,' a sparkling piece of comedy united to superb singing; and Amina in 'La Sonnambula,' a poetic creation only equalled by Madame Carvalho's Marguerite in 'Faust.'

I have often heard actors remark, 'He is not a bad actor for a singer!' What condescension! The dramatic genius and versatility of these two great artists I have never seen excelled, and seldom equalled, by any actor in my day. I once, only once, had the happiness of taking part in an opera with Ronconi, in 'Don Giovanni,' at the New York Academy in 1872, when I played Don Giovanni and he Leporello. His acting in the last scene, when the statue appears, was of itself sufficient to justify all I have said of his genius. With Madame Viardot I never had a chance of appearing on the stage—I was but a crude beginner when she was retiring. Another great artist, great both in bulk and genius, I heard, and I always regret for the only time, at the festival—Luigi Lablache. I have heard many since try to sing Rossini's 'Tarantella,' but his wonderful execution of it remains undisturbed in my memory. Mario, then at his zenith, sang splendidly; in after years we became intimate friends, and many a good lesson I have had from him.

I had only one fault to find with the festival—with

all the rehearsals and performances, it was too short.
How the experience of a few years alters one's ideas!

My first important journey was to London, in 1851,
to see the great Exhibition. I enjoyed myself very
much, except for the Exhibition itself, which I found
an intolerable bore. My great feasts were at the
Opera, where I saw 'Il Profeta' and 'Il Flauto
Magico,' and at Exeter Hall, where I heard the 'Creation.' After these my great delight consisted in
wandering and staring about the streets. I became
enamoured of London, and, probably influenced by the
history of Richard Whittington, conceived a great
desire to become a citizen. My desire has since been
fulfilled. A few years ago I was elected a member of
the Musicians' Company.

In 1851 I was in the second year of my apprentice-
ship to a firm in the American provision trade, at the
termination of which I was engaged as book-keeper in
a branch of the most extensive leather and hide factors'
in the world. All my spare time I devoted to music.
I was a member of the Philharmonic Society, where I
continued to sing tenor in the chorus until I felt
convinced I was injuring my voice. I played the
violin for some time at the Festival Choral Society,
and was a member of a Glee Union conducted by
Joseph Lidel, an accomplished violoncellist, who took a
great fancy to me; it was chiefly through his friendly
disinterested interference that it was ultimately determined I should make music my profession. I also
became a member of the Società Armonica, of which
I have before spoken, conducted by Charles Baader
Hermann. Although I was not a great executant, I

was a good reader, and was elected to the post of principal second violin in preference to some of my more skilful colleagues.   I never enjoyed myself, engaged in music, so much as I did at our practices.   I was 'terribly in earnest,' and on one occasion fell a victim to my zeal.   We were trying Beethoven's Symphony in B flat, always my favourite.   At the end of the first movement I became so excited in my work that I added an extra bar to the score—my second 'domino'—and was rewarded by a burst of friendly ironical cheers, which for a few moments considerably damped my ardour.

My friend Charles Hermann took great interest in me, and, fearing my voice, which promised well (I was only sixteen), might suffer if I continued singing, recommended me to change from the chorus to the orchestra of the Philharmonic Society.   I applied for permission to the secretary, from whom I received a very ungracious rebuff.   As I could not keep aloof from any music in which I had the opportunity of taking part, after two months' cessation I returned to the chorus. I then determined on conversion, and, with the sanction of the committee, took my place among the basses.

My first essay as a soloist was at St. Anne's Catholic Church, Edgehill, where for some time I had accompanied my sister, who was the leading soprano, and assisted in the chorus among the tenors.   They had no professional bass singer, and, as I learned they were looking out for one, I applied to the conductor for the post.   He smiled dubiously, but allowed me to make a trial.   I sang the short solo, 'Et incarnatus est,' in Haydn's Second Mass, reading off the same copy with

Julius* Stockhausen, who, with his friend E. Silas, was at that time residing in Liverpool. I obtained the situation, and soon afterwards made my appearance in public at a concert given by the Glee Union before mentioned. I sang ' Rage ! thou angry storm,' from Benedict's opera, ' The Gipsy's Warning,' which I had shortly before heard Staudigl sing. Of course, I tried my best to imitate him, and I dare say I succeeded— very imperfectly ! No doubt, there was an unmistakable trace of his influence, and Lidel ever after called me young Staudigl. Costa, the first time I sang for him, remarked a great similarity in the tone of my voice to that of Staudigl. I only heard him about three times, and those towards the end of his career. No singer has ever had such a peculiar effect on me, apart from his singing. Each time he stepped on to the platform I felt a thrill run through my whole body, as though he possessed some magnetic influence over me.

* He was called Jules then, as he had just come from Paris, where he learned singing.

CHAPTER III.

I CANNOT now call to mind all the occasions on which I appeared in public. I believe the second was at a concert of the Società Armonica, when I fiddled through the first part, and sang 'Haste nor lose the fav'ring hour,' from 'Der Freischütz,' in the second. Fiddling is not good preparation for singing ; but I did my best, whatever that may have been, and evidently satisfied my public, as they made me repeat the song.

Owing to a misunderstanding between our choir-master and the head priest of St. Anne's, the whole choir migrated to the Jesuit church of St. Francis Xavier, where I often had an opportunity of singing a solo in the evening before Benediction. As soon as I adopted the bass clef, I let my hair grow long, in imitation of Carl Formes, and tried to grunt below the lines of the bass stave ; but my mane never attained the luxuriance of my model's, and my voice was like a penny whistle in comparison to his. I was so struck by Formes' singing of 'In diesen heil'gen Hallen,' from 'Die Zauberflöte,' that, finding an arrangement of the air to Latin words, I was ambitious enough to try it one evening in church. I got on very fairly until I arrived at the final cadence, in which I intended to descend to the lower E. Unluckily, I forgot the organ was half a note below the usual pitch, and, being nervous to boot, failed, to my utter confusion, to produce a sound, and retired to my place cheered by the sniggering of my fellow basses.

I, like most people in England at that time, had not recognised the difference between baritone and bass— baritone was only considered a *light bass!* I had no one to guide me, and sang indiscriminately one or the other; my ambition, as soon as I forsook the tenor clef, being to arrive at the cellar region. Often have I heard the remark, 'You don't call that a bass! Why, he's *only* a baritone!' In Italy I found the *only* was applied to basses, and that baritones were held in much greater esteem, inasmuch as every bass who could ascend by any means to the high F called himself baritone. In England women are sopranos or contraltos, men tenors or basses; the intermediate mezzo-soprano in women and baritone in men, and the different qualities of soprano and tenor hold no position of their own. Still, mezzo-soprano is as distinct from soprano and contralto, and baritone from tenor or bass, as soprano and contralto, tenor and bass are from each other. Beyond this, there is in Italy a distinction between light and dramatic soprano and light and robust tenor, which in England does not seem to be understood. In England a soprano, whatever style of voice she may possess, is expected to sing anything written for a soprano voice; it may be Amina one day and the soprano music in the 'Elijah' another. A tenor, either light or robust, must be prepared to sing the music of Elvino or the tenor music in the 'Messiah,' most of which lies much below the register of a light tenor, as the 'Sonnambula' music is above the register of a robust tenor. In both cases the voice must be forced, and forcing a voice either up or down, beyond deteriorating the quality, may destroy it altogether. This is noticeable mostly in contraltos. As a rule, they force their voices to produce big (ugly) low notes, and by so doing relax the vocal cords to such an extent that they lose their power to produce a full, steady sound in the medium or natural register, the result being a hole in the voice (which no exercise can bridge over) and false intonation. Fine high or low notes produce a very good effect if used with discretion; but if abused to the detriment of the rest of the voice they are better left alone, for good singing does not depend on extraordinary notes, but on the proper use of the ordinary ones.

The quality of the voice alone distinguishes the register—with a young uncultivated voice it is often difficult to decide; and I have known instances where the ablest and most experienced professors have made mistakes.

A notable example of this is Jean de Reszke, who some years ago was a baritone at the Italian Opera, and is now the leading tenor. Mario told me that his first essay before an audience was in the bass part of the trio from 'William Tell'; and it is well known (I believe he relates it in his Reminiscences) that Sims Reeves sang baritone for some time, his favourite songs being ' The Wolf ' and ' The White Squall.'

It is also difficult to judge of the power of a voice ; in my opinion it is a mistake to attempt to do so in a small or empty room. I have heard voices which in the green-room were overpowering, and on the stage, with anything like a full accompaniment, were almost inaudible. I have also heard voices which in a small room displayed but moderate power, that in a theatre or concert-room expanded to a fulness and resonance hardly credible.

In Italy the voice of a singer is said to be an index to his character. Baritone being the natural voice of man, and low bass and tenor being caprices of nature, they argue that baritones are steady characters, whilst low basses and tenors are whimsical and capricious. Out of courtesy, I presume, there is no law laid down for the fair sex.

About the period at which I commenced this chapter I was occasionally subject to an inconvenience, which in after years gave me much trouble and anxiety, caused by a superabundance of saliva, which I was perpetually trying to swallow. The muscles of the throat seemed to relax in consequence of the incessant action, and the voice, instead of issuing with freedom and vigour, appeared to recede, producing a choking sensation, very unfavourable to the delivery of a sustained phrase. For some years after my return from America in 1872 the inconvenience increased to such an extent that at one time I thought I should have to retire from the public exercise of my profession.

I consulted several medical men, who subjected me to a variety of treatments ; one starved me, another stuffed me, and a third dosed me with quinine, strychnine, and iron until I almost lost the sense of taste, and the sight of food nauseated me. This last declared my nervous system was all upset, and, as nothing seemed to set it right, advised me a sea-journey ; accordingly, I crossed to America and back, but without any beneficial result. As a supplementary worry some kind friend suggested I might be suffering from a dangerous internal disorder, and some *kinder* friend spread the report that I was actually a victim to the disease, and that I had only three months to live (I do not know from what date).

I received certainly not less than once a fortnight anonymous letters or pamphlets treating of the cure of the disorder in question, and occasionally old acquaintances stopped me in the street to condole with me on my approaching decease, and mourn over the loss it would entail on the musical world! Highly flattering, but extremely annoying. At the same time I knew from experiment that I not only was not afflicted with the fatal disease, but that there was not the slightest trace of it in my body. I suddenly grew much thinner, losing about two stone in three months. I then consulted my friend, Dr. Owen Rees, who found that my trouble was the result of inactivity of my liver, and, with simple means, in a few months he restored me to health better than I had ever enjoyed. It is curious that, possessed of a strong constitution, and having done more, and more varied work than any singer (except Sims Reeves) before the public, I should always have been singled out as a subject for a premature end.

A short time before I started for Italy in 1855, I met a fellow chorister of the Philharmonic Society, who hailed me with : ' So I hear you are off to Italy.' ' I am,' I replied. ' And what are you going to do ? Study singing ! Why, man, you'll leave your bones there !' I replied, ' Such is not my intention. Why do you think so ?' ' Why, man, you're in a galloping consumption !'

I grew weary of the monotonous routine of keeping a set of ledgers. There was plenty of work to do in them, but work which a schoolboy of ordinary aptitude for figures might learn to do in a week. I felt no interest in it, nor could I see any prospect of altering my position for the better in the commercial world. I had no capital to invest in a business, and I am sure I was not possessed by the spirit of commerce ; but I did my duty faithfully, and had the satisfaction of knowing that my punctuality and zeal were fully recognised by my principal. On one occasion when I asked for a few days' leave of absence to go to the country he told me I was at liberty to go at any time, provided my books were made up, without waiting to ask his permission. And when I told him I was about to leave his employ tо go to study in Italy, he said ' If I double your salary from to-day, will you stay ?' I replied, ' No, sir !' ' Then,' said he, ' I see you have really made up your mind, and although I very much regret losing you, I think you are acting wisely ; here there is nothing for you to look forward to, whilst in the musical profession you have the world before you.'

One day towards the close of May, 1855, as my father and I were returning to business after dinner, I remarked that I did not see any prospect of advancement beyond a modest position at a moderate salary in my present employment. He replied, ' Then why not try Italy? Save what money you can ; go and study in Milan for a time. With your voice and knowledge of music you can surely do something !' I was so dumfoundered at this sudden opening of a path out of the thicket of despair that I could not speak ; but I acted promptly, and set to work that day to find an Italian master. A little before the next quarter-day, June 30, I gave notice of my resolution to my employer, with the result already recorded. Early in October I gave a grand farewell concert at the Lord Nelson Street Rooms, assisted by my elder sister, Mr. W. Ryalls, a very popular tenor, Mr. T. Armstrong, the principal bass singer in Liverpool, and Mr. John Radcliffe, the celebrated flautist, then Master Radcliffe, aged thirteen—my father presiding at the piano as conductor.

I do not remember the exact receipts, but the net proceeds amounted to about £18.

Through Mr. J. Zeugheer Hermann I received some valuable information respecting masters in Milan from Sims Reeves, to whom I was afterwards introduced, during the interval, at one of the concerts of the Philharmonic Society, when he spoke very kindly and encouragingly to me. Some friends in Chester procured me a letter of introduction to a gentleman in Milan, which I was not at all anxious to accept, as I felt shy about presenting it, but which turned out to be of the utmost importance, as I will explain further on.

Besides the few pounds I made by my concert I had saved some £30 out of my year's salary. I had some purchases to make of underclothing, a portmanteau, etc., which reduced my capital to about £40, with which sum I started for Milan on Saturday, October 27, 1855. A friend had jotted down divers available routes, of which I chose the one I conceived would be the shortest and cheapest—*via* Paris, Basle, Lucerne, St. Gothard, and Camerlata. I stopped in London over the Sunday, which I spent chiefly in strolling about the West End, and enjoyed it very much, especially Hyde Park, to my great relief divested of that unsightly Exhibition building which had been my antipathy in 1851.

In my business days a man who had the courage to walk abroad in a turn-down collar or with an unshaven face was set down as a blackleg or a foreigner. By the street boys he was invariably held up to scorn as a Frenchman, and assailed with the opprobrious epithet of ' Mounseer ' or ' Frog.' A clerk with a moustache would not have been tolerated ; with a turn-down collar he would have been looked upon with suspicion, as a probable frequenter of the music-hall or billiard-saloon, neither of which, at that time, were the resorts of respectable youths ; and it was not the custom for young men to smoke cigars and pipes on their way to business—the exceptions to the rule were considered eccentric, if nothing worse.

I was doomed to wear on my neck an instrument of torture, which I conceived must be an invention of the enemy, it was so hideous and inconvenient. But as soon as I found myself in London, released from the fetters of commerce, I turned down my collar and breathed freely. Nature saved me the trouble of shaving by retarding the growth of my facial hirsute appendage, and I could not smoke; nor did I acquire the habit until I was twenty-eight years of age.

I am often asked if I consider smoking bad for a singer. Scientifically I cannot offer an opinion, practically I think I can. Smoking is an art; it may be made useful or otherwise, according as it is exercised. By some it is called a filthy habit. I cannot understand why. Tobacco is as clean a plant as tea or coffee; even its substitute, said to be used occasionally in the manufacture of cigars—the domestic cabbage—is not filthy. An inartistic smoker, like any other inartistic individual, may 'make a mess'; a person who paints may daub his attire and person with the pigments he ought to lay on his canvas, but I should not call him a 'painter.' So a person who smokes may expectorate into the grate or about the room, or scatter ashes in places not intended for their reception, but I would not call that person a 'smoker.'

Being an art, it requires study and attention to make it useful, yet how few people who smoke study their art and can claim to be called 'smokers'! It is just the same with riding. Of hundreds who mount and remain fairly seated on a horse, however vicious he may be, few become 'riders.' Of thousands who cover canvas and paper with colours, and produce pleasant and even striking results, it is not easy to find one 'painter.' Out of myriads who use their voices in various ways according to the strength of their lungs and the formation of their throats, it is difficult to find one 'singer.'

A 'smoker' ought to be able to distinguish between a German cigar, dear at seven pounds a thousand, and a Havana worth eight guineas a hundred, whereas many persons who smoke cannot. He ought to smoke without expectorating. He ought not to chew the end of his cigar or the mouthpiece of his pipe. He ought never to allow a drop of tobacco-juice to pass beyond his lips. He ought neither to puff his tobacco for the mere sake of enveloping himself in a cloud of smoke, nor have to make repeated visits to the match-box. And above all, he ought not to go about the whole day long with a pipe or cigar in his mouth, but confine himself to a moderate use of them. I do not arrogate to myself the right to dictate laws ; I simply recommend these observations to the consideration of those who smoke, as I believe that, with attention to them, any healthy human being may smoke with impunity, and in a good cigar or pipe of good tobacco find a source of enjoyment, consolation, and benefit.

I took to smoking as a preventive of indigestion, and found it a palliative, if not a remedy, and more agreeable than ordinary medicine. As a rule, I do not smoke during the working season until the evening, after dinner, but if I have to sing in a matinée I smoke a cigar after lunch. I find it soothes the nerves and clears away cobwebs.

I have never known a great singer who did not smoke. Mario, for instance, smoked a great deal, and apparently it did him no harm. He smoked from twenty-five to thirty ordinary-sized cigars a day, and in Italy, where real Havana cigars are rarely obtainable, he used to smoke a hundred Cavours a day. The first time he accompanied the Mapleson Italian Opera tour, our luggage was sent on to Dublin by the North Wall boat, which arrived the day after we arrived by the mail. I was wandering about in search of my portmanteau in the morning, when I saw Mario's servant, who told me his master was awake ; so I stepped into his room and sat down on the bed to have a chat. He took a cigar out of his case, which he always kept close at hand, and offered me one. At first I declined, as I was not accustomed to tobacco at such an early hour as eight a.m., and before breakfast. However, he pressed me, and I thought I might as well keep him company, so we both lighted up. We grew interested in our conversation, one cigar succeeded another, and by nine o'clock, when his man announced my portmanteau had been taken to my room, he had disposed of five, and I of three.

I do not advocate smoking, nor do I deem it necessary to smoke to become an artist ; my remark, that I have never known a great singer who did not smoke, I put forward merely as a curious coincidence. Those who feel at all incommoded or unpleasantly affected by smoking had much better leave it alone.

But, indeed, is not every occupation of our lives, be it for amusement, instruction, or gain, an art? Even supplying the inner man with food and drink is an art, which, if properly studied, and exercised with judgment, would go far to abolish gluttony and indigestion, and anger, hatred, and malice would diminish, to the great advantage of the world in general. I do not care how low in the scale the occupation may be, or the person employed in it—a scullery-maid scouring pots and pans, or a groom sweeping out the refuse from a stable—art can be, and often is, brought into requisition, as attentive observation will verify.   I have more to say on the subject of eating and drinking, but it is too early in the day, and there is still a great deal of work to be done before we may sit down and feast, so I will defer further dissertation thereon to a later chapter.

CHAPTER IV.

I LEFT home without regret, except that of parting
with my parents, sisters and brother, with the expectation of not seeing them again for a long time. I had
never before passed more than four weeks away from
my father's roof. Leaving Liverpool did not cost me
a pang. I had never had a great affection for my
native town, nor for many of the people belonging to
it, and the climate did not suit me. I had experienced
no favour from a quarter where I think I was justified
in looking for some. I was a performing member of
the Philharmonic Society from February, 1849, until
the beginning of 1855. Although during the last
three years of that period I had met with a considerable amount of appreciation as a public singer, and
opportunities frequently occurred when the society
might have availed itself of my gratuitous services, and
done something to forward my interests, I never was
invited to take a solo part in any performance. Beside
the subscription concerts, for which artists from

London were engaged, there were minor performances of oratorio with local soloists accompanied on the organ. On one occasion Horsley's 'David'—which was first brought out by the society—was given: the principal bass part was allotted to Mr. Armstrong, and the other less important bass part, which I hoped might be offered to me, was entrusted to Mr. Scarisbrick, a mediocre singer, one of the choir of Chester Cathedral. Mr. Armstrong was prevented from fulfilling his engagement, owing to the death of his father; I then thought, surely I must have a chance! But no: rather than favour me, Mr. Scarisbrick was requested to sing both parts. At the last rehearsal, however, when we arrived at the double quartette, there arose a difficulty. The conductor exclaimed: 'What are we to do now? We have no first bass!' Miss Stott, our leading soprano, who had always displayed a friendly interest in me, spoke out: 'Surely, Mr. Conductor, there can be no difficulty; Mr. Santley is standing there!' The conductor turned round and said: 'If Mr. Santley thinks he can sing the part, I shall be glad if he will oblige us by trying.' I sang it, and that was the only occasion, except when I made the false start in the Amen of Rossini's 'Stabat Mater,' already recorded, on which my voice was heard in the Philharmonic Hall, until I returned from Italy. I was never again asked to undertake the smallest solo part. I felt hurt, and seceded from the society at the commencement of the season 1854-55. When I gave my farewell concert, I purposely chose a Monday evening, being the rehearsal night of the Philharmonic, that they might understand I did not intend to beg any favour of them.   Very foolish, and probably worse, no doubt, but I was piqued at the treatment I had received, and was too young to exercise patience and judgment.

On Monday, October 29, 1855, I started for Paris, *viâ* Southampton and Havre.   It was not until we were clear of Southampton that I felt myself free from a recall home, and I learned some years after that my father had so many misgivings about my undertaking that several times he was on the point of following me to London to beg of me not to pursue my journey. Once out of England, I knew I was safe—at any rate, as far as Milan ; but after my arrival there, I did not know what might happen.   Forty pounds was a small sum with which to start on a course of study in a land of whose customs I knew nothing, and of whose language I knew little more.   I hoped in a few months to be in a position to obtain some small engagement. My views were not ambitious — anything for a beginning, by which I might supplement my capital, so as to keep body and soul together, gain experience, and pursue my studies at the same time.   My father promised to assist me as far as he could, but I had no desire to encroach on his slender means, and I had sufficient pride to wish to keep myself, without being a burthen to anyone.   I can conscientiously say that I never had money-making for an object ; my aim and ambition have always been to make the best use of the talents God entrusted to me.   I dismissed all thought of future provision : I trusted in God for help, and I did not trust in vain !

On board the packet I scraped acquaintance with a

young Frenchman, a teacher at an English school, going to spend a holiday in his native place. He accosted me in French, but soon found that I had not sufficient knowledge of the language to take part even in an ordinary conversation ; he then took pity on me and conversed in English. I owe him a great debt of gratitude for his ready assistance in passing my baggage through the Custom House, and myself through the formalities incidental to the examination and countersigning of my passport—both much more troublesome then than at the present day.

Immediately after our arrival at Havre we were visited by an official, who seemed to be a cross between a beadle and a policeman. He wore a cocked hat, and carried a tall stick, and looked so severe that I trembled, lest, finding any discrepancy between my features and their description in my passport, he might order me to prison or back to my native land. My amiable companion and I went on shore and repaired to a *café* on the quay, where we had coffee and hot milk, such as I had never before tasted, a fine crusty loaf, and abundance of fresh butter, served in the open air by a jolly-looking old woman in a snow-white Normandy cap. She was such a dear-looking old soul, and was so attentive to us, I would willingly have had a little conversation with her, but, for obvious reasons, had to remain dumb. What I failed to express in language I made up for in smiles and attention to the good things with which she supplied us. We then repaired to be examined at the passport-office and claim our passports, which occupied a considerable amount of time ; we saw our baggage registered and properly bestowed, and

then my companion suggested it was time for breakfast. I thought we had breakfasted, but I learned that
a cup of coffee with bread-and-butter does not
constitute a breakfast. We, therefore, betook ourselves
to another *café*, of a better class, in the town, where
we ordered so sumptuous a repast that I began to fear
I should have to dispose of the whole of the money I
had reserved for my journey almost before I was well
on my way. We had oysters! cutlets with vegetables!
salad! cheese and dessert! a bottle of wine each, and a
cup of black coffee!—a Lucullian feast to me, who had
never been accustomed to anything more than an
occasional egg as an addition to my coffee and bread-
and-butter ; and, if I remember rightly, the meal cost
two and a half francs each, including the waiter's tip.

The journey through Normandy is very pretty, and
I enjoyed it much. Rouen passed, I grew drowsy
after the night-travelling, to which I was not accustomed. At the railway-station in Paris I took leave of
my good-natured acquaintance, and crossed the street
to the small hotel to which I had been recommended ;
it was chiefly occupied by English mechanics and
warehousemen in charge of machinery and goods on
view at the Exhibition. I was shown to a small room
without a carpet, and a miserable little den it appeared
to me. A small bed, with the smallest allowance of
bed-clothes possible, a stand, on which were a cream-
jug full of water placed in a large saucer, one little
towel about the size of a decent pocket-handkerchief,
no soap, a looking-glass that made my face appear
longer than even the review of my dormitory, and a
chair, were all it contained. I felt that life was begin-

ning in earnest, and at a very rough end ; but a little thought on what might be before me dispelled the gloom I felt gathering round my spirits, and I descended to the dining-room. After a good plain dinner and a glass (not a bottle this time !) of wine, determined not to waste time, I started off, intending to go to the Italian Opera, but I missed my way, and, as I found it difficult to ask it of the passers-by, and impossible to understand the directions they who con-descended to listen to me favoured me with, I abandoned the idea. I turned a corner to retrace my steps to my lodging, and found myself in front of a large establishment brilliantly lighted, which I knew must be a theatre. I was in hopes it was the one I sought, but it turned out to be the Opéra Comique. I had never heard of the opera announced for that evening's performance; however, I entered the vestibule, paid for a place, and, after ascending three flights of stairs, was shown into a seat at the back of a little stuffy box. The atmosphere was overpoweringly hot, and the theatre was very bad for sound. The voices of the singers were often inaudible where I was perched ; there was a great deal of dialogue, of which I could not make out a single word, so, having nothing to arouse my interest, I fell asleep, and only woke as the curtain was descending. I hurried out into the fresh air. I had lost all idea of my latitude and longi-tude ; I tried first one street and then another. I made inquiries which no doubt were difficult to understand ; received replies which I did not understand at all, but only made confusion worse confounded. I had just made up my mind to pass the night with the stars for my coverlet, when I found, to my inexpressible delight, I was at the foot of the Rue d'Amsterdam where my hotel was situated. The landlord had kindly waited up for me, and, of course, enjoyed the relation of my evening's adventures much more than I had the reality. I went off to bed, packed my overcoat and all my available clothing on the bed to make up for the want of blankets, popped in under them, and was in the arms of Morpheus in the twinkling of an eye.

The next day I sallied forth to call at the English Embassy, to have my passport *viséd*. I asked for the Ambassador—I believe, Lord Lyons—and was ushered into his presence. He received me very affably, probably taking me for somebody connected with the Exhibition ; but when he learned my business, dismissed me promptly, although very politely. I was referred to a clerk, who told me that all that was necessary had been added to my passport ; but I had such a dread of being made prisoner on my journey, that I insisted on something further being done. He smiled, told me to leave my passport and call in a couple of days for it, and he would see that it was all in order. I called, and received it with the stamp of the Embassy added, for which I paid three francs. I filled up my time with a visit to the Exhibition, which had the same depressing effect upon me as that of 1851 and all others I have visited since. I noticed Verdi's opera, the 'Vêpres Siciliennes,' was announced for Wednesday, with Sophie Cruvelli in the cast, and I could not resist the temptation of staying one day more in order to have another opportunity of hearing the goddess who had enchanted me a couple of years before. I knew nothing about the distribution of places, took what was offered me in exchange for my money, and in consequence found myself with the crown of my head almost touching the ceiling, planted behind a row of people who, with that French politeness of which I have often heard, but seldom experienced,* would insist upon standing, and entirely obstructing any view of the stage. Spite of the discomfort, I enjoyed the performance. Obin, the bass, especially pleased me ; I was somewhat disenchanted by my goddess ; the tenor I did not like ; and the baritone, Bonnehée, I liked very much, only, as he did not go down to F, or anywhere near it, I did not take the interest in him I would have done a few years later, when I had learned to distinguish between bass and baritone.

On Thursday evening I left Paris for Basle. The route then lay through Strasbourg, and a very tedious journey I found it, in a slow train, seated for twenty-two hours in a third-class carriage, with only a folded shawl for a cushion, and with travelling companions who had never acquired a taste for soap and water, grimy soldiers, who made the compartment reek with the smoke of vile tobacco ejected from filthy pipes, restless children, and other minor eccentricities. At six p.m. on Friday I reached Basle, and, after a hasty dinner, left for Lucerne. The railway was in course of construction, but was open for a very short distance ; nearly the whole of the journey was in consequence performed by *diligence*. I had taken my place at the last moment, and found I had to ride outside. The night was intensely cold, and when we arrived at

* I speak of Paris.

Lucerne, between four and five in the morning, my legs
were so benumbed I could not stand for some minutes ;
my gums were swollen, and my throat ached, and I
began to fear there was a probability of my having made
my journey for nothing.   However, I walked briskly
about, and in a short time found that my 'bottom G'
was still safe and sound, and my fears vanished.

The journey over the St. Gothard was much more
interesting in 1855 than it is now, spite of the expedition with which it is accomplished and the marvels of
engineering employed in its accomplishment. I passed
over on the 2nd November ; a great deal of snow had
already fallen, and men were constantly employed clear-
ing the carriage-road beyond Andermatt.   At Amsteg
the snow was fairly deep, but not sufficiently to prevent
the use of wheeled vehicles.   I walked a great part of
the way from Amsteg to Andermatt, where we dined.
When I returned to take my place in the *diligence* I
found in its stead a number of small sledges like
children's go-carts, each capable of carrying two persons face to face, drawn by one horse, with a man to
guide the machine.   It began to snow afresh, and soon
grew dark.   We were requested to keep the weight of
our bodies directed towards the side opposed to the
declivity, in order to avoid the possibility of an upset
into the deep snow, from which rescue would have
been difficult, if not impossible.   I felt the cold pene-
trating to my bones.   I was not provided with wraps ;
I had only an ordinary overcoat, and my clothes were
not of the thickest material ; but I was exhilarated
with the mountain-air and the novelty of the drive, and
took little notice of the cold until we halted at Airolo,

and I tried to straighten my limbs. The William Tell who guided my sledge came to levy backsheesh (no need to go so far as Egypt to learn what backsheesh means), in this case well-deserved, for a more tedious piece of work I can scarcely imagine. The horse, harnessed to the sledge with ropes and without reins, was left to his own devices, and the man, sitting on the front, guided us over the slippery, uneven, frozen snow by trailing his left foot along the ground by the side of it. I unintentionally behaved shabbily to the poor fellow. My companion, a French servant-man, with true French polish, gave me a handful of small coins in exchange for a five-franc piece, which I afterwards discovered amounted to about two-thirds of its value. I gave one of the pieces to the driver, who seemed very angry; but as I did not know what it was worth I refused to give him more. Some time after I learned the value of Swiss coins, and I then found I had presented him with a piece worth five centimes. I have often remembered my meanness with remorse when I have been treated with contempt by some embryo Arnold Unterwalten or Walter Fürst, because I did not reward him with half a franc for merely pointing out a road.

At Bellinzona I nearly parted company with all my worldly goods; I made my appearance at the door of the hotel where we stopped to change horses just in time to prevent my portmanteau being carried to some place in a direction opposed to that in which I was journeying. It was broad daylight when we arrived at Lugano; a bright sunshiny morning, such as we occasionally enjoy in May in our native island. The discomfort of a sleepless night in a *diligence* was for-gotten in a moment; I began to sniff the southern breeze, and felt so happy I could have hugged myself with delight. We arrived at Camerlata too late to catch the early afternoon train, and, as we had to wait for another until six p.m., I stepped over to the Station Hotel, and ate my first dinner in Italy. I do not know what it consisted of; I took whatever the waiter seemed to think good for me. I found it excellent; but not having partaken of a proper meal since I left Andermatt, my appetite was so keen I should have enjoyed it had it been a much more ordinary specimen of culinary art.

At about nine p.m. on Sunday, November 4th, 1855, on the feast of my patron saint, 'San Carlo Borromeo,' I found myself at last within the gates of the city of Milan.

As I was approaching the end of my journey I could not but feel somewhat ashamed of my poor attempt at speaking French, and determined, if pos-sible, to prepare myself, that I might make a better show in Italian, to which end I arranged in my mind a series of phrases which I deemed would be necessary and useful on the arrival of the train. What con-fusion! Such a clatter of tongues! That of Babel must have been a fool to it! Rival porters, struggling for a job, literally yelled at each other; passengers calling down the choicest blessings or otherwise on the heads of officious porters carrying off their bags and wraps without orders; and cabmen wrangling over disputed fares. I was almost stunned, and the first question propounded to me finished me off. '*Cos'el voeur lu ?'* What language on earth could that be? For a few moments I fancied I had got in the wrong train and been transported to the wrong country. I replied with a vacant stare at the individual who addressed me. Supposing, probably, I had not heard the question, he repeated it with additions and variations. All my beautifully arranged phrases had evaporated. I threw up the sponge and gave myself up captive, trusting to his tender mercy. He guessed I was a foreigner, I presume, and, as he found speech useless, availed himself of pantomime.

The confusion abated as the crowd dispersed, and I managed to gather my wits and make him understand I wanted my portmanteau and a cab to convey me and it to my hotel. The former was easily found, and instead of a cab he hired a boy with a barrow to convey my portmanteau, whilst I walked. The railway-station lies outside the gates of the city ; on attempting to pass through an official ordered my baggage to be dismounted, and as he could not make me understand in words what he desired, made signs for me to open it, which I was proceeding to do, when the boy offered some explanation, which the official replied to with a shrug of the shoulders and a sign for us to clear out, which we did, and I could not help wondering if it would be as difficult to get out of Milan as it was to get in.

It was dark, and as almost all the streets were lighted by oil-lamps I could not satisfy my curiosity respecting the appearance of the city. We passed by the cathedral, so close that its great size was not apparent, and being in doubt, after a few moments' hesitation, I asked my guide, ' E questa la catedrale ?' He looked at me as though he thought he had a lunatic in charge, and, with a contemptuous grin, replied, '*Ques' chi lè el domm !*' I caught the sound of the words, but I did not comprehend the poetic beauty of his reply until I had made some advance in the acquisition of the Milanese dialect.

At the Gran Bretagna, where I put up (and an exceedingly good hotel it was), to my great joy I was able to let my tongue loose, after being tied up for a whole week. I found a commissionaire who spoke English, not very fluently, but sufficiently well to satisfy my cravings. I made arrangements with him to conduct me to the police office, to claim my passport, which was retained at the frontier, where I had been examined carefully, and made declaration of my profession, object of visiting Milan, etc. ; then to pay a visit to one of the masters recommended to me by Sims Reeves, and arrange about my lessons, for I was anxious to be at work without loss of time. After I had partaken of some slight refreshment, I retired for the night. I opened my portmanteau to make sure all my possessions were safe, and found on the top of my linen a Prayer-book which my mother had placed there after packing my clothes, together with her portrait. I felt so lonely ; I sat down on my bedside and indulged in a good cry, after which I felt more hopeful ! I was not sorry to divest myself of my garments, which I had worn since Thursday morning, and enjoy the luxury of a bed, after three nights spent on the road. Nothing very arduous ; but, remember, I had not travelled much, and never by night, and I had been cared for in my home by the most careful of mothers.

I never indulge in a grumble about the discomforts and annoyances of travelling without reflecting upon what they must have been in those times when mail-clad knights with their followers travelled from the West of Europe to the Holy Land, on horseback or afoot, through unexplored regions, uncleared forests and sandy deserts, among hostile people, and deprived of most of the necessaries which make life bearable, and almost, if not entirely, of its luxuries. Or, again, when Columbus started with his company in open vessels of small tonnage, and in such bad repair that the water trickled through the open seams between the planks ; horses dividing the limited space with men ; exposed to drenching rain, freezing cold and fiery heat ; driven beyond the power of guidance by raging storm, or immovable in a sea of glass under a burning sun, without a breath of air to stir the canvas. When I do this I cannot help contrasting the earnestness of those men, who underwent dangers and privations for the glory of God and the good of their fellow-men, with our impatience in these times, when, provided with luxurious coaches, furnished with lavatories and dining-rooms, where we can partake of an excellent dinner, and retire afterwards to the smoking-saloon and dispose our minds for contemplation with a cigar or pipe and cup of coffee, we arrive at our destination washed, combed, and all in trim order a few minutes later than the advertised time for the arrival of the train, and all because we have missed a bargain ; or with the bobbery we raise and the letters we write to the *Times* if we are called up in the middle of the night for half an hour to undergo a custom-house examination on an excursion of pleasure.

I know women, and some men, whom a journey of four hours by coach or rail overwhelms with fatigue and exhaustion, although provided with sustenance in the shape of cold chicken and sandwiches, and a pocket-flask of strong waters ; whilst their ancestors, male and female, thought nothing of a ride on horseback from London to Edinburgh, or *vice versâ*, except to make their wills before starting in case they were murdered by highwaymen on the road.

How the world progresses! Towards what? Not earnestness, certainly !

CHAPTER V.

My first object was to hire a modest apartment. The proprietor of the hotel offered to let me a room at a very moderate rent, which I would have accepted ; but I wished to make my little capital last as long as possible, and I feared it would not bear the expense of hotel living. The commissionaire then informed me that his wife's sister, a widow, wished to let her rooms. I went to inspect them, found them satisfactory, and the rent being low—twenty zwanzigers a month, a zwanziger being worth about eightpence farthing—I took them, and had my baggage removed, and installed myself the same day. I then paid a visit to Ulrich and Brot, bankers, on whom I had a draft for £35, which they kindly allowed me to leave in their hands and draw out in such sums as I might require.

My guide then conducted me to the police office to have my name and address registered, and receive a paper called a *carta di sicurezza* in exchange for my passport, which they retained until I should be leaving the city.

In 1855 Milan, under Austrian rule, was subject to surveillance so strict that the haunts, business, etc., of every inhabitant and visitor were known to the police. A foreign officer, during his stay in the city, was accompanied wherever he went by a private soldier, who also mounted guard at the door of his hotel or lodging, or of any house at which he might be paying a visit ; spies obtruded themselves on the frequenters of the *cafés*, and joined in their conversation ; and I was solemnly cautioned against discussing politics, wherever or with whomsoever I might be in company. I little needed such a warning, as I never took sufficient interest in politics to care or be able to take part in their discussion. The city was full of military, with whom very few of the Milanese would mix, and those few were invariably treated with the cold shoulder by their fellow-citizens. There was a *café* at the corner of a block of buildings, demolished some years ago to enlarge the Piazza del Duomo, to which the Austrian officers resorted, which no Milanese would enter.

À propos of police interference a ludicrous incident occurred one night at the Albergo del Pozzo, where some students from the Conservatoire were supping and making merry. As the wine warmed their blood the merriment became somewhat boisterous. The sergeant of the patrol, hearing the noise, stepped in and requested to be shown into the room from whence the sounds of revelry proceeded, where he demanded the names of those present one by one: 'Your name?' 'Pollini' (in Milan they call a turkey pollino). 'Yours?' 'Capponi' (capons). Here the sergeant began to look black. 'And yours, sir?' 'Galli' (roosters). Here he could contain himself no longer. 'Come!' said he, 'the police are not to be trifled with ; you will accompany me to the police office.' The landlord was then called, and gave testimony to the fact of the names being correct ; the sergeant bade them continue their revels in a lower key, and departed with a surly grunt. I knew all three. Pollini became a '*Maestro concertatore*' at the Scala ; Capponi frequenters of the Italian opera will remember as a very good bass for some years ; Galli I lost sight of, and do not know where he went to roost.

On giving my name, an official produced my passport and proceeded to question me through my interpreter. First of all he asked me where I was going to sing? At the frontier I had stated I was by profession a singer. I replied I did not know ; I had made no engagement, as I intended to study first. He then informed me I had not described myself properly ; I was a student, not a singer, and could not therefore remain in Milan, and must take my departure within twenty-four hours, unless I could find a citizen of standing who could certify I was a student. 'Well,' I thought, 'now for certain it is all over with me,' and was much annoyed to think that all my arrangements were to be upset by such a ridiculous quibble. I did not know a single soul in Milan ; how was I to procure a certificate ? The commissionaire asked me if I had not brought any letters of introduction. I told him I had one, but knew nothing of the person to whom it was addressed. I had left it in my bag at home, whither we bent our steps immediately—my guide very hopeful, and I very crestfallen. I took out the letter, and was so enraged I literally chucked it at him. He opened it, and exclaimed, 'The very thing! This is a letter to Eugenio Cavallini, the conductor at the Scala, from his brother Pompeo,' then a bandmaster at Plymouth. I forgot all about the police, and saw myself on the instant figuring in some important part on the stage of the august temple of Apollo. I need scarcely add that Austria, through the police official, took me to her bosom and accepted me as a dependent *pro tem.* on the spot.

The next thing my guide insisted upon was that I should pay a visit to the tomb of San Carlo Borromeo, as, during the fourteen days succeeding his feast-day it is shown gratis, whilst during the remainder of the year a fee of three or five francs is expected.

The day following I had an appointment with Lamperti, Catherine Hayes' master, and one of those recommended to me by Sims Reeves. As he could not speak English, and very little French, the commissionaire again accompanied me to act as interpreter. We were shown into a room where the professor was giving a lesson to a somewhat vulgar-looking woman, who emitted the most agonizing shrieks, I thought. I also thought if that were Mr. Lamperti's method of teaching, I would not trouble him for his instruction. However, I bethought myself of Kate's delicate singing, and I concluded the pupil has as much to do with the result of teaching as the master. I was spared the trouble of deciding, for after hearing me, and turning up his nose a trifle—so I imagined—he informed me that his time was fully occupied just then ; but if I could call again in a fortnight, he probably would be able to spare me an hour. I did not return, and have always been glad I did not ; he was an excellent master, but not one to suit my temperament.

My guide then confided to me he had a nephew who was an excellent singing master—he always had a relative ready. I engaged him, but after a few experiences found he knew nothing about singing, so I paid and dismissed him. He was perfectly contented, and invited me to dine with him and his wife, and the commissionaire and his wife, when he treated me to a sumptuous repast—at my own expense. I had engaged an Italian master, who, when I told him I considered Mr. Rosa (the soi-disant singing-master) was a humbug, informed me he was well-acquainted with the gentleman ; that he was a very mediocre fiddler, and never had tried to teach singing before. I mentioned to him that I had determined upon the master I preferred, and at my request he made an appointment with and introduced me to Gaetano Nava.

I do not intend to insert a biography of my master, I will merely relate what I personally know of him, and what he told me about himself.

His grandfather was a celebrated professor of and brilliant performer on the guitar ; his father was also an accomplished guitarist. He himself, although not a heaven-born genius, was possessed of refined taste and feeling and love of music, to which from childhood he devoted himself.   His leaning was towards the vocal branch, but as he was not gifted with a voice, he did not become a practical singer.   He had the advantage which the youth of France and Germany, in common with that of his native country, enjoyed, of hearing the best music of the time executed by the best singers and players, at a trifling cost.   While still under twenty years of age, he was engaged at the Scala and other theatres as '*Maestro concertatore*' (the professor who superintends the pianoforte re-hearsals), and learned how such singers as Pasta, Malibran, Grisi, Pesaroni, Rubini, Donzelli, Filippo Galli, Tamburini, Luigi Lablache, and other brilliant artists, although stars of inferior magnitude, by dint of study imbued themselves with the spirit of the music they had to interpret, and whose beauties they had to develop.

How he profited by this experience can be seen on perusing the numerous studies, *solfeggi*, etc., he wrote for every voice.

He was a diligent student of the history and theory of music, as may be gathered from his numerous anno-tations to many works upon these subjects, which, together with masses and other compositions in MS., were bequeathed to me, and are still in my possession. Moreover, he was well versed in Italian literature, which cannot be said of many of his fellow professors.

I loved him as a master for the pains he took, and the knowledge he displayed in my instruction, and I loved him still more as a man ; he was a kind father to me whilst I was under his care, and a true friend to me as long as he lived.   My sincere admiration of his abilities and love for himself do not cause me to think it impossible that there have been and are other masters quite as competent as he ; but that I had the good fortune to enjoy his friendship and profit by his tuition is one of the many boons for which I thank God. We were united in sympathy, and hence he found no difficulty in imparting, nor I in comprehending, his instructions.

I hope to let fall hints occasionally, from which young people may derive advantage. I have, however, no intention of obtruding 'a method of singing' on those who may deem it worth their while to read these memoirs ; at the same time, a few of my master's remarks made during 'breathing time' may not be out of place.

At the Conservatoire, where, during the time I was his pupil, he was master of the girls' singing-class, he was obliged to teach all those who were accepted as pupils by the directors ; privately, he would not accept as a pupil, on any terms, a youth of either sex with whose musical disposition he was not thoroughly satisfied. Often he dismissed girls with advice to turn their attention to knitting stockings or other domestic works, and so become useful members of society, instead of wasting their time in the study of an art for which they had neither taste nor aptitude, and of which the small smattering they might acquire, instead of amusing, would only distress themselves and their friends.

He insisted that the object of music was to give greater expression and emphasis to the words, and for this reason never allowed a syllable to be neglected.

' I must hear what you are singing about,' he would say, ' or I cannot tell how you are singing, and, consequently, cannot help you!' When I had mastered Italian sufficiently, he made me learn the buffo parts in Rossini's comic operas, ' La Cenerentola,' ' L'Italiana in Algeri,' ' Il Turco in Italia,' etc., and also in Mercadante's operas and those of other composers whose names I cannot now call to mind. He made me *sing* them, not gabble them, as I have heard many Italian *buffos* do ; he said, ' Luigi Lablache and Luigi Galli (brother of Filippo, for whom many celebrated *buffo* parts were written) never gabbled ; they sang, and they were grand artists, who ought to be taken as models by all students who are striving after perfection.' To this study I owe the clear pronunciation which I believe is one of my good qualities. During the first years after my return to England I used often to sing *buffo* duets with Giorgio Ronconi and Belletti, and many an unexpressed challenge I have accepted and deadly combat fought in the arena of words. At one of Chorley's parties Belletti and I sang the duet 'Che l'antipatica vostra figura,' from Ricci's opera, ' La Chiara di Rosemberg ' (on the same subject as Balfe's ' Siege of Rochelle ') after some long instrumental pieces, of which, spite of their classical propensities, English fashionable audiences do grow weary sometimes. Virginia Gabriel accompanied. In the last movement Belletti, thinking it about time to rouse the slumbering enthusiasts from their lethargy, started off at a headlong pace. I girded up my loins and followed him, and we bore Miss Gabriel along between us at such a rate she could scarcely see the notes. Fortunately, she was an excellent reader, and well-versed in Italian music, and we landed at the end all safe and sound, when, amidst the deafening applause and hearty congratulations of the now wide-awake classicals, we congratulated each other on having come in with un-broken necks.

Incidentally, I may remark that women, who are generally supposed to be faster talkers than men, seldom acquire the facility of men in uttering 'word and note'; at least, such has been my personal ex-perience.

One of the best lessons Nava ever gave me was on progress. I had received (about July, 1856, I think) a very serious letter from my father in reply to an appli-cation for assistance, in which he said that, after my remarks upon the singers I had heard at the Scala, he had hoped that by that time I would have made my appearance there ; that he clearly saw we had made a mistake, and I had better return home. He would send me money for that purpose, but not to enable me to remain ; as regarded what he had already lent me, no doubt I could soon obtain a situation, and refund it. I felt much cast down ; I had worked hard, and was making progress rapidly, both in singing and the language. I went to my lesson ; Nava saw I was out of spirits, and asked me the cause. I told him what my father had written, whereupon he said, ' Your father is in too great a hurry ! Progress is not made at the rapid rate he evidently expects ; it must be made step by step to make it secure ; you cannot judge of progress from day to day, or from month to month ; work steadily, and at the end of six months compare what you can do then with what you could do at the beginning, then you can estimate the advancement you have made. There must be time to receive instruction, and time to digest the instruction received. We see young people after a few weeks' exercise of the voice set to cram a few parts (in operas), and in a few months from their leaving some other occupation, thrust upon the stage. The consequence is, that the strain on the imperfectly-trained voice impairs its quality and strength in a short time beyond the power of any master to remedy. I am perfectly satisfied with the progress you have made, and am also perfectly satisfied that, the necessary time being allowed you to make sure of every step you take, your father, too, will be fully satisfied with the result.'

It is a lesson which may be equally well applied to any other study, I take it. The painter's perspective, colour, grouping ; the surgeon's anatomy ; the sailor's ropes and sails ; the soldier's gun, sword, and bayonet exercises, and so on throughout the range of human occupation, are no other than scales and *solfeggi* in another form—the foundation, which must be formed of solid materials firmly and carefully welded if the student's ambition is to become a ' tower of strength,' capable of defying the storms of jealous rivalry which are sure to assail him, and a place of refuge for those who require protection and help.

Nava wrote a kind and sensible letter, placing his views before my father, with the result that, fortunately for me, the necessary funds to prosecute my studies were forthcoming.

Besides the affection of my master, I had the good

fortune in a short time to win that of his family ; so much were they attached to me, that all events which occurred subsequently were dated from the day I paid my first visit to their house.

Now began the happiest phase of my existence ; it was of few months' duration, but it was a happy time while it lasted. I lived in a world of which I had dreamed, without any hope of my dream being realized ; now, the study which had been my solace in the few hours' respite from toilsome, because unpalatable, work, had become the pleasurable occupation of my life. I was under the care of one who was at once my teacher and friend, and I looked forward with hope to win an honourable place in the arena I had chosen. An occasional moment's reflection on my slender means, and the probable necessity of having to apply to my father for assistance, was the only bar to my complete happiness.

I had a lesson every alternate day, and they were red-letter days ! Nava took great pains about my speaking, as well as about my singing, and, unless he had urgent business to call him away, used to keep me long after the stipulated singing hour conversing. He did not know a word of English, so I was not shy, and blundered on as best I could, he correcting my mistakes. I also became acquainted with his family, especially with two of his sons, the younger a student of law, and an exceedingly good scholar ; the elder a professor of the pianoforte, a clever youth, but idle and negligent with his pupils.

Lombardy, like all the other Italian provinces, has its dialect, which undergoes variations of form in each town of the province.   In Milan there are, or were, three forms—that of Porta Ticinese (the low part of the city), where they spoke the dialect which Porta, a very humorous Milanese poet, has made famous ; that of the middle-class, tradesmen and shopkeepers ; and that of the gentry and aristocracy.   In one form or another all the inhabitants converse in dialect ; many know Italian well ; few, however, can hold a conversation in it, in consequence of which I had few opportunities of exercising my ear, until I became intimate and had frequent conversations with my master and his family, and made slow progress in conversation.   In music or language I never could pick up anything from mere sound ; I must distinguish in my mind's-eye the note or the word, or the sound leaves no impression.

I was always a slow worker, slow at taking instruction, and slow at digesting it.   I never could work well shut up in a room—I must be moving.   I have done a great deal of work travelling by rail, but I prefer walking, and in the open air.   In a few minutes' strolling about Hampstead Heath I can work out an idea over which I have pondered for hours in my own study without success !   Mechanical work, such as scales, *solfeggi*, or transcribing, I can do at home, though I have wakened the echoes many a half-hour on the hills about the Italian lakes and in the pine-woods of the Black Forest, exercising my voice.   I was always fond of walking ; perhaps I might have preferred riding, had I possessed sufficient means to purchase and keep a horse.   For the first few months of my residence in Milan, to avoid the nuisance of the octroi inspection, my daily walk was round the bastions,

about seven miles. During the day they were little
frequented by pedestrians, so I could take my exercise
and study in peace. I might have learned military
drill, both cavalry and infantry, as all the available
space on the bastions and Piazza d'Armi was in constant requisition for drilling troops, had my taste leaned
that way. The Hungarian hussars alone attracted my
attention, they looked so picturesque in their handsome uniform and mounted on their fiery little black
steeds. The little military ardour I possessed would
soon have been quenched by the bullying of the
Austrian officers, at times very rough.

The Scala was open only during the Carnival and
Lent, from the 26th of December until Easter-Eve.
Under the same management, the autumn season, during
the months of October and November, was held at the
Cannobiana, a much less spacious theatre, and not by
any means so good for sound. The operas in course
of representation when I arrived were ' Gli Ugonotti,'
' La Favorita,' and ' I Puritani,' and a few nights
towards the close of the season were devoted to selections from these and other operas not included in the
répertoire. Of the singers, the only soprano I
remember was Madame Angles Fortuni, whom I only
heard in a scene from one of Donizetti's or Bellini's
operas. I liked her, and she was evidently a great
favourite with the public, as she was much applauded,
both on her appearance on the stage (an unusual thing
in those days) and at the termination of her scene.
The principal tenor was Antonio Giuglini, this being
his first season in Milan, I believe. He had created a
perfect furore. Wherever music happened to be the

subject of conversation, Giuglini was the hero, a curious fact, considering that powerful lungs are supposed to carry the day. Giuglini was a proof that physical force does not always win; his voice was not powerful, but it was of sympathetic quality, although slightly throaty, and his phrasing was perfect; any ornament he introduced he invariably executed with precision and elegance. He was not a clumsy man, but as an actor he was ungraceful, and lacked intelligence. In the part of Raoul, the part in which I first saw him, he sang charmingly, but manly bearing and fire were entirely wanting, with the result that his performance was dull and insipid. In 'I Puritani' he was quite at home; his rendering of Arturo's music, than which more delicious love-strains have never been written, rivetted the attention so completely, that the actor was lost sight of. On one of the selection-evenings, he, with a very good *buffo*, Scheggi, and Marini, a world-renowned bass, sang the splendid trio 'Pappataci,' from 'L'Italiana in Algeri.' It was a perfect treat, and was vociferously redemanded (encores were not then in vogue in Italy), and, by general desire, repeated on subsequent nights. Enrico Delle Sedie, who sang in London some years ago, was the principal baritone, and deservedly a great favourite. The basses were a Spaniard, named Pedro Nolasco Llorens, who possessed a sonorous voice, with a rough, energetic style of using it, and Marini, who, except Formes, was the best Marcel I ever saw. He had at that time, after a long and arduous career, a fine trumpet-toned voice of greater compass than Lablache's, but of similar timbre, and was an excellent actor.

The chorus was good ; the orchestra, that of the Scala, with a slightly-reduced number of strings, under the direction of my friend Eugenio Cavallini, was very good. Two qualities it displayed which struck me forcibly —the superior way in which the stringed instruments 'sang' their music to what I had been accustomed, and the superiority of the double-basses in refinement, execution, and solidity ; they were never heard except when playing alone, but the fine effect they produced was invariably felt.

I saw Ristori in ' Maria Stuarda.' I recognised in her a noble actress, but my enjoyment of her performance was greatly marred through my imperfect acquaintance with Italian—I had not been a month in Italy.

CHAPTER VI.

At my first interview with Nava, to give him a notion
of my capabilities, I sang one of his own *vocalizzi*
at sight.   He was greatly pleased and astonished, not
only that I could read it off, but also execute the
passages with facility—thanks to the early training I
went through with my father.   For the information of
those who are not versed in musical phraseology, a
vocalizzo is 'a song without words,' vocalized to the
vowel *a*, the exercise of which enables the student to
unite the various combinations of notes he has learned
in his preliminary studies, previous to the final study
of interpreting language through the medium of
music.   The *solfeggio* differs from the *vocalizzo* in that,
as each note is sung, its name is pronounced ; this
serves to facilitate the acquirement of reading music—
as there can be no guess-work—and of a clear pro-

nunciation, more especially of the pure sound of the Italian vowels, a most difficult task for an English-speaking student, as anyone who considers the careless manner in which we treat vowels will readily understand.

Only one vowel in Italian possesses two sounds : *o*, pronounced sometimes as *oa* in moan, *e.g.*, *amore*, and at others as *o* in got, *e.g.*, *rosa*. The *e* and *i* at the end of a syllable require great attention ; English singers invariably, unless carefully corrected, add an *i* after the *e* or *i* already belonging to the syllable, and thus *be-ne* becomes *be-i-ne*, *Di-o* becomes *Di-io*, etc., a barbarous defect to an Italian or Italianized ear. The Italian *u*, equivalent to our *oo*, is frequently pronounced like *u* in ' curious ' by our singers.

I have often heard English vocalists say they preferred singing in Italian, because it is so much easier than singing in English. It may be pleasanter to them, and seem easier, but to those of their audience whose ears are accustomed to the beauty and delicacy of the Italian language, the gibberish they utter entirely mars any effect they might make with their vocalization ; much better would it be if they converted their songs into *vocalizzi*. Like many other things, singing in Italian is ' easy to get through,' but it is difficult to do properly. It is only a question of intelligence and application ; ' what man has done, man may do '—if he has but the will. The words! the words!! the words!!! Without the words there is no accent ; without the accent there is no singing. I once heard a man say (he was an English professor of music who did not understand a word of Italian) that he preferred

Italian to English opera. I suggested, 'What about the words?' 'Oh,' said he, 'I would rather not hear the words.' It is not for such as he I write *my* words.

I would impress on students the necessity for refinement, delicacy, and finish in the execution of all detail, whether of music or language ; attention to these distinguishes the artist from the artizan.

I commenced my lesson always with preliminary vocal exercises, taken in progressive order as I mastered them ; the whole course, from the simplest combination of notes to the study of the shake, with which I concluded, occupying twelve months. I then sang one or two *solfeggi*, which, after a few weeks, as I was already a good reader, were replaced by *vocalizzi*, though I still worked at *solfeggi* for the exercise of pronunciation at home ; and I finished with the study of detached pieces from operas, in which the facility of vocalization I had acquired was most available. ' Semiramide ' was my master's predilection, an opera full to overflowing of excellent study for a vocalist, but to my mind tiresome, now that singers, for what reason I am not prepared to say, are rarely to be found who possess the facility and precision of execution necessary to enable them to take part in such a work.

The first piece I was entrusted with was the great duet from ' Semiramide ' for the Queen and Assur, commencing with the fine introductory recitative, in order that I might sing it with one of Nava's pupils at the Conservatorio. It was a favourite practice of his to bring his pupils together in the study of concerted music—a study the value of which, I think, cannot be too highly estimated. It moderates the exaggerated zeal of one, and rouses the apathetic indifference of another ; it leads two or more people to blend a multiplicity of sentiments and characteristics, so as to produce a result apparently conceived by one mind. What is more miserable than to hear a duet where the singers are at variance in accent, in expression, in all that makes the absurdity of two people saying the same thing, at the same time, to or at each other, tolerable ?

The study of subservience in concerted music is of infinite value to the true artist ; he must stoop with the weak and mount with the strong. He can compare his own powers with those of other artists, greater, equal, or inferior to himself, and he cannot fail to pick up occasionally important ideas which never struck him before, and which he can and will use to his advantage, or, by observing them in others, discover defects in his own performances which he will study to avoid.

The pupil with whom I sang the ' Semiramide ' duet, Amalia Peroni, possessed a soprano voice of very good quality, flexible, and sufficiently powerful ; she lacked animation, however, and her companions called her Donna Pacifica. Nava gave her the duet to induce her to rouse herself to some enthusiasm, but except on one or two occasions her performance was purely mechanical—technically perfect, but colourless in expression. Her features were beautiful, but her face, like her singing, was without animation. I believe her apathy was due rather to want of physical strength than of feeling, for she died of consumption shortly after making her first appearance on the stage. During the term of my studies I sang with others of my master's pupils, only two of whom I met with afterwards. Luigia Perelli, also a soprano, had a quite opposite character to her class-mate. She possessed charm both of feature and voice, and was full of animation and sentiment. We sang together a duet from Mercadante's ' Zaira,' but only a few times as a study, as she never liked it, preferring the somewhat exaggerated pathos of Verdi to the dry sentiment of Mercadante. She made her first appearance in public at the Cannobiana during the autumn season of 1856 as Adalgisa in ' Norma,' very successfully, and after appearing at some of the principal theatres in Italy, she was engaged for several seasons at St. Petersburg. In 1872 I met her again at Nava's house, grown into a plump, handsome matron, when we sang, accompanied by our master, and to his great delight, one of the duets from ' Rigoletto.' The other was Luigia Pessina, a handsome brunette, with a magnificent mezzo-soprano voice, which she used well. We studied and sang together on divers occasions a fine duet from Rossini's ' Maometto Secondo,' better known as ' The Siege of Corinth.' When I was singing at the Scala during the Carnival 1865-66, she was playing Adalgisa in ' Norma '; since then I have lost sight of her.

On the evening of the 27th of December a concert by Nava's pupils and his son David, the pianist, was given in the house of Signor Giovanni Marani, whose eldest daughter was under Nava's tuition, to celebrate his saint's day. In Italy, as in all Catholic countries, they keep up the saint's day, not the birthday, as we do. A rehearsal was held the day before at Signor

Marani's house, when at his request and that of his wife I was presented to the family. I was too shy to attempt much in the way of conversation, so retired into a corner, where, undisturbed, I could enjoy the music and observe the audience. I could not help contrasting the lively way in which they amused themselves with the 'sad' way in which, as a rule, audiences enjoy themselves at home. During my stay in Milan I was a constant guest at the Maranis. I owe them a debt of gratitude for the intimate friendly intercourse to which they admitted me, and the almost parental interest they took in my welfare. They used to hold a *conversazione* every Sunday evening during the winter and spring months, which consisted of conversation, interspersed with vocal and instrumental music, concluding with an informal dance. At one of these I sang for the first time to an Italian audience, and was so well received by their extensive circle of friends and relations, that for the remainder of my stay I had to do my share of singing and dancing each evening—a grateful task, as I had the satisfaction of at once affording amusement to my hosts and their company, and deriving profit myself—exercising what I learned. I had also the advantage of joining in promiscuous conversation. Generally, as the guests were assembling, I found myself the centre of a group of merry girls, who discovered a great fund of amusement in the grotesque mistakes of *Il Signor Inglese*, the title by which I was invariably addressed. How odd we should think it, were we to hear a group of English girls addressing a foreigner as 'Mr. Italian!' They had many a 'roar' at my expense, in which I joined heartily ; for it was impossible to feel offended—they took such pains, and were so patient in correcting my blunders.

The announcement containing the *répertoire* of operas and ballets, names of artists and instrumentalists, prices of subscription and admission, etc., for the Carnival and Lent season of 1855-56 at the Scala appeared on the walls about the end of November. The works promised were : operas, ' L'Ebreo ' of Apollini, ' Giovanni Giscala ' (I forget the composer's name), ' L'Assedio di Leida ' of Petrella, and ' I Vespri Siciliani ' (' Giovanna de Guzman,' under which title it was represented) of Verdi—all new to Milan—' Il Profeta ' (Meyerbeer), ' Rigoletto ' (Verdi), ' Lucrezia Borgia ' and ' Marino Faliero ' (Donizetti), and three ballets. The singers were Marianna Barbieri-Nini, Scotta, Eliza Masson, and a contralto whose name I do not recollect, a pupil of the Conservatoire, her first appearance on the stage, and a very promising artist. Lodovico Graziani (brother of the baritone), Bernardo Massimiliani, and Carlo Liverani were the tenors ; Leone Giraldoni and Giovanni Corsi the baritones ; Eugenio Manfredi and Cesare Nanni the basses ; Caterina Beretta was the principal dancer ; Effisio Catte principal *mime*. The orchestra, under the direction of Eugenio Cavallini, numbered about ninety performers. The season extended over about three months, during which there were five performances each week, except Holy Week, when two concerts—one secular and one sacred—were given in lieu of opera. The first concert included David's cantata, ' Il Deserto,' overture to ' Guglielmo Tell ' (Rossini), a concert-overture by Jacopo Foroni, and other pieces; the second included the 'Stabat Mater' of Rossini, and selections from the 'San Paolo' of Mendelssohn, and other works.

On the recommendation of my master, I became a subscriber for the season, my ticket for the pit costing me sixty-five zwanzigers (about forty-five shillings), a reduction of fifteen zwanzigers on the full price being accorded to musical students and officers, civil and military. The Scala and the Cannobiana, the two patent theatres, were held under the same lease, the lessees receiving a subsidy from the Government of (I think) 250,000 francs per annum, in return for which they were bound to carry out certain stipulations, the most important of which were as follows : To produce a certain number of operas never before represented in Milan during each Carnival and autumn season ; to provide a double company, one of which must be of singers of acknowledged celebrity (*cantanti di cartello*) ; to retain sufficient accommodation in the stalls for the officers quartered in and about the city ; to engage orchestra, chorus, and corps de ballet, and supply scenery, wardrobe, and other stage accessories and appointments of standard excellence. The whole business was carried out under the supervision of two gentlemen holding a Government commission, who were likewise responsible for the mutual fulfilment of engagements between the management and artists and others employed in the theatre, and the deciding of all disputes according to established laws and customs, equally binding on both parties.

Gardoni told me an amusing anecdote *à propos* of this

Government supervision. Having become involved in a dispute with the management in the course of an engagement at the Scala respecting what he deemed an imposition on their part, he took the law into his own hands, and, without notifying his intention, escaped in the *diligence* for Paris. At the frontier he had to descend with his fellow-passengers to have his passport examined. He had not visited the police office to obtain it, knowing he would have been stopped at once, and hoping to elude the vigilance of the officer at the frontier. He had only his '*carta di sicurezza*' to show, and was, accordingly, requested to step into a side room, whence he had the felicity of watching the *diligence* depart, and of returning to Milan, accompanied by a couple of *gens d'armes*. He was lodged in the prison of Santa Margherita for a week, and each evening he had to sing, being driven to the theatre and back with a similar escort, who, besides, kept a careful watch over him during the performance. It seems a hard case, but similar treatment would have attended the managers had they, on their side, committed a breach of contract. I remember a baritone, Luigi Valle, being engaged to play Nabucco at the Carcano, an excellent artist, but a victim to extreme nervousness. He had not even the courage to leave his house the first night the opera was announced, excusing himself on the plea of suffering from hoarseness. An incompetent singer was substituted, the consequence being a row in the house ; the second performance was a repetition of the first, except that the row became a riot ; the third night the police called for the affrighted baritone, drove him to the theatre, kept guard outside his room whilst he dressed, and forced him on to the stage. The house was packed, and Valle was so paralysed that they had to lift him off the horse on which he made his entry. The opening notes betrayed the anguish which oppressed him, and were listened to in dead silence. In desperation, pulling himself together, he delivered his first important phrase magnificently ; it shot through the house like a flash of lightning, followed by a peal of thunder such as only excited Italians or Spaniards know how to fire off!

The word '*libertà*' was expunged from the Italian stage - vocabulary by the Austrians. In the duet 'Suoni la tromba' ('I Puritani'), on one occasion, Giorgio Ronconi gave the words '*gridando libertà*' with such vigour and emphasis that the audience were excited to the pitch of frenzy, and a great commotion ensued. Next morning he received a reprimand for using the prohibited word, accompanied by a request to use the word '*lealtà*' on future occasions in its stead. Shortly after, playing 'Il Sargente' in 'L'Elisir d'Amore,' in deference to the request, for '*perdè la libertà*' he substituted '*perdè la lealtà*,' which was received with shrieks of laughter by the audience, to the great discomfiture of the advocates of ' loyalty.'

The season commenced with ' L'Ebreo.' There was a great rush on the first night, but, having been warned, I was at the doors an hour or more before they opened, and so secured a seat. The theatre looked dull and dismal ; the glimmer of light afforded by a single lamp suspended from the top of the proscenium only served to make darkness visible. The Scala in 1855 was lighted, stage and auditorium, with oil-lamps; the chandelier, formed of a large cluster of them, was lowered to the floor of the pit, lighted, and hoisted back to its place about half an hour before the performance commenced. In 1865, when I sang there, it was lighted with gas; and in 1883, when I took a friend to see it, the electric light was used throughout the entire building. It is a beautifully-proportioned theatre, its acoustic properties perfect; the stage, already spacious, was enlarged a few years ago. The custodian informed me they have had as many as 1,200 persons, besides horses and an elephant, on in one ballet scene.

I do not think a detailed account of the season would be interesting after the lapse of so many years, so I will merely note a few of my recollections.

'I Vespri Siciliani' had a great success; with the exception of the *basso*, I liked the performance quite as well as that I witnessed in Paris. Nanni, Obin's representative, was so bad he was replaced after three performances by Giorgio Attry, since known at the Royal Italian Opera; but neither of them came within a long distance of the original. Of 'L'Ebreo,' only one number, a romance for the tenor (Graziani) sung behind the scenes, interested me; the rest I found very weak in substance, though noisy in expression. 'Giovanni Giscala' was a failure, and played only one or two nights. 'L'Assedio di Leida' I did not hear. During the performance of the ballet I had an opportunity of learning how emphatically an Italian audience can express disapprobation. The ballet was a failure; I did not discover why. The grouping of the '*corps de ballet*,' the dancing of the principal executants, everything appeared to me very good, but evidently my taste and knowledge lacked cultivation. From beginning to end, with very slight cessation, and that seemingly made by mutual consent, in order to take breath and begin again with renewed vigour, the audience hissed, screamed, yelled, hooted, and shouted '*basta! basta!*'—in fact, they behaved like so many demons in torment. I could not help thinking it was 'Much ado about nothing,' but it must be remembered that there were a limited number of works announced for performance during the season, any of which, having passed the ordeal, would be served up for an unlimited number of nights. It might not seem necessary to make such a hubbub; but managers are notoriously afflicted with chronic deafness, and Italians are vehement in demanding an adequate return for their money. I do not blame them; on the contrary, I think there are occasions on which their example might be followed, both in theatre and in concert-room, with great benefit to musical society, by my compatriots. The opinion of the Italian public may be just or unjust, but, undoubtedly, it is decided. They manifest it clearly; nor do they always wait until the end of a number, as is the rule with us. How often do we hear poor stuff, badly sung, applauded vociferously on account of some high or low note introduced at the end of a cadence? Without interrupting the performance, they express their approbation with a murmur of satisfaction, or a short sharp '*bravo*,' very encouraging to the performer. When they disapprove they show little mercy, except to modest young artists suffering from stage fright, to whom they express their sympathy by an insinuating '*coraggio.*' Anything like conceit or arrogance they resent; woe betide the unfortunate individuals whose vanity or ambition overrides their discretion! 'There's rue for them'; the first slip is greeted with a salvo of hisses, not readily forgotten, and generally topped up with a recommendation to go home and study. Occasionally Italian audiences indulge in little eccentricities; a young handsome *prima donna*, whose talent is too meagre to meet their approval, in place of applause will receive a shower of kisses (in the air) mingled with exclamations of '*Bella! Bella!*' After singing a low note on one occasion I heard a voice murmur patronizingly, '*Ohè! Cantina!*' ('Hallo! Cellar!')

Startling as at first I found their violent demonstrations, much more annoying I found the incessant chattering and laughing carried on during all parts of the performance uninteresting to the general public. The Austrian officers, who occupied the two front rows of stalls, were the ringleaders; they talked as loud as though they were addressing their men on parade, accompanying their clatter with that of their scabbards and spurs; the Italians, in emulation, followed suit, the result being a fair representation of Chaos. At times the voices of the singers could not penetrate as far as the pit. The scene between Oberthal and the two Anabaptists in 'Il Profeta' was always a piece of dumb show; not a sound, except an occasional loud chord in the orchestra, did I ever hear of it.

At times, whilst there was nothing going on which

interested them, almost the entire audience left the theatre, returning in time to hear a favourite number. 'Lucrezia Borgia' proved very attractive; during the first and last acts the theatre was crowded; during the second it was nearly deserted, the few who remained indulging in audible conversation varied with occasional sarcastic remarks upon the performance and performers. Certainly the appearance of the three principal singers gave ample food for mirth. They were all squat and fat; Barbieri-Nini, whose singing of the two great airs was superb, in all else was as unlike an ideal Lucrezia as could well be imagined. Liverani, the Gennaro, looked like a hogshead on castors, and bellowed like a bull. Corsi, Alfonso, could not bellow, but played fantastic tricks with his eyes to a ludicrous extent. The performance, the only one, of 'Marino Faliero,' however, bore away the palm for amusement. It was a perfect burlesque; the only number that escaped the gibes of the public was Barbieri-Nini's great air, which, like those in 'Lucrezia,' she sang to perfection. In the second scene, towards the end of an orchestral prelude, I beheld protruding from the wings what I took for a red banner, waving a little above the floor; it moved forward, followed by a pair of very fat legs, supporting a portly paunch; a head appeared next, and then the entire body of Signor Carlo Liverani stood revealed; very uncomfortable and uneasy in his mind he looked. What I had mistaken for a banner turned out to be a mantle, worn over one shoulder, which glided off at a tangent from the globe of flesh it was intended to drape. This ludicrous figure roused the spirits of the audience, which had been gradually flagging from the commencement of the opera ; they saw there was no pleasure to be derived from the performance, so they determined to get all the fun they could out of it. Spite of their chaff, the poor tenor struggled through an air, one of Rubini's *chevaux de bataille*, but no sooner had he touched the last note than, terror lending him wings, he bounded off the stage at a hop, step, and jump, followed by a peal of laughter which made the house vibrate.   Giraldoni was, as we say in the north, like a ' chip in porridge ' ; Corsi, Faliero, undertook a part (written for Luigi Lablache) for which he did not possess a single qualification.   It was a disgraceful performance, and well deserved the derision with which it was condemned.

CHAPTER VII.

I ATTENDED the performances regularly for a few
weeks, but the constant repetition of the same operas,
and the annoyance I underwent from the chattering
and other disturbances, damped my ardour. I looked
about for some other way of passing the long winter
evenings. The weather was bitterly cold, and as I
had no means of warming my room, it was impossible
to remain indoors reading or studying with any comfort. I had a small stove set up, but found the
remedy worse than the disease. Though I used little
fuel, the heat it generated affected my throat and head,
so I was forced to abandon it ; and I had not yet
learned that for the price of a cup of coffee I could
enjoy the warm shelter of a *caffè* the whole evening.
The most convenient warming apparatus, I discovered,

was a handful of hot roasted chestnuts carried in each pocket of my overcoat; they imparted a genial glow to my outer surface, and made a comfortable, though slightly *stuffy*, lining to the inner afterwards.

There was an opera at the Carcano, a second-rate theatre, which had seen palmy days when 'Norma' was first produced with Pasta, Giulia Grisi, Donzelli, etc., and 'I Puritani' with Grisi, Rubini, Tamburini, and Luigi Lablache. The productions were on a scale much inferior to the Scala, but for a time they proved an agreeable change. The company, with two exceptions, consisted of mediocre singers, either beginners, or of small provincial celebrity; some of the oracles of the Caffè Martini, the trysting place at all hours of the day, and a great part of the night, for musicians of every class, and others connected with the operatic world—composers, librettists, orchestral directors, singers, instrumentalists, chorus-masters, prompters, ballet-masters, dancers, *mimes*, managers, and theatrical agents. There could be seen—except during the Carnival, when, save those employed at the Milan theatres, all the artists had departed to fulfil their various engagements—the celebrity, in solemn dignified repose, crowned with his well-merited wreath of laurels gained in a recent campaign; the young impetuous *débutant*, fresh from the scene of his first great triumph; the blatant, swaggering nincompoop, boasting of victories he had not won; and the modest, earnest youth, overshadowed with doubt about his success, and fears for the future. It was at times an interesting scene to behold, often amusing, and sometimes a very sad one, when the eye rested in some retired corner on a haggard, careworn face, watching with avidity to lay hold on a few crumbs of comfort in the encouraging glance of agent or comrade. I have witnessed re-unions of artists of various professions, but for contrast no parallel to that of the Caffè Martini. The engagements, not only for the theatres for Italy (and they were legion), but for all the European opera houses and for those of America, North and South, Havana, Africa, India, etc., were almost all made through the Milanese agencies.

The Caffè Martini was the exchange where artists in search of employment were wont to meet managers, or agents commissioned to negotiate for them. With celebrities, to whom places were always open, it was only a question of arrangement of terms ; with the great concourse of the less famous and inexperienced, eager to find a place somewhere, negotiations were more protracted, and carried on with as much commercial strategy as between merchant and broker. For the Carnival, the principal season, when every theatre in Italy was open, the strife, except for the better places, was not so furious, demand and supply being about equal. It was for the off-seasons, fair times in Bologna, Bergamo, and other cities that the fight became deadly. Some of the most noted singers who were not engaged for the foreign theatres were at liberty, and could afford to accept moderate terms, and so debar those who had made headway during the Carnival from following up their successes in desirable spheres. Salaries were not great in those days ; there were no £200 per night artists. The result was that to live, the minor stars had to fall back on less important and less lucrative engagements ; they in turn drove those of lower rank to take what would procure the barest necessaries of life, and often to the confines of starvation. This is no exaggeration. I used to visit a fellow student, who had a monthly allowance from home, at his modest lodging ; in the same domicile lived a tenor, who afterwards arrived at a position of eminence in Italy, and a bass, who was one of my comrades during my first season. Both these poor fellows were without the means of paying their *pension.* Their landlady good-naturedly allowed them to lodge on promise of future payment, but was too poor herself to provide them with board ; so they used to sit like two hungry wolves looking on whilst my friend took his meals, and gladly accepted any morsel he in pity bestowed on them. Any Christian heart must be moved to compassion, reflecting on the deprivations endured by such as are brought up in poverty ; but that pity must be surely deeper for those who, having been brought up amidst plenty, are reduced by untoward circumstances to the very verge of death from starvation. Do those who pay their franc for an evening's amusement ever reflect on the terrible wound they are inflicting on a fellow creature, striving to entertain them against lack of bodily strength from want of nourishment, when they meet his efforts with contempt and derision ? It *may be* just. It *is* brutal! Thank God, it is not our practice in England!

At the Carcano I heard Pacini's ' Saffo '—to say the least, a somewhat dry work—with Carolina Sannazzaro, one of the exceptions I mentioned above, a talented artist, with a small but sympathetic voice, who played and sang the part of 'Saffo' exceedingly well, especially the last scene. The tenor in the same opera, as also the Manrico in 'Il Trovatore,' was a corpulent gentleman, with a well-developed nasal organ of roseate hue ; and a podgy baritone (I noticed that the tenors and baritones had a decided inclination to obesity), whom the English students nicknamed 'Punch,' from an unmistakable likeness he bore to that famous personage, played the Conte di Luna in 'Il Trovatore,' and Ezio in Verdi's 'Attila.' They were two Stentors ; they literally hurled the notes at the ears of the audience, who clearly showed that they did not appreciate such wanton waste of energy. I felt sorry their efforts were thrown away, yet it was a consolation to me to find that mere volume of sound did not suffice to captivate the sympathy of the public ; my pipe of itself would have stood little chance against such clarions as theirs. The other exception was Giovanni Battista Antonucci, a very good bass, who succeeded in gaining a high position in Italy ; he was a member of Mapleson's company the last year I belonged to it, when he played Beltramo, Marcello, Sarastro, etc., with great success.

I considered it my duty to hear as much music as possible, but so much of the same class became monotonous. I always had more affection for the dramatic than the lyric stage, and it occurred to me that, by paying a little attention to the drama, I might combine instruction with amusement as well there as at the opera. A dramatic company, under the direction of Gasparo Pieri, occupied the Teatro Rè.

Among its members it numbered several good actors and actresses, notably Pieri himself, one of the best eccentric comedians I have seen ; Giuseppina Casali, the leading lady, afterwards Pieri's wife ; Carlo Romagnuoli, a good juvenile tragedian ; and the now world-renowned tragic luminary, Tommaso Salvini, who only appeared for a few nights. I saw him in a melodrama entitled ' I due Sargenti,' and I shall ever regret I missed seeing him in his grand impersonation of ' Saulle,' in Alfieri's tragedy. He could not have been more than twenty-five, but with his noble voice and commanding presence, united to rare histrionic genius, cultivated under Modena, the Italian Edmund Kean, he had already become one of the greatest tragedians the world has produced. The company, always good, were especially so in the representation of some of Goldoni's comedies. As the hero in ' Il Bugiardo,' and Paon Togn in ' Le Baruffe Chiozzotte,' Pieri was inimitable ; as also in ' Box and Cox,' which farce I saw then for the only time in my life. One of the dramas, which I enjoyed very much, was founded on an episode in the life of Goldoni, who is the principal character in the piece, entitled ' Goldoni e le sue sedici commedie.' The first scene takes place in Goldoni's study, the second in a *caffè*, the third on the stage of a theatre during the rehearsal of one of his comedies, and the last in the green-room, whilst the first performance is going on. It is full of the flavour of Venice, minus that of her canals. My ardent desire to see it acted on its ' native heath ' was fulfilled a few years ago. I arrived in Venice one evening with some friends ; whilst enjoying a fragrant weed at a *caffè* I mentioned my desire. The next morning, the first thing which attracted my attention as I started out of the hotel was an announcement that 'Goldoni e le sue sedici commedie' would be played that evening by Bellotti-Bon's company. We booked places, went, saw, and enjoyed it thoroughly, and oh, what a crowd of recollections it conjured up!

I took a stall at the Teatro Rè for the half season, about six weeks, where I could enjoy myself at my ease every night in the week, including Sunday, at a cost of about threepence per night. At first I had some difficulty in following the play, but after a fortnight my ear became so accustomed, I could catch every word, and I no longer perceived I was listening to a foreign language.

Except for the performance of 'Giovanni Giscala,' and that of the unhappy 'Faliero,' I had neglected my operatic friends entirely. The Teatro Rè closed after Tuesday in Holy Week, so I was free to attend the two concerts at the Scala. The secular concert was not remarkable in any way. I thought 'Il Deserto' a trifle dull, but I fancy the performance cannot have been good, as on hearing it again more recently I found it a very interesting work. At the second concert the 'Stabat Mater' was fairly well executed, in spite of the conducting, which amused me highly. The chorus was conveniently arranged on the stage, divided by a gangway through which the principal artists passed in and out ; the orchestra occupied its usual place, Cavallini at his post at the back of the orchestra, not close to the stage, as with us ; while in front of the stage sat the '*maestro concertatore*' at the piano, and in front of each wing of the chorus stood a sub-conductor.

Cavallini and the *maestro* at the piano beat time throughout, and all four in the choral parts—and not always together. The result I leave to the imagination of those who know something about choral performances. The selection from Mendelssohn's ' St. Paul' was a decided ' frost'; nobody concerned in the execution seemed to have the slightest idea of movement or expression ; the chorus ' How happy and blest are they ' was dragged so fearfully that the theme was entirely lost ; and the air ' O God, have mercy' was simply murdered.

I put in an appearance at one of the masked balls, which are given towards the end of the Carnival, dressed as a ' *débardeur*,' at least, so the tailor said from whom I hired the costume for five zwanzigers. I wore a mask, and thus could observe without being observed, and hear without being accused of eavesdropping ; and I observed and heard several curious things. The merriment was at times boisterous, but it was at all times good-humoured. There was no horse-play and no drunkenness. A great part of the time I stood in a retired nook listening to the music. Those who have not heard a fine Austrian band play dance music have no idea what charm dance music can effect. I was spell-bound, and forgot all about dancers, masks, everything, until my attention was aroused by the sweet sounds of my native idiom. They proceeded from a masker dressed in what I took to be a quartermaster's uniform ; for a mask he wore a huge pasteboard nose, which covered a great part of his face ; his hat-band bore the name of H.M.S. *Lion.* He was amusing himself talking English to some ladies in a box, who evidently did not understand a word he said.

I followed him until he joined some companions, then accosted him (they were all English), and was introduced to the group with ' I say, boys, here's a compatriot with a devil of an accent '—the Lancashire lad would peep out. I did not know them, nor did they know me, so we agreed to meet at the Caffè dell' Europa the following Sunday, and scrape acquaintance. The day after the ball my nautical friend received notice to quit Milan within twenty-four hours. When he called at the police office to learn the reason why, they told him that foreign officers were not allowed to remain in Milan without depositing certain necessary documents and receiving a 'permit' in exchange. In vain he endeavoured to convince the officials that he was a student, and the dress he wore, except the hat, was the uniform then adopted by the students of the Royal Academy, Hanover Square. Like me, he had to produce a satisfactory certificate to that effect, when he was sent off with a recommendation to discard the suspicious costume and avoid playing pranks for the future.

I kept my appointment the following Sunday, and made myself known to the party I met at the Scala ; two of them I still number among my intimates. Until then I had only met one Englishman since my arrival in Milan; and, to make a bull, he was an Irishman and an adventurer ; he forced himself on me at a *caffè*, where I was in the habit of breakfasting. I should not have been inclined to entertain his acquaintance, but for the opportunity it afforded me of letting my tongue loose after a couple of months of comparative silence. We arranged to meet next day, to take a walk together, when he promised to point out to me some of the places and objects of interest; we had a long stroll, and parted near his domicile. The same afternoon I received a note from him, begging the favour of a loan, and enclosing me a ring, a valuable heirloom, which I was to retain as security. It was a well-worn specimen of real ' Brummagem.' I sent him a five-franc piece and returned the heirloom in a note, in which I explained concisely my objection to a continuance of his acquaintance. I saw no more of him.

Although I was at all times on friendly terms with the English students resident in Milan—never more than eight or ten at that time, now a regiment of goodness knows how many hundreds—I kept aloof from their society, as I was bent on learning to speak and think in Italian. It is not difficult for those whose taste lies in that direction, and who are possessed of a good memory, to acquire the grammar and words of a foreign language from books; but to acquire the accent and idiom, conversation and the power of imitation are absolutely necessary. Naturally, for reasons I have already given, the acquisition of a pure Italian accent is scarcely possible in Milan, but a short residence in Tuscany or Rome will suffice to correct any provincialisms. For the rest, I have found my acquaintance with the Lombard dialects, the result of hearing them so much, and reading Porta's and other works, very useful in my wanderings about the lakes.

I can understand and make myself understood where a native of Rome or Florence could neither do one nor the other. Yet I confess I love to hear the pure language. Tuscan I prefer, though I know I am in the minority ; the language of a Tuscan peasant is a combination of poetry and music.

I had to change my lodgings. I learned from friends that the neighbourhood I resided in was infested with shady characters ; in fact, I often noticed unmistakable specimens of the brigand species prowling about the courtyard (there was no porter's lodge), especially at night. I dined at a little eating-house close by, in the kitchen, an honour conceded to frequenters, a salon being set apart for casual guests. One evening, as I was taking my place, after giving my instructions to the cook, the landlord asked me if I had lost anything, pointing to my side pockets. I felt them, and replied in the negative. ' Because,' said he, ' there was a gentleman trying them just now, and, as I did not wish to make a disturbance, I collared him and put him out quickly into the street !' After that I deemed it quite time to clear out. Through the instrumentality of my Italian master, I found a comfortable apartment, consisting of two rooms on the fourth floor of a house close to the Biblioteca Ambrosiana, exactly over the rooms occupied by Verdi when he wrote ' Nabucco,' for which I paid thirty zwanzigers a month. My landlady was a stout little Jewess, who perpetually talked about her triumphs in various theatres ; she had a daughter, a singer ; her mother acted as cook, and, like Sairey Gamp, dropped more snuff into the victuals than was actually necessary for seasoning purposes. This I learned from future experience, as I did not board in the house until a year later. All my fellow-lodgers were theatrical artists of one class or another; amongst the number, the knight of the 'red banner' in Marino Faliero. When I afterwards became a boarder, we had at one time a male dancer, a nice-looking young fellow who could bound I don't know how high in the air, but totally ignorant of everything beyond his steps; he was accompanied by his mother, who took as much care of him as though he had been the Koh-i-noor. At times the atmosphere of the mansion was charged with music; I remember one morning (I do not know how I could possibly forget it) there was a rehearsal of ' Il Trovatore ' in the landlady's private apartment; two other singers and I were practising scales, etc., in our several rooms; while an organ on wheels and two smaller ones were stationed immediately under the windows, all working away full blast simultaneously. It was rather like Bedlam, but nobody seemed to mind the confusion of sweet sounds; and, after all, it was not worse than a Royal Academy or Conservatorio.

Early in January I made acquaintance with the Lake of Como. It was hardly the season for a visit to the lakes, but I took the opportunity offered by my Italian master to accompany him to Rovenna, a village situated about half-way up Monte Bisbino, where he had a small property, consisting of a comfortable dwelling-house and a few acres of land, covered chiefly with chestnut-trees. It was arranged that we each paid our share of the expenses, and it turned out the

most inexpensive holiday I ever took. As we had to
start early in the morning, and to make sure of being
in readiness, I took a room at an inn near my host's
house. Between anxiety about being up in time and
the noise of some bacchanalians playing at ' Mora ' in
an adjoining room, I scarcely got a wink of sleep, and
felt very loath to turn out at six, on a bitterly cold
morning, with a north wind sharp enough to shave me,
to walk to the railway-station, acting as my own
porter. At the station another companion joined us.
Three hours' journey in a third-class carriage in the
cold and darkness was not a pleasant prospect, but I
improved the time by finishing my night's rest, and
only awoke on our arrival at Camerlata, where the sun
was shining bright and warm, and I soon forgot my
woes in the delightful balmy atmosphere. My host
laid in a supply of comestibles on the way to Como,
where we took a small boat, and crossed the lake ; an
hour's climb landed us at our destination. A sister
and niece of the professor made us welcome, and I
soon found myself perfectly at home. We remained
four or five days—the two other men busy marking
trees to be cut down for timber, and I rambling about
the hills, than which, for me, there is no greater enjoyment. The weather continued very fine, during the
day, from ten until four, like fine spring weather in
England ; indeed, when the sun was high it was more
like summer. I regretted very much I could not
prolong my holiday ; but I found comfort in the reflection that I had not to return to an office stool. The
brief change did me good, and I went to work again
with renewed vigour. My share of the expenses,

including railway and boat fares, amounted to eleven and a half zwanzigers, or eight shillings!

I seldom allowed a day to pass during the whole of my stay in Milan without paying a visit to the cathedral. Frequently I attended High Mass on Sunday. As I had been accustomed to sing in the Catholic church at home, I *went* to hear the music, but I *remained* to hear the sermon. The music was shocking, both composition and execution; how it could be tolerated in such a temple I could not conceive. The conductor was a great nuisance. For *bâton* he used a piece of music twice doubled and folded flat, with which he beat the first two beats of every bar on the book in front of him. In a quick three-four movement the constant flip-flap engrossed the attention; but perhaps that was providential : the wretched singing might have done worse! The sermon I always enjoyed. On several occasions I heard a Capuchin monk, a handsome man, with expressive mouth and eyes full of the fire of enthusiasm. He had a rich, sonorous, and well-modulated voice; he was a master of elocution, and his enunciation was so distinct that, even in that vast area, I never missed a word of his sermon. At times he would make a sweep from one end to the other of the pulpit, which half encircles one of the great columns supporting the dome, so as to command the attention of the whole of his auditors. He made free use of gesture, which was always noble and elegant, without the slightest touch of theatrical display. He was one of the few preachers who have left a lasting impression on me. I hope I profited by his discourse ; I know I did by his oratory.

San Carlo and Sant' Ambrogio, as far as I can recollect, were the only churches at which full choral Mass was performed regularly every Sunday; in the others, except on the feast-day of the saint to whom the church was dedicated, there was seldom any musical performance worthy of attention. Generally, the organist played at intervals music supposed to be appropriate to the different parts of the ceremony; anything more inappropriate than what I have often heard it would be difficult to imagine. Passing the Carmelites one day, I heard the sound of the organ, and entered. About twenty-five girls were receiving confirmation; the organist enlivened the proceedings with selections from ' La Traviata.' In the country places all attempt at propriety was discarded; the organist simply played whatever he could get through, sacred or profane. I have heard the favourite galop from the last new ballet and the last movement of the overture to ' William Tell ' played as voluntaries. At Baveno a few years ago, on the occasion of a wedding, Mass being performed, at the Elevation (the most solemn moment) we were regaled with ' Largo al factotum,' from ' Il Barbiere di Siviglia '! The music in our Catholic churches at home would bear reformation, the execution generally leaving a great deal to be desired; however, we try to find compositions appropriate to the solemnity of the Holy Sacrifice.

CHAPTER VIII.

APART from the religious observance of Church
festivals, there are others, sometimes very curious ones,
whose connection with the subject of the festival
would, it appears to me, be difficult to trace. What
has plum-pudding to do with Christmas Day? The
inventor of it must have been copper-lined, or have
had wicked designs upon his fellow-creatures. It is a
stodgy complement to a solid dinner of roast beef and
goose, or turkey with plenty of stuffing, sausages, etc.
I have seen a clerical gentleman dispose of about a
couple of pounds at half-past one lunch, and, after
a walk of five miles, dine at five. He exists still, a
living wonder! One of the best plum-puddings I
ever partook of was at the Fonda de las Cuatro
Naciones at Barcelona. It was made by an Italian
cook, who had evidently modified the recipe given

him by an English traveller ; it did not require a
'patent digester' to convert it into wholesome food
(chyle). At Easter, in my youthful days, before
digestive pills formed a part of my 'domestic economy'
(perhaps one of the reasons for requiring them), we
were regaled with 'bun-loaf,' a baked edition of plum-
pudding, and about as digestible.

The feast of San Giorgio in Milan was kept on
bread-and-milk, an improvement, as far as digestion
and nourishment are concerned, on the cloying Christmas pudding. The feast was celebrated in the different
osterias outside the city, and I was conducted to one
enclosed in an extensive garden. On entering we
were presented with a bowl and spoon each for our
use whilst we remained. We wandered about armed,
until one attendant filled our bowls with milk, and
another handed us a hunk of bread, whereupon we
joined in the revels. The grounds were crowded,
everybody laughing and chatting with everybody else,
no introduction necessary, all the time plying their
spoons as if preparing for a famine. I could not help
wondering what my parents would have said, could
they have beheld their infant distending himself with
bread-and-milk (to which they knew he was not
partial), instead of consuming the evening candle over
his studies. There were only a few, otherwise indis-
posable, children ; there must have been some
hundreds of adults assembled in that place alone.

The lay observance of the feast of Sant' Angelo
struck me as being still more curious. From dawn
until after midnight every available nook and corner,
every *piazza*, intra- and extra-mural, was covered with

booths and stalls piled up with whistles of every description. I could not have believed it possible to produce so many at one time. Nobody dreamt of being satisfied with a single instrument of torture; they bought sufficient to cram their pockets, besides as many as they could hold in their hands and between their jaws. The boys seemed to vie with each other in stretching their mouths so as to hold and perform on the greater number at once. In the quarter of Sant' Angelo the traffic was incredible and the noise excruciating. The 'nonconformists' were all provided with cotton-wool to stop their ears; I was advised to do the same, but I thought it was a joke, and, neglecting the precaution, had to adopt the more inconvenient and ineffectual plan of jostling my way through the crowd with my thumbs stuffed in my ears. It was worse than passing through an avenue of trees infested with cicalas on a hot summer day. I must confess I am not sufficient of a poet to imagine what connection exists between whistles and Sant' Angelo.

Turning from the ridiculous to the sublime, the feast of Corpus Christi was celebrated with great pomp. On that day and the two following all shops were closed and business suspended. Two or three days previously a crowd of workmen was employed decorating the Duomo, and erecting a *baldacchino* from the doors to those of Sant' Ambrogio, about half a mile long. Pontifical high mass was celebrated in the presence of the whole clergy, secular and regular, belonging to the diocese, and a crowd of worshippers and spectators. The steps and a great part of the *piazza* were filled with people who were not fortunate enough to gain admittance. Mass ended, the clergy-men and religious orders, headed by the Archbishop bearing the Host, the monsignori, canons, deacons, and sub-deacons, followed by the united bands of the two principal Austrian regiments and a vast concourse of people, marched in solemn procession bareheaded to Sant' Ambrogio, the clergy and people singing the hymn 'Pange lingua,' and the bands playing alternately. I saw the start, and taking a short cut, arrived at Sant' Ambrogio in time to secure a place in the church. The procession entered by the cloisters, and passed slowly along the nave, and out at the opposite end ; as the band followed, they played the march from 'Il Profeta.' It was the most imposing and impressive ceremony I ever witnessed.

Picture-galleries, museums, libraries, or exhibitions never possessed much attraction for me. I did not visit the Ambrosian Library nor the Brera Galleries until I returned to Milan in 1865. I delight in open-air recreation, of which I had enjoyed very little during my school and business days. My daily routine was as follows : The morning I devoted to study ; about mid-day I turned out for my 'constitutional,' whatever the weather might be. Unless very wet, I made my round of the bastions, and generally made a short halt at the Piazza d'Armi to rest and feast my eyes on the grand panorama of the mountains about the Lake of Como, backed by the snow-clad peaks of the loftier mountains beyond. In the foreground I had the ' Arco della pace,' which, spite of its artistic beauty, irritated me, as it obstructed in some measure the view of what gave me infinitely more pleasure. In the afternoon I had a lesson three times a week ; the other days I did some work at home, and then amused myself strolling about the city for a couple of hours, avoiding the aristocratic neighbourhoods, a monotonous series of stone walls, embellished with occasional grated windows, all that might be interesting being hidden from the public gaze. Many of the fine mansions (*palazzi*) of the nobility possess gardens of considerable extent, small parks in fact, hardly conceivable in a city built so compactly. Through the courtesy of a lodge-keeper, I have had my curiosity gratified with a peep at one or two. My favourite haunts were the plebeian quarters, where I found an infinite variety of entertainment : the shops, the names over them, the wares sold in them ; the odd variety of articles on sale at the same shop, for instance, salt, tobacco, stamped paper and postage stamps ; the stalls of fruit, fried fish, *polenta*, roasted chestnuts, ices, drinks cold or hot, according to the season, haberdashery, ironmongery, toys, etc. ; the bargaining between buyer and seller, often assisted by disinterested lookers-on ; the hunch-backs and other deformities, for which, until I had seen more of the South of Europe, I imagined Milan held a patent ; the canal boats of antediluvian construction ; the altercations, which I always expected to end in murder, but which were 'all sound and fury, signifying nothing.' One thing I never saw during my two years' residence, neither a man nor a woman drunk.

During the hot weather in July and August I used to rise early, from five to half-past, and stroll about in the public gardens until breakfast-time ; then, in the afternoon, I took a siesta before dinner. As the days grew longer, I preferred passing the evening in the fresh air rather than in the close atmosphere of a theatre. One moonlight night I discovered, or think I did, as I never found anyone else who had noticed it, the most advantageous view of the cathedral I know— from the bastions, almost in a line with the Conservatorio, besides which, and a few small dwelling-houses nearer the walls, there was no building to be seen except the Duomo, every pinnacle and ornament clearly defined, and white as snow.

An accident happened to me one summer morning that caused me no little grief when I reflected on my limited banking account. At Easter I mounted a 'darlin' pair o' bags,' as Mickie in the gallery of the Theatre Royal, Dublin, remarked to the late Charles Mathews on the stage one night : ' Them's a darlin' pair o' bags, Charlie. Who's your tailor ?' They were of a light colour, and designed to make havoc on the Corso on Easter Sunday, when the female sex all turn out in their best ' bibs and tuckers.' A month or two of wear had shadowed their brightness ; they were sent to the cleaners, who returned them almost restored to their pristine splendour, at the cost of some three shillings. I went to breakfast the first time I wore them again very satisfied with my 'get-up.' I ordered a ragout, with macaroni and tomato sauce. It looked like a juvenile golden sunset, and, oh, what a bouquet ! sufficiently inviting to lead an anchorite astray. Being hungry, I fell to with great vigour ; the table was covered with a cloth, and I had not remarked that the sides were hollowed out, and my plate was simply balanced on the edge. I had only demolished half my breakfast, when I made a dive with my fork, and overturned my plate and its contents into my lap. I lost the tit-bits I had reserved for the last, the golden sunlight illuminated my 'darlin' bags' in a most unpleasant fashion, and I had to walk half-way down the Corso on my way home, a subject of merriment to an unfeeling crowd, and of commiseration to myself.

We do not live to eat, but we must eat to live ! We do not, like other animals, instinctively choose one aliment; and what is food for one is poison for another, so it behoves each of us to observe what quality and quantity of food suits us best, and adhere, as far as lies in our power, to that *régime*. That this study is neglected there is abundant proof in the innumerable pills, powders, tablets, and mixtures used to promote and aid digestion. How often we have to listen to the complainings of the 'martyr to indigestion'! I have been a so-called martyr; I can therefore speak feelingly.

The following remarks I especially address to my young brother and sister singers. How the voice is produced or where, except that it is through the passage of the throat, is unimportant ; it is reasonable to say that the passage must be kept clear, otherwise the sound proceeding from it will not be clear. I have known many instances of singers undergoing very disagreeable operations on their throats for chronic diseases of various descriptions ; now, my observation and experience assure me that, in ninety-nine cases out of a hundred, the root of the evil is chronic inattention to food and raiment. It is a common thing to hear a singer say, ' I never touch such-and-such food on the days I sing.' My dear young friend, unless you are an absolute idiot, you would not partake of anything on the days you sing which might disagree with you, or overtax your digestive powers : it is on the days you do not sing you ought more particularly to exercise your judgment and self-denial. I do not offer the pinched-up pilgarlic who dines off a wizened apple and a crust of bread as a model for imitation ; at the same time, I warn you seriously against following the example of the gobbling glutton who swallows every dish that tempts his palate. I am neither philosopher nor law-giver ; I have no intention of laying down rules for your guidance. Study to know, and adopt those aliments which your own good sense will suggest are good for you *at all times;* protect yourselves from cold or damp, but beware of muffling yourselves like mummies ; avoid talking and laughing in the cold air, especially after singing, and you will not need to trouble the doctor much.

People often ask me, do I believe in alcohol ? As it exists, more or less, in everything I eat and drink, I am bound to believe in it. I presume, if they would speak plainly, they would ask do I drink wine, beer, or spirits ? Wine and beer contain alcohol, but I object to their being called by that name. They contain, besides, many elements beneficial to the human system, and are entitled to an important place among foods. Beer I never liked, and very rarely take. Spirits I care little for, but I find a little ' nightcap ' soothing. Wine I like very much, and took whenever I could get it, which was seldom before I went to Italy; since then regularly, both at lunch and dinner.

I find it does me good; but I cannot undertake to prescribe for others; I leave you to learn and adopt what your own sense will suggest is good for you.

I used occasionally to indulge in a day's relaxation—I cannot call it holiday, for every day was to me a holiday then—and take a run into the country, accompanied by one or both of the young Navas. Monza was our favourite resort; it is a pretty, clean town; the cathedral is a fine church, containing some objects of interest, among the rest the iron crown with which Napoleon I. crowned himself. The greater part of the day we spent in the royal park, wandering about admiring the numerous specimens of plants and trees, native and foreign, or lolling in their shade enjoying a pleasant chat. About five we adjourned to an inn, and after a good dinner returned home in the cool of the evening. We used to hire a horse and trap for the day, which cost some five shillings and the horse's feed; one of us drove, and though we were not great whips, we ran no risks, as the road was pretty straight and level, and the horse required little management beyond keeping him on his legs. It was not an extravagant outing, the whole expenses amounting to ten or eleven shillings. My English friends were in the habit of making similar excursions, and a ludicrous adventure happened to a party of them one night returning from Pavia. They did not start until ten o'clock, and, as the roads were not lighted and there was no moon, they had to drive slowly; suddenly the horse went lame, and at last came to a dead stop; one of them jumped out to see what was the matter, and in doing so kicked something lying in the road, which jingled like metal ; he stooped and picked up a horseshoe. The mystery was solved : the horse had cast a shoe ; and so they all dismounted and led the poor beast until they came to a forge. After half an hour's knocking and parleying (it was then past midnight), the blacksmith came down and prepared to repair the damage, when, to his rage and the travellers' astonishment, he found all four shoes intact, and the one they found big enough for a horse twice the size of that they were driving. A stone had got embedded in one hoof, which caused the animal's distress. It was speedily removed, and after appeasing the smith's wrath with a few zwanzigers they started afresh, and arrived in Milan at six in the morning.

My summer work terminated with the close of the Conservatorio for the vacation. The examinations occupied some days, after which there was an exhibition by the advanced students, vocal and instrumental. Once every three years the pupils who were leaving to commence their public career had an opportunity of appearing in an opera. In 1856 an opera was expressly written by Pollini (one of the party disturbed by the police at the Pozzo, described in an early chapter), entitled ' L'Orfana Svizzera,' a melodious, unpretentious work.

The principal parts were sustained by Isabella Alba, soprano, L'Orfana ; Christoforo Fabbris, light tenor, the lover ; Giuseppe Limberti, robust tenor (as there was no baritone sufficiently advanced to take it), his rival ; and Capponi, bass, a hermit. The chorus consisted of the younger scholars, and the band of the instrumental students and their professors, under the direction of Cavallini.   The opera, followed by a short concert, in which Luigia Perelli and others performed, was given three times.   I was present twice, and was much pleased with the performance, which, on the whole, was highly creditable.   Isabella Alba, a very charming singer and intelligent actress, I thought was destined to rise to a high position, but an affection of the throat compelled her to abandon the stage after a short career, when she married Angeleri, the head of the pianoforte school, and devoted herself to teaching.   The two tenors were fair singers, but being in bad health, unfortunately, could not do themselves justice ; they both sang with success some years after in South America.   Of Luigia Perelli and Capponi I have already spoken.

I had several acquaintances among those who took part in the performances.   My most intimate was Luigi Rivetta, flautist and pianist, whom I constantly met at the Maranis', where he took part in our musical entertainments.   He was one of the best-tempered individuals I ever knew.   After the excitement attendant on the breaking-up had subsided, he and I arranged to take a little trip ; he suggested Lecco as an inexpensive place within our means. Accordingly we decided on passing a week there together.   I was desirous of taking a longer holiday, and as he could not stay more than a week, I arranged with Davide Nava to join me as my guest for a day or two, and on our return journey spend the remainder of an additional week with the Maranis at Desio, where they had a country residence.   Strict economy being necessary, we made the journey from Milan outside the coach, a rickety machine drawn by three bony steeds; barring the dust and an occasional shower of stones, with which the rude young villagers we passed on the road saluted us, we enjoyed a very pleasant drive for half-a-crown each. We put up at the Croce di Malta, a good old-fashioned, rough-and-ready inn; the bedrooms scantily furnished according to English notions, but perfectly clean and comfortable. They would have had us take our meals in the *sala*, as honoured guests, but we preferred the lower regions, among the familiars, where we could select our dishes in the raw state and superintend their preparation, and so sharpen our appetites, if need were, with the contemplation of the delicacies we were about to consume. We had more fun, too; we were soon on familiar terms with the proprietor, frequenters, cook, household, and the dog that turned the spit; the cook was as pleased to attend to our elaborate instructions as we were with his attentions to our creature comforts, and fed us well; the master, seeing we were interested in and satisfied with his endeavours to please, took interest in us, and placed us on a familiar footing with regard to charges; our expenses, for bed, two substantial meals with wine, lights, and attendance, did not exceed five zwanzigers—three shillings and six-pence—per day.

I have done a fair amount of travelling, and had much experience of hotel life in Europe, America and the Australasian Colonies; but for comfort and good living, combined with economy, I never fared so well as in Italy. I must add, however, that latterly English and American travellers have spoiled the large hotels in the principal cities to a great extent. Three years ago I made a short hasty tour in the North of Italy. At Venice, where I arrived after the *table d'hôte* was over, as I wanted to dine immediately, I was served from what remained. Ox-tail soup and roast beef and Yorkshire pudding are very good fare in England, but who that has ever eaten a good Italian dinner could relish ox-tail soup and roast beef and Yorkshire pudding in Venice? I remonstrated with the waiter, who told me my countrymen would not touch Italian dishes, so it was useless to provide them. However, he made amends next day; at his instigation the cook sent me up a dinner after his own heart—and mine! At Bologna nobody in the hotel knew the names of ordinary Italian dishes (the cook was not Italian), let alone how to prepare them; and at Florence the food was as limited in quantity as it was inferior in quality; the fowls seemed to have been born with half a dozen legs apiece, and reared on pebbles.

Except one very wet day, we were out in the open air from breakfast until dinner-time on the lake; or roaming about the hills, or visiting the spots made famous by Manzoni in 'I Promessi Sposi.' It happened to be the time of the *fiera*, so we were able to while away the evening at the opera. The theatre was very pretty, and the company very fair for a place numbering some 4,000 inhabitants; the admission was only seventy-five centimes, with a small additional fee for reserved places. I have heard and taken part in worse performances, although with better artists, in many of our provincial towns, more than ten times the size of Lecco. The wet day we were obliged to pass in doors, as it rained in torrents ; we had no books or other means of amusing ourselves ; cards I abominate, and I never learned to play billiards. Rivetta was a smoker, so to pass the time he proposed I should join him in a weed ; I did not like to attack a strong Virginia, and procured a couple of choice Havanas (' Regalia de Cabagio '), which kept me employed for some time ; we had still two or three hours to get through before dinner-time, so as my friend wanted shaving, and could not perform the operation himself, I proposed that I should do it for him. After some demur he submitted ; he had a nice fat face suitable for a first attempt, but I suppose I must have been slightly nervous, for, in finishing off the first side, I managed to take off a slice of cheek ; he would not allow me to proceed, and as he could not appear at dinner 'half done,' he ran over to the barber's to have his wound plastered and the other side shaved. I had the taste of choice Havana in my mouth all day, and dreamt I was making a meal of it in the night, which put me off smoking for some years. I have never tried to shave anyone except myself since.

At the week's end Rivetta went away and Nava joined me. He had never been near mountains or on the water before, and lived in the constant dread of being crushed by the one or drowned in the other. He was struck with astonishment at the sight of a barge with her only sail set, making about two knots an hour, and asked me if we had such large vessels at Liverpool. I am afraid I was somewhat cruel to him ; he was not shod for mountain climbing, and preferred mooning about in a *caffè;* however, I induced him to accompany me part of the way up Monte Bara; he was greatly impressed with the scenery, which he acknowledged amply repaid him for the fatigue he underwent.

According to promise, we stopped at Desio. The Maranis had a number of mutual acquaintances staying at their house; there were no walkers among them, so by day I had to be my own companion; in the evening we sang, danced, or played round games of cards or dominoes; the few days we spent there made an agreeable finish to our little holiday.

The last time I met Rivetta, he was conducting a very good orchestra at the Caffè Cova, in Milan. Davide Nava died of consumption a few years after I returned to England.

CHAPTER IX.

My holiday time had now come to an end; I had to turn my attention seriously to business. Before the vacation I had sung to Bonola, the principal agent, in the hope of securing an engagement; the theatres for which he catered, however, were beyond my capabilities, consequently I had to aim lower. A lady who was about to make her *début* at Pavia the ensuing Carnival, and with whom I had sung occasionally at a friend's house, hinted at the possibility of my being engaged at the same theatre. I called upon the agent who was forming the company, and sang Zaccaria's air from 'Nabucco,' accompanied by my master, whom I left to hear the result. I felt much disappointed and depressed when he told me the agent did not approve either of my voice or my singing. I could not expect my father would supply me with any more money, and as my funds were fast dwindling away, I began to feel my position was growing desperate. I did not know then, and I believe never shall know, the tricks of the trade. After a week or two of suspense, I had the felicity of signing my first engagement, not a fat one, barely enough to subsist on, but I was truly thankful for it. The terms were three hundred zwanzigers (about ten guineas) and half a clear benefit; the Carnival lasted seven weeks, and I had to be at Pavia two weeks before for the rehearsals. Salaries were paid in quarters; the first on arrival, the second after the third performance, the third on completion of half the season, and the fourth three days before the close of the engagement. The benefits were to be taken in rotation, beginning with the *prima donna* and ending with the bass. The theatre at Pavia would have been handsome if tastefully decorated; being entirely constructed of stone, it was difficult to sing in; the stage was not overclean and the dressing-rooms were like pigsties, a common fault in almost all the theatres I have had anything to do with. It is strange so little attention should be bestowed on the health and comfort of those on whose work artistic and pecuniary success both depend.

There were only three operas to be given during the season, ‘La Traviata’ and ‘Ernani’ (Verdi), and a new opera written and composed expressly by two students of the university, entitled ‘Lamberto Malatesta.’ The lady I mentioned was our *prima donna*, and proved very successful; at the close of the season she married a gentleman of Pavia and gave up the profession. The last opera required two *prime donne*, for which another lady was engaged; being somewhat *passée*, her efforts were not appreciated. There was no contralto part in any of the operas.

Our tenor was the most conceited donkey I ever encountered, and I have met with some fair specimens. Had the baritone and I changed places, it would have been the better for both of us ; but he was averse to coming down, and I afraid of going up, so we kept to the colours we had chosen. He could not sustain the baritone register in Verdi's operas, though he was a fair singer. After we had played the ‘ Traviata ’ a few nights his voice gave way, and I was asked by the manager to take his place, in order to avoid closing the theatre. I had heard the music performed and rehearsed so often that I already knew the part fairly well ; however, I declined to sing it unless requested by the baritone himself. I called to see him, and, after a few unpleasant remarks, he told me I could not sing it. I was nettled, and I determined to prove he was wrong. I sang it the same evening, and obtained such a success that the manager desired me to supplant him altogether, and take the part of Carlo Quinto in ‘ Ernani.’ This I would not listen to—he was a struggling beginner like myself ; we were good friends, and I did not feel inclined to assist in any tricks to get rid of him. He did not attempt Carlo Quinto, so another baritone was expressly engaged for the part ; this was the only member of our company that ever appeared in London, where I saw him at the end of 1857 at St. James's Theatre, during a season of Italian *opera buffa*, of which Alberto Randegger acted as conductor. We had also a second lady, who looked fifty, and said she was not out of her ‘ teens ’ ; a second tenor, and a second bass, who used to recount to me in confidence his numerous triumphs in *buffo* parts. His appearance was anything but jovial ; indeed, he seemed as though ' Melancholy had marked him for her own ' ! The chorus, except three ladies from Milan, was native, and the orchestra was composed chiefly of semi-professionals—the principal oboe was a student of law.

The *seconda donna* and I journeyed by the same *diligence* from Milan to Pavia, she an inside and I an outside passenger. I had been introduced to her by my landlady, whose comrade she had been in her professional days ; if her own statement of her age had been correct, she must have been a baby in arms when she made her *début*. My landlady, with a knowing twinkle in her eye, begged me to take care of her on the journey, though I thought it would have been more natural for her to take care of me, seeing she looked old enough to be my grandmother. She was evidently relieved from great anxiety on my account when she found we were to be separated ; I was delighted, though I hypocritically concealed my joy. Her appearance was, to say the least, grotesque. I could not help fancying her hip-joints had grown outside the flesh ; they turned out to be two flat-irons, which, to save room in her trunk, she was in the habit of carrying attached to the waistband of her petticoat under her dress when travelling ! On our arrival at Pavia they were produced at the barber's, where she lodged, amid a great deal of blushing and giggling.

I took a room in the house of a respectable lady, another lambkin, who had seen some sixty summers. She was a dark-complexioned, shrivelled little being, with jet-black hair so like a horse's tail that it reminded me of the sofa-coverings of my youth. She, too, evidently feared the power of her attractions on me. Her coyness highly amused me, but I seldom had the chance of enjoying a bit of fun at her expense, as she objected to receive me *en tête-à-tête*, on account of the danger to our youthful hearts. Her name was Luigia (I forget what). Once when I told her Luigia was one of my most favourite names, she was so startled she nearly tumbled into the fireplace. My room was on the ground-floor, and seldom cheered by the sun's rays ; the weather was bitterly cold, and we had snow at times, knee-deep. I preferred passing my evenings at home, and tried lighting a fire, to make myself comfortable, but I had to open the door and windows to avoid being suffocated with smoke, so after a few nights I reluctantly availed myself of a snug corner at the *caffè*.

We commenced the rehearsals of the ' Traviata,' in which I was to make my *début* as the Doctor, immediately. They were numerous, long, and irritating from the small amount of earnestness displayed by the singers, excepting the *prima donna*. I had very little to do, and soon grew weary of going over the same few bars twice a day. On account of the absence of the students during the vacation, we did not open until the 1st of January, 1857, by which time, to my astonishment, although we must have had between thirty and forty rehearsals, we were all ready. First nights I have always found depressing ; unless I am engaged in the performance I always avoid them. On this occasion I had no fear on my own account ; I had no responsibility, but I was very anxious about my nervous comrades. I had not a hair on my face, and, when made up, looked more like a youthful page than a staid doctor, spite of my sombre costume.

The audience, a very capricious one, expressed their satisfaction with vigorous applause ; the *prima donna*, who sang and acted the part of Violetta very well, at once established herself as a favourite, a position she maintained and strengthened as the season advanced the tenor 'got through '; the baritone showed he possessed talent, though the music was too high for him. Whilst he was indisposed I sang the part of Germont (father) three nights, after which the tenor induced me to join him in sending a notice of our success to a musical journal in Florence, his native place, in which, for the sum of five francs, my share of the cost of insertion, I figured as the legitimate successor to Tamburini. In 'Ernani' I essayed the *rôle* of Don Silva. The costumes were provided by the manager, but the small articles of dress we had to find. I laid in a stock in Milan, which consisted of one imitation lace and one plain linen collar ; two ballet shirts ; one black and one white ostrich feather ; one pair black and one pair white silk, and one pair red worsted tights ; a pair of black velvet shoes ; and a pair of shiny leather leggings, fitting on my ordinary walking boots to imitate high boots, all of which, except the red tights, I pressed into the service of Don Silva. The barber made me up very red, as he said I must look like a fiery old gentleman. At first I wore a moustache and imperial, held by elastics round my ears, but they felt very insecure. I was afraid of swallowing them every time I opened my mouth wide, and I did not approve of the mark the elastic left on my face, so I resorted to ordinary gum (spirit gum was not known there); washing it off scarified my lips, but, finding it safer, I suffered in silence. I do not know what impression my singing made on the audience—not unfavourable, I think, as they applauded me when opportunity occurred; but I feel sure they must have found ample food for merriment in my representation of a Spanish grandee. Dick, Tom and Harry were not photographed in those days as they are now; besides, I doubt whether there was a photographer in Pavia, or I might be able to amuse myself and friends still with my 'make up.'

The third opera, 'Lamberto Malatesta,' came to grief. The libretto was not bad, but the music was wretched. We had plenty of rehearsals, but the tenor never learned the third act, and had but a hazy notion of the first and second. The season was drawing to a close, but the managers were bound to fulfil their obligations to the subscribers, and the opera had to be performed, perfect or imperfect. Being the work of two students, nobody doubted that their schoolfellows would ensure its favourable reception; but students, comrades though they be, are not to be conciliated with chaff; there must be a few grains of wheat mingled with it. Throughout the first two acts the rumblings of an approaching tempest grew louder and more frequent; the curtain fell on the second amid tumultuous expressions of disapprobation; at the commencement of the third I was discovered in the centre of the stage between the rival *prime donne;* each had a short passage to sing, which was uproariously applauded by her partisans and outrageously hooted by her enemies. The storm then burst in all its fury. For twenty minutes we stood unable to proceed with the opera ; at length, finding there was no possibility of restoring order, the Commissioner of Police came round from the front and ordered the curtain to be lowered ; he very politely expressed deep regret that we should have been subjected to such violent treatment, and dismissed us. The sequel threatened to be most disastrous ; my benefit did not come off ; the subscribers would not be satisfied with the reproduction of the ' Traviata ' and ' Ernani,' nor was there time to prepare another opera ; the managers made this an excuse for not disbursing the last quarter's pay. What was to be done ? After various suggestions, the baritone and I agreed to wait on the Mayor and plead for his intercession. We found him at home, a very genial, kind-hearted old gentleman. He listened patiently to our story, and requested us to call again in the evening, by which time he would arrange what he could do on our behalf. On our return he informed us that there were four or five masked balls still due to the subscribers, which would also be a source of great profit to the managers ; he had, therefore, sent them notice that, unless all money due to the singers and others employed in the opera were paid, and their acknowledgment sent to him by twelve o'clock next day, the police would not allow the theatre to be reopened that season. The order was complied with, we were all paid, and, after calling to thank our friend in need, I returned to Milan.

My first Christmas Day in Italy I spent alone at

Milan.   Except the respective waiters at the *café*
where I breakfasted, and the *osteria* where I dined,
I did not speak to a human being the whole day.   I
had a solitary walk in the afternoon, dined alone,
returned home, and read until bed-time.   My second
I spent more socially at Pavia.   The landlord of the
inn where I dined regularly invited me and any others
of the frequenters who were not otherwise engaged
to eat our Christmas dinner with him.   Everybody
belonging to the household sat down to table with us,
from the landlord to the stable-boy ; the cook joined
us during the intervals when his presence in the
kitchen was not necessary, the landlord's sons and
daughters waited on us.   Dish succeeded dish, until
I found my waistcoat growing uncomfortably small.
There was abundance of excellent wine of various
kinds from the vineyards on the other side of the
Ticino, to which all were free to help themselves
without restriction as to quantity ; yet not one indulged in the slightest excess.   The food was of first-
rate quality, well cooked ; and the 'made' dishes
cunningly prepared to tempt the most delicate appetite.   It was a bonny feast, given with a welcome that
would have gladdened the heart of the veriest churl ;
it was no spurt to inveigle guests.   The daily table,
although less elaborate, was equally well served ;
there were always ample rations of the best kind at a
small cost.   For my dinner, with a pint of good wine,
I paid, except on rare occasions, from 10d. to 1s.
True, the tables were of plain deal, the table-cloths
and napkins were of coarse linen ; but they were
invariably clean when we sat down to dine.   The

medical students were fond of airing their scientific knowledge with regard to aliment. A young curly-headed philosopher, fresh from a lecture in which the professor had touched on the digestibility of flesh-meat, entered one day, and, with an air of great wisdom, ordered a veal cutlet, raw, to be served up with oil, vinegar, and fine herbs—a cannibalistic order which made us all stare. The cutlet came. It could not see, or it would have pitied the poor youth making desperate efforts to hide his nausea; but it conquered! After bolting a few small mouthfuls he had to throw up the sponge, and, with a pale countenance, acknowledge his defeat. I need hardly say for some time he was a butt for the shafts of his companions' playful sarcasm.

I presume modern taste and the exigencies of increase of traffic and speed of travelling necessitate the change which has been made in hotels of late years; yet I cannot but regret the gradual disappearance of quiet, comfortable hostelries I used to frequent—most of them have either been demolished or else so modernized as to be no longer recognisable. Hotel-keeping is a business, and one ought not to murmur if it is managed strictly on business principles; but I miss the host's cheerful welcome and attentions, and I do not find in modern hotels any compensation for their loss. Nearly all our large railway stations are fronted by hotels; I do not find that any means whatever are adopted, or even tried, to deaden the noise of the rolling of trains and screeching of engine-whistles! The traveller is still annoyed by the porter thundering at the door of a neighbour starting by an early train ; surely it would not be difficult to contrive a plan for abolishing this nuisance ! If he arrive late at night and hungry, most probably he will have to be content with the hacked remains of a cold joint, or a limb of a dried-up fowl ; or perhaps with nothing more than a dry biscuit and a glass of spirits, or go to bed fasting. If he wants a bath, he must wait while the chambermaid or porter prepares it, and pay 1s. 6d. or 2s. for it. If he drinks wine, he must pay an exorbitant price for it ; and the contents of the bottles are not always accurately described on the labels. He must pay attendance charged in his bill, and fee the waiter and chambermaid besides.

Advancement in extent of accommodation ought to be accompanied by proportionate advancement in appliances for the traveller's comfort and repose, and in the regulation of the scale of charges according to the entertainment he receives.

CHAPTER X.

I RETURNED to my old quarters, where I arranged to
board and occupy a single room for one hundred
zwanzigers a month.   I had little more than one
hundred zwanzigers in my possession, seventy-five of
which I handed to my landlady on account of my first
month's board and lodging.   I called immediately
upon the friends through whose instrumentality, in-
directly, I obtained my engagement ; they were going
to a masked ball at the Scala, and pressed me to
accompany them.   I tried to excuse myself ; I felt too
depressed with the dismal prospect before me to be
inclined to make merry, and it was hard to part with
five zwanzigers out of my limited store.   However,
false shame prevented me acknowledging my position,
and I joined them.   The Emperor and Empress of
Austria, accompanied by the Emperor and Empress of

Mexico, were present. The theatre was '*illuminato a giorno*' (illuminated to day-light) ; and when the imperial party entered their box, a shower of small parachutes of various hues, weighted with packets of bonbons, descended from the gallery, and were eagerly seized by the crowd below. The costumes of the maskers were more than ordinarily striking, and the band played exquisitely, forming altogether a brilliant and interesting *spectacle.* I forgot my troubles in the contemplation of the lively scene, though not for long. I was tired after my journey, and distressing thoughts would obtrude themselves, spite of the distractions around me ; so I retired early.

My living was secure for three weeks, and I had still a little money in my pocket, out of which I hired a piano, paying a month in advance, so that I might continue my studies. I believed I had made a step in my career—albeit a small one—and I determined to do my best to conquer difficulties which at that time I feared were almost insurmountable. My voice, though clear and sonorous, was not of sufficient volume to satisfy agents and others to whom I looked for engagements. I sometimes felt thoroughly disheartened, and inclined to give up all thought of making a name ; yet, when I called to mind instances such as I have cited of singers whose position was the result of artistic execution and feeling, not power of voice, I resolved to make them my models, and, as far as lay in my power, follow in their footsteps. The agent from whom I received my engagement for Pavia gave me great encouragement. I owed him his commission —fifteen zwanzigers. I asked for some money from

home, which was refused.   I then parted with some
of my worldly goods to my Italian uncle (and was considerably done by the friend who transacted the business), and called to pay my debt.   I was very much
taken aback by the agent's kindness ; he told me, if I
were in want of money, he was content to wait until
I could pay him without inconveniencing myself, and,
which gave me much greater satisfaction, that he had
seen me twice or thrice in ' Ernani,' and was much
pleased with my performance.   He then offered me
an engagement for a month at Padua, which, after
looking through the operas to be performed, and
finding some passages in one of them, as I thought,
too high for me, I declined.   I acted very foolishly, I
admit, but I feared being over-venturesome with a
public so ready to give expression to its feelings.

The three succeeding months were a time of great
trial.   I had only myself to blame, for I might have
made the money sent me go much further than I did.
I was not extravagant on my own account, but my
companions cost me more than I was justified in
spending.   I continued visiting the Maranis, but I
did not let them know my position, or, I feel sure,
from the unvarying kindness with which they treated
me, they would have helped me out of my difficulties.
I confided in one person only, who had several times
offered me assistance in case I ever found myself in
need of it ; I asked him to lend me a very small sum
to enable me to pay the hire of some music I wished
to study, which he made some lame excuse for refusing.   My board was frugal : a cup of coffee and milk
for breakfast at nine, dinner at four—a fair repast, but

scarcely solid enough for such a hungry stomach as mine ; occasionally I supplemented it with a roll before turning in at night.

One Sunday, returning from the *caffè* where I had called after spending the evening at the Maranis', I met the patrol at the corner of the street where I lived. The sergeant stopped me, and after making sundry inquiries as to who and what I was, finally demanded my *carta di sicurezza*. I had changed my dress before starting out, and left the document at home. I begged him to accompany me to my door, where I would fetch it for him ; but he declined, and I was marched off to the police office like a malefactor by six *gens d'armes*. There, after he had roused a sleepy official, I was detained to undergo a cross-examination which would have been entertaining had it not been so late. The commissioner, more tender-hearted than the sergeant, at last threw on his cloak, and the two accompanied me to my lodgings. They ransacked my drawers, and took away all my papers, requesting me to call for them next morning, when they were returned to me with a caution against re-peating the offence. It is possible I might have saved myself the trouble and annoyance had I tipped the sergeant, but all I was possessed of was one five-franc piece, which I could not make up my mind to part with.

Day after day I called on one agent or another, until I was weary, the invariable answer to my beggar's petition being : ' Nothing for you to-day !' I sang for them if they expressed a wish to hear what I could do, but my youth and voice were everywhere against me.

At times I felt my situation so keenly that I contemplated putting an end to my existence. An occasional gleam of light in the shape of a possible small engagement shone on me ; but some more fortunate or more enterprising individual overshadowed me, and made the darkness gloomier than ever. Sick at heart, after making my rounds, I returned one day to my lodgings ; my landlady, with a beaming countenance, rushed out as soon as she heard my step, and informed me that Orlandi, an agent I had not called on for some days, wished to see me immediately. I did not wait to be told twice, and ran off in a wild state of excitement to find out what slice of luck was in store for me. I accepted his offer before I knew precisely what it was—an engagement for a month at a small theatre, Santa Radegonda, terms one hundred zwanzigers. I then hurried to the theatre and saw the manager, who informed me I was to sing in a new opera, written and composed by a lady, an ex-pupil of the Conservatorio, Carlotta Ferrari. I would have preferred appearing in an opera already known, but the state of my finances would not admit of any dallying. Except that it was entitled ' Ugo,' and that three very good artists took part in it, I recollect little about the work. I was very happy during the rehearsals, for the composer and my comrades all treated me with the greatest kindness and consideration. Achille Errani, the tenor, an excellent singer, and a great favourite with the Milanese, took great pains in assisting me. I afterwards renewed his acquaintance in New York, where he had established himself as a teacher. Each theatre kept a carriage at the disposal of the artists to drive them to and from the rehearsals and performances. After one of our rehearsals, the attendant, closing the door suddenly, crushed one of my fingers ; I did not notice it was bleeding, it was so benumbed, until I arrived at home and found one side of my same 'darling bags' (again restored) smeared with blood, which cost me a heavy sigh. The next time we met, I was horrified to find that my accident had been the cause of ruining the *prima donna's* gown of pale-blue silk beyond redemption. She knew I was poor, and begged me not to be troubled in my mind, at the same time expressing her sorrow at the pain I suffered with a hearty good nature I can never forget. The opera was played three nights ; it contained some effective numbers ; one, a duet for tenor and baritone, created a sensation, and was redemanded each night. My three companions were received with great enthusiasm, and I acquitted myself fairly well. After this I was to have played Germont in the 'Traviata.' The lady who was to play Violetta, however, entertained views which did not coincide with those of the manager—at any rate, he said so ; a dispute arose, which through my impatience terminated in my throwing up the engagement and losing the little pay I might have claimed.

The advent of the long-desired supplies from home relieved me from anxiety. I also received advances from another agent who was desirous of entering into an engagement with me for a period of five years, to sing in any theatre in Italy with which he might contract for the use of my services. The terms proposed were one hundred zwanzigers per month for the first year, with an increase of one hundred zwanzigers per month each succeeding year until the termination of the engagement, out of which I had to pay all my expenses, travelling as well as living, and find the minor wardrobe.   Fortunately for me, the engagement was never concluded.

In the midst of my distress during the three months of 'hard times,' I was not without some consolation ; I found friendly sympathy where I had no reason to look for it.   My landlady behaved most generously ; she never by word or act implied she thought I was imposing on her hospitality, though I was actually living at her expense.   She tried all she could to persuade me to accept the engagement for Padua, and offered to lend me the money to pay my expenses ; and she took the trouble to visit some of the agents with whom she was acquainted to endeavour to excite their interest in my behalf.   I sang one evening at a concert in the crush-room of the Scala, given by a horn-player named De Paoli ; and though I had not paid her a farthing for several weeks, she insisted on preparing a dinner expressly for me, such as she deemed advisable for a singer ; and when at length I was able to clear myself of debt, she was much more rejoiced at my relief from anxiety than at receiving the money I owed her.

I had received my last supply, which with the most rigid economy would not last long ; the prospect of an engagement on which I could subsist was very remote.   I could not afford to share my little with anybody ; therefore, much against my will, I was forced to give up intimacy with my Italian friends.   I had kept aloof from my English ones, and I could not expect they would entertain any regard for me. Here again, however, I met with unlooked-for sympathy, displayed in various friendly actions, mingled at times with a slight degree of pity, which, spite of myself, irritated me. They evidently looked upon me as a weakly traveller, trusting to an obstinate guide, who insisted on leading him by an abandoned path so steep and rugged that, if he reached his destination, it would only be with strength exhausted, instead of the newly-constructed smooth highway, by which he could accomplish his journey without fatigue. I was pained, though I am sure they harboured no ill-natured intentions, at the slighting way in which they spoke of my master. He was behind the time, he was too slow, he was all very well for Rossini, Bellini, Donizetti and the old school, where there was little scope for declamation ; but for the sensational operas of Verdi and the new declamatory school he was of no use. I would like to know how many baritones of that or any time were capable of declaiming (if they could sing them) the parts of Assur ('Semiramide'), Fernando ('La Gazza Ladra'), Maometto Secondo, Dandini (' La Cenerentola') and 'William Tell.' Do people who talk so much about declamation know what they are talking about ? I doubt it in most cases ! Declamation is the art of uttering language, with just emphasis accompanied by appropriate gesture, in order to produce dramatic effect. An isolated scene of a drama may produce a 'sensational effect' if played with extraordinary vigour, pathos, or brilliancy, but unless that scene bears relation to those which precede and those which follow it, it is not a 'dramatic effect.'   So also with a poem or narration ; any isolated passage may produce a sensational effect, but it must bear relation to the remainder of the poem or narration, otherwise it is not a 'dramatic effect ' ; the declamation is false, or, in other words, not declamation at all.   In order to declaim, the dramatic intelligence must be concentrated on the drama, poem or narration as a whole, not as made up of various scenes or phrases. In fact, declamation is the art of 'holding the mirror up to Nature,' which can never be achieved by paying attention to any particular scenes in a drama, however sensational or startling may be the effects produced in them.   Such effects may please the general unthinking public, and draw crowded houses, but they can never satisfy people of artistic intelligence.

Let any member of the latter class examine the parts I have mentioned above, and I feel sure he will acknowledge they all demand declamatory talent of the highest order to do them justice.

Fortunately the engagement for five years was not concluded.   I might have been starved to death before the expiration of the first year, or had I contrived to escape that fate, and fulfilled the contract, the wear and tear would probably have destroyed my voice. However, as I then felt, I would rather have faced those risks than return to England—as I knew I must, unless I could earn sufficient to support myself. I left no stone unturned ; I persecuted the agents, until they must have been as sick of my importunities as I was of importuning.   I thought of turning my fiddling to account ; but there were already plenty of violinists, willing to accept two or three zwanzigers a night without finding employment, to whom I could not hold a candle. I could not afford to attend theatres, so occupied myself indoors studying singing and thorough-bass, and out of doors studying Nature and my fellow-creatures.

At last the time arrived when it was evident I must decide on the course I intended to pursue ; all hope of an engagement for the autumn season had vanished long before—the theatres were already open or about to open. I would have struggled on through three months preceding the Carnival with the smallest certainty in view, but I had not received even the offer of an engagement ; I would have accepted small parts —any parts within my means—by which I could have earned my daily bread, so unwilling was I to leave Italy. With all my troubles, the two years I spent there formed the happiest period of my life. I have no desire to make much of my troubles—thousands of people have had to endure far more than ever it was my lot to suffer ; but they were great troubles to me, inasmuch as they kept ever present in my mind the dread of not being able to pay my way. My ambition was to sing in opera ; I had studied for it, and I desired to remain in Italy, where there were numerous small theatres in which I could have gained stage experience before attempting those of greater importance—in fact, I wished to return to my native land with something of a reputation to back my pretensions to favour.

Early in October, Henry F. Chorley, who was making a tour of recreation, called on me. I had heard a great deal about him, but had never seen him. I expected to find a dark, stern man, with a tendency to domineer ; I was surprised, therefore, to meet a delicate-looking being, with light, sandy hair, a thin, rather squeaky, voice, and a hesitating, shy manner, which I soon discovered was only manner. There was no lack of decision in the expression of his opinions ; he entertained the strongest prejudices of anyone I ever knew, but he was one of the best friends I ever had. As I was not at home when he called, he left a message, in accordance with which I joined him at breakfast next morning, Sunday. It poured with rain, which gave him the opportunity for airing one of his pet prejudices—that the climate and weather in England were as fine as those of any other country in the world. We walked to and fro inside the cathedral for about a couple of hours, discussing my plans and my probable chances of success if I returned to England ; also the state of music in Italy. He did not like the idea of my remaining ; but there was nothing peremptory in the way he urged the advisability of my return to England. I passed the whole of that day with him, and, by appointment, we called together on my master the day following, when I sang several pieces for him—to his satisfaction, I believe, as he then advised me to return with great earnestness ; however, he recommended me to weigh the matter well before deciding. Knowing the position he held in the musical world, I had great faith in his opinion, and made up my mind on the spot. He gave me a letter of introduction to John Hullah, told me he would let me know as soon as he returned to

London, and offered me the use of his purse, which I with heartfelt thanks for his courtesy and thoughtfulness declined. We then parted, he to pursue his journey southward, I to prepare for my journey northward.

I had very few friends to take leave of, the Maranis having gone to the lakes. The day before I left, I met an English student, a baritone, supposed to be the 'coming man'; he was quite irate when I told him I was about starting for home, just as I had placed my foot on the ladder of fame. What could I expect in England? If I could take a part in a glee, I might procure a few engagements, and earn a five-pound note now and then at City dinners, or I might give lessons; but to make a name and position with my meagre talents was out of the question. I think we differed on the subject, but I did not tell him so. When he found I was obstinate or foolish, or both, he poured a flood of pity over my deluded soul, and gave me his parting blessing.

The journey was very tedious; the line by Culoz had only just been opened, of which I did not know, so I took the old route, by rail and *diligence* alternately, to Lyons. Owing to floods, a bridge had been carried away between Novara and Turin, which caused me a delay of twenty-four hours in the latter city, and the expense of food and lodging, which I could ill-afford. A rascally waiter at the hotel where I put up robbed me of five francs, which he declared he had paid for the French *visé* to my passport. When I arrived at Lyons late in the evening, I had scarcely enough money left to pay for a bed; a friendly fellow-traveller, however, shared a room with me, and offered to pay my part if I could not. I was relieved from the necessity of borrowing ; for when I applied at the office of the Messageries Imperiales, instead of a second-class ticket to Paris, they handed me the amount of the fare. I paid my bill, made a substantial breakfast, and travelled third-class. Just as the train was about to start, a labouring man with his wife and seven children entered the compartment I had made up my mind I was going to have all to myself. The day I passed in tolerable comfort ; but between having no pillow myself, acting as one to at least two of the youngsters, and an occasional squabble, I passed a very uncomfortable night. I had not sufficient money left to pay my journey from Paris to London, and threw myself on the mercy of the agents for the route *viâ* Dieppe and Newhaven, who courteously advanced me the ticket on my leaving my portmanteau in pledge with them. The cab-fare from London Bridge to my destination drained my purse. I was back in my native land without a penny to bless myself with, my portmanteau in pawn, tired and hungry—for, with the exception of four meals, I had subsisted on a Milanese sausage and dry bread since I left Novara, five days *en route ;* yet I had only one regret—that I had been obliged to leave Italy.

CHAPTER XI.

I WAS so anxious to be at work that I deferred paying a visit to Liverpool to see my relations and friends until I had taken some steps towards making an appearance in public. My father came up to meet me, and we called together upon John Hullah to present the letter of introduction Chorley had given me. He received us very courteously, and made an appointment to hear me sing. At the time indicated we went to St. Martin's Hall, and were ushered into the large concert-room, where a class was struggling with a *solfeggio.* The novelty and innocence of the proceeding amused me ; I observed that a large number of those present did not open their mouths, and those who did did not produce many musical effects. The class dismissed, I went on the platform to stand my trial. I was introduced to Mrs. Hullah, who accompanied me exceedingly well; she was a very talented woman in her profession and most amiable in private life. I sang the same piece by Rossini I had sung for Chorley in Milan. At the end of it Hullah remarked that, sung by Tamburini, no doubt it would be very interesting; evidently, from his manner of saying it, he found it uninteresting sung by me. He requested me to sing something from an oratorio, suggesting the recitative and aria from the 'Messiah,' 'For behold darkness,' etc., with which I complied. He then said I was better prepared than anyone coming from Italy he had heard for some years, but added the original remark, 'You have still a great deal to learn.' It is now thirty-four years since the observation was made, and I find I have still a great deal to learn, so I am convinced Hullah was right.

When taking leave he told me he would give me a chance of a public hearing as soon as an opportunity occurred, but at present, etc., etc.—the old, old story, as usual, I thought, and did not feel at all elated. My father was much annoyed at what he considered the cavalier, off-hand way in which I had been criticised and dismissed, but he had never had any experience of managers. I sang for J. L. Hatton in the green-room of the Princess's Theatre one morning before rehearsal; I felt much more angry at his offer to put me in the programme at a City dinner than I was at being told I had a great deal to learn.

Chorley returned to London shortly after I came back

from a visit to Liverpool. I frequently dined alone with him, and afterwards accompanied him to the theatre or a concert. One morning I received a message to go round to his house immediately, as he had something of importance to communicate. It was to the effect that Hullah was going to perform the 'Creation,' and was desirous of having different singers for the parts of Adam and Eve from those who represented the angels in the first two parts of the oratorio ; he could not offer me any terms, but if I was satisfied with this opportunity of making an appearance in public he would be pleased to accept my services to sing the part of Adam. Although Chorley begged me to take a few days to consider the offer, I decided at once ; I knew the part well, the music suited me, and I cared nothing about its comparatively minor importance. I went to try over the duet with the lady who was to represent my *malheureuse cotelette ;* I found a lady seated in the drawing-room, who made me a distant though graceful bow on my entrance. After a few moments' hesitation I ventured to remark, ' Miss ——, I presume.' ' No,' she replied, ' I am not Miss —— ; I am Miss Messent, and I understand I am to have the pleasure of singing the duets in the last part of the " Creation " with you ; Miss —— was to have sung them, but for some unexplained reason she has given up the engagement.' The reason, which I only learned some years after, was that Miss —— had made a small reputation already, which she declined jeopardizing by singing duets with a young man fresh from Italy. I dined with Chorley on the evening of the concert, and met Manuel Garcia, who accompanied us to St. Martin's

Hall. I succeeded better than I had dared to hope
I walked home with Chorley and Garcia after the per
formance; the latter expressed himself pleased, anc
pointed out certain defects to be overcome, at the
same time offering to render me any assistance in hi:
power, an offer of which I promptly availed myself
and with great profit. One consequence of my succes:
was an engagement for three concerts at the Crysta
Palace, for which I received ten guineas. The las
took place on Christmas Day, 1857; Molique playec
two solos, and furnished me with an amusing example
of pedantry. The orchestra played the overture tc
'Der Freischütz.' I happened to be conversing with
Molique when it was about to begin, so I begged him
to excuse me leaving him abruptly, as I wished to heai
it; it was such beautiful music. 'It is very effective,
said he, 'but it is not music.' 'How do you mean it
is not music? I always thought it was very fine!
'No, no; listen, and you shall hear it is not music!
I listened, and enjoyed it very much. When I re
turned to the artists' room, Molique looked at me with
a knowing twinkle in his eye, and said, 'Well, you
have heard?' 'Yes,' said I, 'and I was delighted.
'Ah, but that is not music,' he repeated; 'did you no
hear?' humming the violin passage in the *stretto*
'Yes,' I said, 'what about it?' 'It is wrong; the
B must go to C, not back to G.' 'But,' I exclaimed
'that would ruin the passage.' 'That may be, but I
cannot allow it; it is not music.'

At the first concert of the three I was very much
disappointed with myself. I sang the Count's air from
'Le Nozze di Figaro,' 'Vedro mentr'io sospiro,

which did not rouse the audience to any enthusiasm, and, by Chorley's desire, the old English song, 'When forced from dear Hebe to go'—a dull song, quite out of place in a Crystal Palace Saturday programme. It had been scored, too, by somebody who had much better have left it alone. The small applause which followed my 'rendition' was bestowed out of compassion, I believe.

I sang at several concerts in London and the suburbs during the winter, but was obliged to admit that I did not make much impression on my audiences. I should have liked to introduce songs I had sung before I went to Italy, or something suited to popular taste, which need not be of inferior quality; but my friend and monitor, whose kindness and generosity bound me to study his wishes, insisted upon my selections being submitted to him for approval. One song in particular, which I was anxious to sing at the Surrey Gardens, he rejected with indignation, and told me if ever I sang it he would cut my acquaintance.

I may as well introduce here two short anecdotes of Chorley, which may prove interesting, and certainly serve as a warning to those of my readers who are apt to be rash in stating their convictions. On the first occasion, when I paid him a visit on his return from Italy, among other incidents, he told me that at Naples he had seen an opera by Donizetti announced for performance, of which he never before heard; but he did not attend the performance, as he was sick of Donizetti, and he presumed the opera would be full of his usual maudlin sentiment. I was curious, and asked the name of the work. He replied:

'Elisa Fusco.' 'But,' said I, 'you must have heard it often.' 'No, never!' 'Why,' I said, 'do you not know that is "Lucrezia Borgia," the title being changed by order of the Government for political reasons, as "William Tell" is rechristened "William Wallace," and "The Sicilian Vespers" "Giovanna de Guzman"?'

During the Pyne and Harrison management at Covent Garden, Longfellow's poem 'Hiawatha,' with music by Robert Stœpel, was represented in pantomime by the Payne family, the poem being read by Miss Matilda Heron. Chorley was so pleased with the music that he determined to submit a libretto of his own to Mr. Stœpel, in the hope that he might be induced to set it to music. He invited Stœpel to dine with him to discuss the matter. In the course of conversation, Chorley told me, after extolling the musical merits of his work, he asked Stœpel what on earth could have induced him to jeopardize his success by allowing such an incompetent person as Miss Heron to attempt to read the poem. I stopped him abruptly, and asked 'if he knew who Miss Heron was?' 'No,' said he. 'Well,' I said, 'she is Mr. Stœpel's wife.' 'Good God!' he exclaimed; 'what have I done?' and after a few moments' uneasy reflection he added: 'I don't care; people have no right to sail under false colours!'

Soon after my appearance at St. Martin's Hall Costa returned to town, and, to my great joy, Chorley informed me he had consented to hear me sing. At the same time I felt great diffidence, for I could not help meditating on the contrast between the great singers he had been accustomed to hear and accompany and a beginner like myself; however, I determined to do my best. Chorley accompanied me to his house, and presented me. I sang the cavatina 'All' invito generoso' from 'Maometto Secondo,' and at Chorley's suggestion the air 'If Thou should'st mark iniquities' from 'Eli.' Costa expressed himself pleased, and kindly directed my attention to some points capable of improvement. Thirty years of intimate professional acquaintanceship did not change the impression then made on me by the great conductor. Somewhat cold and distant in manner—an attitude he always maintained in business—he was quick even to curtness in his remarks and directions, by which he acquired the unmerited name of 'tyrant'; he had an impassive countenance, in which it was impossible to read his thoughts; the only visible sign of approbation or the contrary which he ever vouchsafed was a peculiar twist of the back of his neck. Clear·headed, systematic, and punctual, he never wasted a moment of time at rehearsals; the work once arranged was carried on by clockwork. Out of business he was affable, or merry, according to the society in which he found himself. He liked a good dinner and good wine, and knew how to enjoy them; and in a quiet *tête-à-tête*, of which I have had many with him, he delighted in a bit of gossip or mild scandal. He made me no promises, but told me he was sure I should make a good career, and if at any time it was in his power to do me a service, he would do all he could for me. This he carried out; I found him always a staunch friend, adviser, and monitor.

He had two hobbies—watches and horses. Of the latter I do not think he was rich enough to own many, but of the former he possessed several, some of them valuable as curiosities. He also possessed a chronometer, a very appropriate and necessary article for one who prided himself on his punctuality. I believe only one instance is recorded of his retarding the commencement of a performance, and that was in consequence of the delay of a train. On one occasion, when I sang the 'Elijah' at Exeter Hall, I was delayed some time in the cab-rank before I arrived at the entrance, and I could not get out of my vehicle to walk up, as the rain was pouring in torrents. I arrived at the foot of the staircase as the clock struck half-past seven. I rushed up, and was in the orchestra at two minutes after the half hour, but the second bass was already singing the opening recitative. I expected a reprimand, but Costa smiled as I took my place, and told me to keep calm and think of my work only.

He had a method of reading a score for the first time in the orchestra, which, as far as my observation goes, was peculiar to himself. It is the usual practice to read a bar or more ahead of, but he read a bar or more behind, the orchestra. I remarked it at a rehearsal for Birmingham festival some years after the period on which I am now engaged. I had to sing a hymn by Rossini never performed before, and as I had not been provided with a copy, I was reading from the full score from which Costa was conducting. I, of course, had to read a bar ahead, and as he did not turn over in time, and I could not very well guess what was coming, I was forced to leave out a bar or two each time we arrived at the bottom of a page. I then noticed it was a systematic plan, which I think is well worth the consideration of young conductors. It is much easier to correct mistakes after hearing them than before.

In the evening, after my first appearance at the Crystal Palace, I had an invitation to a party at Chorley's to meet Miss Gertrude Kemble, who was about to make her *début* at St. Martin's Hall in the Christmas performance of the 'Messiah.' I would have much preferred staying at home with a book; I felt depressed with the poor impression I had made in the afternoon, and tired after a long day in that dreary place; but duty called, and at ten o'clock I made my way to 13, Eaton Place, West. The party, which had been arranged to give Miss Kemble an opportunity of singing before a small assembly before confronting the larger audience at St. Martin's Hall, included Mrs. Sartoris (Adelaide Kemble), Virginia Gabriel, John Hullah, Mr. and Mrs. Henry Leslie, Miss Kemble, myself, and a few others. I felt great sympathy for the poor trembling girl who was about to undergo an ordeal for which she was not physically prepared. I learned afterwards her voice had been much strained by an incompetent professor during her long residence in Hanover. Manuel Garcia had done wonders with it since her return to England, but she had still great difficulty in controlling the upper register, which naturally added considerably to her nervousness. Nevertheless, she sang 'Rejoice greatly,' and 'I know that my Redeemer liveth,' exceedingly well, and with great intelligence.

I did not feel very happy myself at the idea of singing before the great Adelaide Kemble, whose manner when I was presented to her did not inspire me with much confidence. I sang a song by Angelo Mariani, the conductor of the opera at the Carlo Felice, Genoa (and at Bologna during the season of the *fiera*), called 'Il Contrabbandiere,' and fortunately had the advantage of Miss Gabriel's assistance at the piano. I flattered myself I had acquitted myself honourably; everybody complimented me, but some time afterwards I heard that Mrs. Sartoris criticised my performance very severely, and prophesied I should never be a shining light. This party, which I would willingly have shirked, proved a very important event for me—in less than eighteen months Miss Kemble became my wife.

For the performance of the 'Messiah,' Hullah had already engaged the solo singers, but being desirous of including my name in the programme, he asked me if I would care to sing 'The trumpet shall sound,' as it was the only song he could ask Thomas to give up. I said certainly, I was quite satisfied to help in any way I could. I was too interested in the young *prima donna* to pay much attention to the other solo singers. Although she suffered considerably from 'stage fright,' she sang with true artistic feeling and perception; all the roulades were clearly and firmly executed, and her voice was bright and in tune throughout. Her reception was most enthusiastic. As I was about to go on the orchestra, Hullah informed me that the trumpeter had been called away suddenly, and asked me whether I would prefer omitting the song, or singing it with the trumpet part played on the organ. I chose the latter, and sang it so much to the satisfaction of the audience that they wished me to repeat it ; however, I thought once without the trumpet was sufficient, and I simply bowed my acknowledgments. Miss Kemble afterwards informed me that an old and intimate friend of her family, who came to town expressly to be present on the occasion of her first appearance. said that I reminded him forcibly, both as regards voice and singing, of Bartleman, the predecessor of Henry Phillips.

I had a desire to continue my theatrical career ; the Italian opera was the object of my ambition, but I was sufficiently modest to comprehend that with such artists as formed the staff there, there was no chance for me. When I first returned from Italy, I saw an announcement of an operatic tour with a number of eminent artists, Sims Reeves being one of them, under the management of Willert Beale. I had not the pleasure of his acquaintance, nor did I know anyone who could have introduced me to him, so I wrote him a polite note, asking him whether he could find a place in his company for me, to which I received no reply. I do not blame him, for I know what it is to be deluged with similar applications. The Pyne and Harrison Company had already begun its career at the Lyceum. so for that season I could not hope for an engagement. In January, 1858, there were three state performances at Her Majesty's Theatre during the week in which the Princess Royal was married. One of the evenings was devoted to ' Macbeth.' Benedict had the direction of the music, and engaged me to play Hecate, but when the dates were arranged, the performance of ' Macbeth ' was fixed for a night on which I had promised to sing for Hullah, so with no small feeling of disappointment I gave up Hecate. Early in the year I sang in ' St. Paul ' at the Gentlemen's Concerts in Manchester. I was engaged to sing in Haydn's ' Seasons,' at which I worked hard, as I had never either heard or read the oratorio. A week before the performance, Hallé wrote to me saying they had found it necessary to change the work ; would I sing in ' St. Paul ' instead ? I was only too pleased, as I had once sung the part at a private performance in Liverpool before I went to Italy, and it suited me much better than the part in the ' Seasons.' After this I made my first appearance in my native town at the Philharmonic Hall.

I essayed the part of ' Elijah,' the first time, for the Sacred Harmonic Society at Exeter Hall early in March. I had only twice heard the oratorio, and I had not contemplated the difficulties of the part. Musically, I had little to fear, but as I proceeded with the study of it, its histrionic exigencies (if that expression may be allowed in speaking of a drama represented without action) overwhelmed me. The three episodes in the first part—the resuscitation of the widow's dead son, the confounding of the priests of Baal, and the calling down of the rain which ends the part—demand the greatest possible amount of force, not physical so much as mental, by far the most trying. The mind must be absorbed in the scenes represented, or the performance, however good as a vocal display, cannot be a portrayal of the character of

Elijah ; consequently, to those who are able to discriminate, it will be totally uninteresting. I grant there are but few who care to discriminate, or are capable of doing so, but it is to those few a true artist will address himself. The second part contains an episode no less exacting than the three already quoted, and of a totally different nature, in the picture of Elijah's despair of fulfilling his mission, his declaration of his unworthiness, and his longing to die. Here the vocalist is prone to forget the intense dramatic interest in the execution of one of the finest examples of vocal writing. And it must never be forgotten that the recitative which opens the oratorio, like the first line Hamlet speaks, ' A little more than kin, and less than kind,' is the keystone to the whole character. My first essay was a failure, but the performance was repeated a week after, when I recovered my lost laurels. As I came off the platform, Charles Lucas* patted me on the back, and said, ' You were Elijah to-night, my boy ; last week you were nothing like him.'

I was invited to the annual dinner of the Royal Society of Musicians, and to take part in the musical proceedings. I chose Hullah's song, ' I arise from dreams of thee,' which Cusins kindly accompanied for me. When dinner was concluded, I noticed a commotion amongst the professional gentlemen seated in my vicinity. There was evidently a hitch somewhere, so I asked my neighbour what was the matter. Winn,

* Charles Lucas was a first-rate musician and violoncellist. He succeeded Lindley as principal violoncello at the Italian Opera, Covent Garden, the Sacred Harmonic, and all the principal festivals, and was for some years principal of the Royal Academy of Music.

who was to have taken the first bass part in the glees, 'The tiger couches' and 'Queen of the Valley,' was unavoidably absent. I volunteered my services in his stead, which seemed to surprise the other singers, as they only knew I was a young singer fresh from Italy, by no means a sufficient passport to their confidence. However, under the circumstances, they agreed I might try, and we began with 'The tiger couches,' as the least exigent of the two. I looked it through, and took my place. and evidently satisfied my comrades. I afterwards sang in 'Queen of the Valley,' and received high eulogiums for what I did not deem a great exhibition of prowess.

Sight-reading is a mechanical process, which, though not absolutely necessary, ought to be cultivated by all singers, if for no other reason than to save time and trouble to themselves and those with whom they are studying. A singer who reads at sight can form a good estimate of what he can do with a song or work by glancing over it without the aid of an instrument ; whilst the non-reader must either pick out the notes on the piano, or procure a capable person to play the song or work over until he becomes imbued with the spirit of the music he wishes to become acquainted with. I say it is not absolutely necessary—I speak of solo-singers ; it does not matter whether the artist read his music at sight or take months to study it if the result be a finished performance. Though incontestably reading at sight has its advantages, it has at least one disadvantage ; it offers an inducement to study hastily. I know, at the beginning of my career, I depended too much on my capability of reading, and my performances were often crude ; whereas had I been obliged to spend more time in mastering the music, I should certainly have presented a better digested, and hence more refined and artistic, execution. Berlioz, in his letters, finds fault with Staudigl for trusting almost entirely to his ' sight-reading '; and, speaking of his performance of Mephisto in the ' Damnation de Faust,' says that he consequently gave no colour to the part.

For all that, singers, bearing in mind that singing is their principal study, ought to study, as far as their leisure and facilities will allow them, all branches of music, and learn an instrument, giving preference to a stringed instrument. It exercises the ear, and does not require the physical exertion the pianoforte exacts, which is sure to fatigue the voice.

In the autumn of 1858, the New Town Hall at Leeds was opened by her Majesty the Queen, and the ceremony was followed by a musical festival, for which I was engaged. The only important music I had was the bass in Rossini's ' Stabat Mater.' I sang the duet, ' The Lord is a man of war,' from ' Israel in Egypt,' with Weiss ; and I also sang the quartets in ' Elijah,' and one or two pieces in the miscellaneous concerts. My hopes revived of gaining a footing on the stage, but for a time were again frustrated. I received a note from Harrison asking if I would entertain an engagement for the English Opera for the season 1858-59, and on what terms. I replied stating my willingness, and demanding what I considered moderate terms ; his ideas, however, were so much below mine that I closed negotiations. I also received a request from Douglas, the manager of the Standard Theatre, to let him know what terms I would require to play Count Arnheim for a week with Sims Reeves. I again asked what I thought a modest sum, and again opinions differed ; the sum he offered, ten pounds, after paying for hire of dress and other expenses, would have left me little remuneration for the trouble of learning the part, rehearsals, and six performances. There was some intention of engaging me for the Birmingham Festival ; unfortunately, the chairman and one of the members of the orchestral committee came to London to judge for themselves whether they could engage me.   The performance they attended was one of Leslie's 'Immanuel.'   I was not in good form, and sang very tamely ; so they decided to forego the honour of introducing me to Birmingham.   One of the choral societies of that town wished to avail itself of my services in a performance of the ' Creation ' in the early part of the year, holding out as an inducement, instead of terms, a chance of making a favourable impression on the Festival committee with a view to an engagement, an offer which I respectfully declined.

I attended the Festival, although not engaged, as Chorley's guest.   Sims Reeves was in grand form, and sang splendidly ; and Madame Viardot Garcia made a great impression on me by her singing of ' Oh, thou that tellest' in the ' Messiah,' an air too often treated with indifference, and in the morning and evening prayers in ' Eli.'

In private concerts during the season, I had the honour of singing with many of the greatest singers of the day, both belonging to the Italian Opera and my own compatriots. I felt very like a minnow among a shoal of whales, but was not inclined to be cast down. Their example inspired me with earnestness and perseverance ; they could not all have been great when they began—why should not I rise, too ? Sims Reeves and Clara Novello had taken me by the hand from the beginning ; so had Costa. Mario and Grisi, with whom I had sung several times, gave me great encouragement.

As I was returning one day in the early part of the year from a rehearsal at St. Martin's Hall, I met J. G. Patey, just returned from Turin, where he had been singing at the ' Teatro Rossini,' Madame Lancia being one of the company. We had been chums for some time in Milan, and I was very glad to meet him and renew our intimacy. He hailed me with ' Hullo ! have you gone into the Church ?' I was attired in a highly respectable black suit and tall hat, and probably presented somewhat of a clerical appearance—maybe the result of my connection with St. Martin's and Exeter Halls. He certainly had nothing of the clerical about him ; he looked rather like a cross between a modern Fra Diavolo and a pigeon fancier, dressed in a velveteen jacket of eccentric cut, and trousers of a flashy hue. He could not find lodgings at a moderate price to suit his taste, so I suggested he might find such in the house where I lodged. He accompanied me home to make inquiries and an inspection, which ended in his taking up his residence in Stafford Place with me. We lived together for about twelve months, almost inseparable companions. We frequently went to the theatre and opera in the evening, or, in the summer, for a stroll in the country. During the week Sims Reeves was playing at the Standard (mentioned in the previous chapter), being curious to know what an East-end performance was like, we paid them a visit, arriving about the middle of the first act. We could not find seats in what were denominated the 'stalls,' and ensconced ourselves in a passage which ran round the pit, where, by standing up, we could just obtain a glimpse of the stage. At the conclusion of the act, we sought a more convenient spot ; but the theatre being crammed full, we were obliged to make the best of the places we had. There was only one other occupant of the passage, and he seemed to be enjoying a nap leaning on the balustrade. Behind, we discovered a doorway, approached by a step from the floor. Patey mounted the step so as to have a better view of the stage, when he suddenly called out to me, 'There's something here under my feet!' 'Take care!' said I. 'Oh, it's quite hard,' he replied ; 'see what it is!' I groped about in the dark, and found the object. 'It's a lobster!' I informed him. No sooner had I mentioned the fact than our slumbering friend woke up, and, in a voice indicative of abuse of stimulants, exclaimed, 'Yes, sir ; that's my lobster.' I remarked it was unsafe to leave anything good to eat where it might easily be trodden on and spoiled. He made no further reply, but now bestowed his attention on the opera. He asked several questions about the singers on the stage. At last, when Reeves was singing the duet with Miss Ternan (Arline), he asked, 'What is that gentleman's name ?' I said,

'Mr. Sims Reeves.' 'Mr. What, sir?' said he. 'Mr. Reeves,' I said, a little louder. 'I am very glad to hear it, sir,' said he, looking greatly relieved in his mind. 'I took him for Mr. Galier' [so he pronounced Mr. Galer's name], 'and I am very glad it isn't ; for I thought if it *was* Mr. Galier, he'd fallen off considerably since last I heard him.'

CHAPTER XII.

Soon after Christmas, 1857, my landlady came to my
room one morning with a very grave face, and informed me she had a subject of great importance
about which she wished to consult me. I had paid
my rent regularly, and was a little curious to learn
what other subject could be of much importance to
her. I requested her to let me know in what I could
be of service to her, on which she informed me that
her Majesty's piper wished to take a room in her
house, and before letting it, she would like to know
whether a bagpiper would be an agreeable fellow-
lodger. I confess my affection for the pipes did not

extend to a performance on them in a small house in a room immediately over my head, yet I did not wish to be in the way of my landlady securing a good tenant. I suggested that if she had no fear of his blowing the roof off, and he would arrange to get through his practising whilst I was out, I had no objection to her accepting him. *That* she had already arranged, so we were forthwith honoured with a royal piper's company. I did not suffer any inconvenience from his pipes; he practised for an hour or two generally whilst I was out in the evening, but I suffered from a dreadful fright he caused me the last night he resided under the same roof. It was the night of the ball at Buckingham Palace after the Princess Royal's wedding. The noise of the carriages kept me awake for a long time when I went to bed, but at last I dropped off to sleep. I was awakened suddenly by a horrible row going on on the staircase leading up to my bedroom. I heard somebody, evidently very drunk, shouting: 'Let me at him; I'll soon pull him out!' interlarding his threats with certain epithets which I do not think were of Highland origin. Then I distinguished the mild voice of my landlady beseeching the drunken scamp to have some consideration for her other lodger. More epithets ensued, and a tussle in which MacSnifter, or whatever his name was, rolled down a few stairs. After a great deal of coaxing and pushing, he was at last landed at the door of his bedroom, into which he fell head-foremost, and as I heard no more of him I concluded he slept off the effects of his potations in his kilt on the floor. He was very penitent next morning ; he insisted he had only drunk one glass of whisky—it must have been a mighty big one—but my landlady was inexorable, and insisted upon his vacating instanter !

I was engaged to Miss Kemble in the summer of 1858, and in consequence became a frequent guest at her aunt's house, where I made the acquaintance of Henry Greville, in whom I found a warm admirer and staunch friend. He gave very select musical parties in which I was always invited to take part, having the good fortune to be associated with Mario, Grisi, Gardoni, Ciabatta, Schira, Pinsuti, etc., with whom I was soon on terms of intimacy and accepted as their comrade and friend. H.R.H. the late Duchess of Cambridge was always present, attended by one or both of her daughters. The guests included the highest in culture, rank and wealth ; the programme was of moderate dimensions, and the little reunion of intimates in the supper-room, after the bulk of the guests had departed, was delightful. On one occasion I arrived very early, Mrs. Sartoris arriving soon after, while there were still very few people in the room. I was to sing a duet with her, and we were having a little conversation on the subject, when suddenly she exclaimed : ' Good God ! Santley, what shall I do ?' ' What's the matter ?' I said. ' My petticoat's coming down,' was her response. ' Well,' I said, ' I don't see how I can help you !' ' *I* do,' she said ; ' stand before me and spread out your coat-tails as wide as you can !' I obeyed, pretending to be absorbed in the study of the duet, which was lying on the piano. In a few moments she whispered : ' It's all right, but what on earth am I to do with it?' I looked at the bundle and saw it was impossible to pocket it ; at that moment Leighton made his appearance, carrying his hat in his hand. 'Just in time to save me!' exclaimed Mrs. Sartoris. 'Here, Fay, put that in your hat and keep it till we get away!' 'What is it?' 'My petticoat!' 'Oh!'

One evening I sang the romance 'O Lisbona,' from 'Don Sebastiano ;' the Duchess of Cambridge was so pleased, she asked me to repeat it, which I did at the end of the programme. Grisi turned to Mario and remarked : 'What a splendid voice, eh, Mario?' He replied quickly : 'Say rather he has made good use of the voice given him, and sings well.' I felt very proud of and greatly encouraged by praise from the two most prominent singers of the day.

The London season finished, I accompanied Patey to Plympton, Devonshire, on a visit to his father. We passed the time very pleasantly, walking and fishing (I do not think I caught a single fish) during the day, and generally spending the evening at a pleasant party at one neighbour's house or another. The last day of our visit we went to breakfast at the house of a doctor, a particular friend of Mr. Patey, and an eminent physician. We were ushered on our arrival into the drawing-room, where, to my surprise, I found a large number of guests assembled. At breakfast I was placed alongside of a stout middle-aged gentleman, who occupied himself, during the repast, in carving a huge round of beef, with a knife half a yard long. I conversed with him about the beauty of the country, the fine walks, etc. ;

he and everybody present seemed to be exceedingly cheerful and chatty, and the doctor, our host, very attentive and hospitable. On our road home, I remarked upon the number of guests invited to meet us. 'Oh!' said Patey junior, 'they are chiefly his patients.' I remarked it was rather strange to ask all his patients. 'But they live there,' said he. 'How extraordinary!' I replied. 'Not at all,' said Patey; 'don't you know where you have been breakfasting?' 'At your friend's house.' 'Why,' said he, 'that is a private lunatic asylum!' 'And my neighbour who carved the beef?' 'One of the patients.' I ruminated.

As I could not come to terms with the managers of the English Opera, I had again to turn all my attention to concert and oratorio singing. My second season was somewhat of a repetition of my first, with an increase of public favour, as my name became better known, and a consequent and considerable increase in my work.

On the 9th April I was married to Gertrude Kemble—on expectations—for all I possessed was £10, and I had still the greater part of my debt to my father to pay off. I fortunately had a large number of engagements, public and private. I also sang in a great many benefit concerts gratis, which I now consider a great mistake. To help an unfortunate deserving comrade, or assist in the cause of charity, is the duty of everybody; but gratuitously to assist adventurers for their own benefit, or ostensibly for that of a charitable institution, is not the duty of anybody. London during the season was infested by a band of marauders from foreign climes, who came down like 'wolves on the fold,' ready to give their services (Save the mark!) in any house where they might gain an introduction—not a difficult matter—the insinuating and not easily abashed stranger finding favour and patronage where a native would never obtain recognition. They gave lessons—at least, they called them so—and ended by giving a concert, generally in the drawing-room of some rich patron, when all those in whose parties they had assisted gratuitously were bound to take tickets; thus they netted a more or less considerable profit, afterwards returning to their 'lares et penates,' very often to descant upon the gullibility and lack of taste of the barbarous Briton. There were, of course, some foreign artists whose visits to London during the season were always welcome, who exercised their talents in a legitimate way, and who, unless on terms of sufficient intimacy to expect it, or in a position to offer adequate services in return, would not stoop to make importunate demands on their fellow-artists. Why should artists be called upon to give their services for the benefit of charitable institutions? Those who purchase tickets for such entertainments receive ample return in amusement for the amount expended; that is not charity, and the promoters do little more, if anything, than enlist the sympathies of those who provide the entertainment. In some cases the promoter is a neglected genius, who, seeking a field wherein to display his talents, importunes every artist of position with whom he may have a bowing acquaintance, to assist him in the cause of charity, that he may reap the benefit derived from cheap (for him) and wide-spread advertisement. In both cases the charity is entirely on the part of the artists who sing or perform ; this surely is not just.

I do not share the opinion of many that a foreigner has no right to come to England to take the 'bread and butter' out of the mouth of the native. I do not believe any foreign artist ever deprived me of an ounce of food. An artist has no nationality ; he is the property of the world, and has a perfect right to exercise his profession in any country where he finds a public desirous of hearing or seeing him. It is not of such I have spoken above ; it is of the impertinent interloper, who, unable to make a position in his own country, with audacious pertinacity throws dust in the eyes of the foolish but benevolent would-be patron of art in England.

Negotiations were pending for my appearance at the English Opera during the season of 1859-60, to open with Meyerbeer's 'Dinorah,' translated by H. F. Chorley. I learned afterwards there were some doubts about entrusting the part of Hoel to me, which were dispelled on my singing for Meyerbeer at a party at Lady Molesworth's house. He expressed himself perfectly satisfied, and a desire that I would undertake the part, with the result that my engagement was arranged.

The last Bradford Festival was held in August. I was engaged as second to Belletti ; my work was light. I sang in the quartets in 'St. Paul,' a portion of the bass music in 'Judas Maccabæus' and 'The Messiah,' and in some concerted music in the evening programmes. The most remarkable feature in the Festival was the devotion of the 'White Roses' to the 'ould gal,' as Mrs. Sunderland* was familiarly styled.

After a short holiday in the North of France, I returned to London full of my new venture. I was not over-sanguine about my success, yet hoped all would go well, and that the great desire I had of gaining a footing on the operatic stage might be realized. I had seen 'Dinorah' at the Italian Opera, and was charmed with the music. I became still more enthusiastic about it when I came to study my part; but I also grew more diffident about my powers as I discovered the histrionic difficulties it presented. I received the first act and a call for rehearsal for the next day simultaneously; I spent the whole of the intervening time studying hard, and was able to go through my part almost perfectly by heart. In the two following days I did the same with the concerted music of the second and third acts, and by the end of the week had no longer need of the score. The dialogue cost me infinitely more labour; I had not much difficulty in learning the words, but between hearing the sound of my speaking voice in the large theatre and attending to the stage-manager's directions, I grew so confused that I almost despaired of being able to deliver them. With patience and perseverance I accomplished it at last, and went through the opera the first night without a slip. Histrionically I know my performance was feeble, though I hardly merited

* Mrs. Sunderland was a native of Yorkshire; she possessed a pure, brilliant soprano voice, and sang well, although her style lacked polish. She was a great favourite all over the north of England, but, for some cause I cannot explain, did not find a place amongst the singers in the capital.

the sweeping condemnation of a celebrated critic, who announced that 'Mr. Santley sang his music well, but has neither stage face, stage walk, nor stage anything, and never can become an actor.' My father came to London to be present at my first appearance unknown to me. He came to my dressing-room at the conclusion of the second performance. His remarks were few, but telling—'You need not have made such a guy of yourself' (it was not my doing, but the barber's who made me up); subsequently adding, 'Well, lad, you are not an Edmund Kean yet' (not even a Charles ditto, I thought to myself).

After I had been playing the part every night for a week—we had not arrived at the halcyon times when two artists play the same part on alternate nights—I received a visit from an intimate musical acquaintance— one of those kind friends who insist upon giving a candid opinion, 'the truth, the whole truth, and nothing but the truth,' according to their lights—who came to condole with me on the unfortunate mistake I had made in quitting the concert-room. He also was of opinion that I could never make an actor. I ventured to suggest he might be mistaken; it was rather early to judge, and I told him I did not expect to become an actor without experience. He then asked how long I intended to give myself to gain the necessary experience. I said that if in ten years I could feel myself at home on the stage I should be well satisfied. Only three years later, or little more, the same gentleman acknowledged he had been mistaken. It certainly was not intended I should be spoiled by flattery. I am quite aware, as I have said, that my performance was tame, but it was the tameness of diffidence about my execution of what I had conceived, not lack of spirit or energy. I had a long and difficult part to sing, had had slight experience on the stage, and the major portion of the opera I had to play with a man who, though not an accomplished, was an experienced actor, and was wont at times to take advantage of the inexperience of a comrade. But I think excuses are unnecessary. A man cannot become an actor any more than he can become a barrister or a preacher without much experience, however gifted he may be. I have heard of born actors, but I never saw one ; I have seen some who were born to be actors, and fulfilled their destiny by unceasing toil and perseverance ; and I have seen others born with great natural gifts who ought to have become actors, but lacking earnestness and industry, have never risen above mediocrity.

After thirty nights of ' Dinorah,' by way of rest I sang in the English version of ' Il Trovatore,' ' The Rose of Castille,' ' Satanella,' etc. At Christmas we brought out a small opera by Alfred Mellon, entitled ' Victorine.' During the run of this work Hallé produced Gluck's ' Iphigénie en Tauride,' English version by Chorley, at his concerts in Manchester, with Catherine Hayes, Sims Reeves, myself, and Winn. I was able to accept the engagement, as during the pantomime season I was only engaged four nights a week at Covent Garden. To close the season Wallace's ' Lurline ' was produced, which proved a great success, both artistically and financially. One morning, whilst we were rehearsing it, I found the scene set for the second act, supposed to be under the Rhine. Noticing what appeared to me to be a quantity of magnified sticks of red rhubarb hanging about, I asked Fitzball, the author of the libretto, who was standing by, if they were really intended to represent that wholesome plant. He replied they were to represent coral! 'But,' said I, 'do they find coral in the Rhine—red coral?' 'Of course dot,' he replied (he had an infirmity of the nasal organ); 'that is all robadce; I ab very robadtic. I was brought up a huddred biles frob the haudts of bad, that is why I ab so robadtic.' We had as usual, a stage-manager, who did not deem it necessary to study the drama and prepare the situations. At one of the last rehearsals we all got into a muddle in the finale of the second act; nobody seemed to know what to do, so we all stood still, which gave promise of a most thrilling effect on the audience. Suddenly Harrison was seized with an inspiration. 'Stop! stop!' he cried out. 'Stirling!' 'Yes, sir!' 'Cannot we have a Huguenot rush here?' 'Certainly, sir, the very thing I was thinking of myself!' 'Now then, all of you, be ready,' and at a given signal we all rushed down to the footlights as though we had been going to annihilate Mellon and the whole of the orchestra. It brought the house down every night we played the opera. I nearly came to a premature end in this scene. I had to catch Lurline, Miss Pyne, in my arms as she swooned on the departure of her lover; she stopped short of the usual spot one evening, and I did not notice it until I received a gentle hint on my crown from the roller of the curtain. Fortunately my head was bent down, and did not receive the full force of the blow ; everybody screamed and thought I was killed. I saw all the constellations in the firmament, so it appeared to me. I was stunned, but in a few moments I recovered myself and finished my part. Her Majesty the Queen expressed a wish to witness one of the performances, and requested to be furnished with a list of the operas we were playing. She chose ' Dinorah,' for which I had a new dress and a more respectable make-up. I was gratified to learn that her Majesty and H.R.H. the Prince Consort both approved of my performance. I was engaged, in consequence, I presume, for the next royal concert which took place at Windsor Castle, when Haydn's setting of the seven last words of our Saviour was performed. After the close of the season, Louisa Pyne, Harrison, and I sang at Augustus Harris senior's benefit at the Princess's. Wallace accompanied. He had spoken to me more than once about taking up his song ' The Bellringer,' so, deeming this a fitting opportunity to try it, I asked him to send me a copy, which I received on the morning of the benefit. I did not feel very confident about doing it justice with so little study, but it turned out to be my first great concert success.

For the winter of 1860-61 I was engaged at Her Majesty's Theatre to sing with Madame Lemmens-Sherrington and Sims Reeves ; Mlle. Parepa, Swift, George Honey, and J. G. Patey were also of the company, and Charles Hallé was conductor. We produced Macfarren's ' Robin Hood ' to open the season, and Wallace's ' Amber Witch ' to close it. In the interim, whilst the pantomime was running, we brought out 'La Reine Topaze,' and also played 'The Bohemian Girl,' 'The Trovatore,' and 'Fra Diavolo.' 'Robin Hood,' with Sims Reeves, who returned to the stage after some years' absence, was a success; the 'Amber Witch,' although it contained some fine music, was not.   I sang in it at Drury Lane for some three or four weeks after the season at Her Majesty's Theatre had closed, to almost empty benches. 'Queen Topaz' might have proved a fair success if some care had been taken in its production.   Swift, who played the hero, never knew his part, neither music nor dialogue.   There was no attempt at stage-management; we all wandered on and off and about the stage as we pleased.   The effect produced was very curious —neither players nor audience seemed to have the remotest notion what it was all about.   The stage-management throughout that season was the most perfect—of its kind—I ever knew.   At one performance of 'Fra Diavolo' matters were so well arranged that principals, chorus, supers, etc., were all left outside the curtain at the end of the first act.   At one of the rehearsals of the 'Amber Witch' the stage-manager showed off to peculiar advantage.   In the last act, the so-called witch, finding herself menaced by a number of peasants who believe her really to be a sorceress, to rid herself of the annoyance, conceives the idea of acting on their superstitious fears, and sings or recites a Latin prayer; this they take for a spell, and hurry away, leaving her in peace. Mr. Stage-manager, hearing the prayer, called out, 'Don't you hear, she's praying? down on your knees!' I happened to know the situation from Chorley, the author of the libretto, and took upon myself to point out the mistake. The stage-manager merely remarked, ' How the devil should I know anything about it? I have never read the book! Here, you chorus, it's a spell to frighten you, so as soon as you hear the first words clear off as fast as you can !'

One evening we were playing 'The Bohemian Girl,' with Parepa, Parkinson, etc., to a meagre house. Everything was very dull, and the audience was very apathetic. At the beginning of the last act Parepa and I were singing the duet ; she had just concluded her opening phrase, and I was preparing to upbraid her, when a dog which belonged to the *répétiteur*, and accompanied him always to rehearsal, trotted on to the stage, and squatted on his haunches in front of me, staring me in the face. The enthusiasm of the audience was roused immediately. I felt horribly indignant, and tried to drive the beast away with my foot ; my kicks he treated with silent contempt. There he remained until I concluded my cadence, when he rose up, wagged his tail, and walked quietly into the wings.

For the summer season of 1861 E. T. Smith, the then lessee of Her Majesty's Theatre, had engaged a company such as had never been heard of. Grisi had retired from Covent Garden, and was bound not to sing again in London ; Mario had signed a contract with Gye, so the two were engaged by Smith to sing in an opera at the Crystal Palace. The host of talent included Adelina Patti, who was to make her first appearance in England. I was to make my first appearance on the Italian stage, and, amongst other operas, was announced to sing in Verdi's 'Macbeth' with Grisi. I was greatly troubled when I read this, and remonstrated with Brizzi,* who had much to do with the arrangement of the programme, on the folly of my undertaking to play such a part as ' Macbeth.' My fears were soon dispelled, for Smith came to grief, and the monster programme ended in smoke.

Mapleson then took the Lyceum, for which he had secured a good card in the ' Ballo in maschera,' new for England. He asked me to transfer my engagement with Smith to him, and make my *début* in Italian opera in the part of Renato ; but I was not satisfied that I had had sufficient experience to do it justice, so I declined. I had read that Delle Sedie, whom I had heard in Milan in 1855, was in Paris ; I recommended him to Mapleson. Whether in consequence of my recommendation or not, I do not know, he was engaged, and made a great success. He was afterwards engaged at Covent Garden, where he sang several seasons, and became a great favourite.

This year I made my first appearance at Birmingham Festival, Belletti being principal bass. He declined to sing in ' Elijah,' so it fell to my lot. I had studied the part a great deal since I first sang it in London, and I thought I had made a considerable improvement, both in my conception and execution of it. Costa expressed his satisfaction to me at the conclu-

---

* Brizzi had been a tenor singer of some repute. At the time I knew him, he had almost retired from public singing and gave lessons. He was on terms of intimacy with most of the celebrated Italian artists, and in consequence was of great service to Smith in his negotiations with them.

sion of the oratorio. The following morning I found a newspaper lying by my plate on the breakfast-table. I incautiously opened it and read, in a notice of the performance, ' From the opening bars of the first recitative we knew Mr. Santley in " Elijah " was a mistake ; to do justice to the part requires a bass, and Mr. Santley is a mere baritone. Mr. Santley endeavoured to make up for lack of voice with energetic declamation, but it was of no use,' etc. I had read very little in the way of criticism on my performances before, and I then made a resolution, which with rare exceptions I have adhered to, to avoid reading any in future. There evidently was some discussion about my performance. Costa told me he had had an altercation with a gentleman at dinner, who contended that, because I was *only* a baritone, I could not sing the part of ' Elijah.' Costa was not a talkative man on such subjects, but he said sufficient to lead me to understand that his antagonist got the worst of the argument.

I returned to Covent Garden for the season of 1861-62, which opened with Howard Glover's ' Ruy Blas.' On the Saturday it was to have been produced I had not received the whole of my part, Don Sallust, nor did I until the Tuesday following, the opera being first performed on the Thursday, two days after ; the parts for the overture were given out for rehearsal that very day at half-past four, after the general rehearsal was finished. The opera contained one or two effective numbers, but was not a success ; however, it proved of great benefit to me, as owing to the advice and hints of my friend Walter Lacy, who had played the part, with great success, with Fechter at the Princess's, I made my first step histrionically. I met with an accident in this opera which nearly ended fatally. Harrison and I played the last scene as arranged by Fechter. Ruy Blas at the end of the duel stabs Don Sallust and throws him through a window at the back of the scene. Harrison incautiously used a real dagger, and one night stabbed me in the side; I had the presence of mind to put my hand behind me as I fell, and draw the dagger away. I did not take any notice of the wound until the next day, when it pained me; I then showed it to my doctor, who, after probing it, told me it was very lucky I was so well covered with adipose tissue, otherwise the dagger would have pierced the lung. A reproduction of 'Robin Hood' with Madame Guerrabella (Genevieve Ward) Haigh, Honey, and myself followed; it did not prove attractive and was played alternately with operas of the *répertoire*, until the production of Balfe's 'Puritan's Daughter,' about the beginning of December, which had a run of fifty-seven nights. I found it very tiresome singing the same music night after night, especially the ballad with its inevitable 'encore.'

The other novelty produced was Benedict's opera, the 'Lily of Killarney.' There was so little to do in the first act that I was inclined at first to refuse the part, whatever the consequences might be, and they were dire, according to the rules of the theatre, a copy of which was attached to each engagement, all one-sided in favour of the manager. But my indignation was set at rest when Benedict showed what he had done for his 'dear boy' in the second act; I was cut out of the third for reasons which it is not necessary to explain. I was fortunate in having the assistance of the only capable stage-manager I ever had to work with, William, or as he was always familiarly called, Billy West. He gave me a lesson at one of the rehearsals I never forgot. I was always nervous and fidgety at stage rehearsals, to cover which I assumed a vivacious nonchalant air which I did not possess. The first day we rehearsed the 'Lily' on the stage I was playing the fool somewhat, whilst Billy was eyeing me very gravely. At last he stepped up to me, and said quietly : 'My boy, you have the finest part in this opera ; if you set to work steadily, and attend to me, you will make a great part of it ; but if you insist on playing the fool in that manner, you will make nothing of it. Remember there is one step from the sublime to the ridiculous, and if you are not careful you will make it.' I put aside my hat and cane, and set to work in earnest, and never again was I tempted to indulge in fooling at rehearsal. We played the 'Lily' for five or six weeks, every night. Danny Man is a very exigent part, and I was not sorry when the season came to an end, for I was beginning to feel fatigued. I had sung every night of the season from the end of September until the week before Easter except two—one night when 'Maritana' was given with Madame Guerrabella, and one night when I had a violent cold.

CHAPTER XIII.

THE year 1862 proved a very eventful one for me.
As I have said before, I found singing an opera every
night very fatiguing; not the physical exertion—though,
besides the singing on a large stage like that at Covent
Garden, the mere going through a long opera entails
no small amount of bodily exercise—but on account of
the expenditure of nervous force. I could never do
anything by halves; if I went down to the theatre
determined to spare myself except in the more important points, I had only been a short time on the
stage, and got warmed to my work, when all idea of
saving myself was cast to the winds. Five months of
such continuous excitement, with the addition of study
and rehearsal of new parts, and the worries which it
would appear are inevitable in a theatrical career,
would tell on the most robust frame. Towards the

end of the English opera season I called to have a chat with Costa, in the course of which I mentioned this subject, at the same time explaining the difficulty of altering the system ; nobody would believe in the feasibility of breaking the run of an opera even for a single night. He asked me why I did not turn my attention to the Italian opera. I said I would, willingly, but I doubted if an opportunity would present itself whilst I continued to sing in England regularly. He advised me to go back to Italy for twelve months, and make a reputation there in some of the good theatres, and then there would be no difficulty in finding a place for me at the Italian Opera in England. I liked his proposal, and talked it over with my wife, who was also pleased, and advised me to give the plan a fair trial. I saw Costa again and told him I had decided upon taking his advice, whereupon he gave me a letter of introduction to Rossini, begging him to recommend me to his friends in Italy, and one to Mario, asking him to introduce me to any agent in Paris who was likely to be able to further my interest. Mario had removed to a house somewhere in a new street near the ' Arc de l'Étoile,' and I tried in vain to find him. I called on Rossini, sent in my card with Costa's letter, and was shown into a small room where Rossini was seated, with his face lathered, a towel round his neck, waiting for the barber to apply his razor. Of course I called to mind the scene in the ' Barbiere ' on the spot. After a cordial salutation he begged me to step into the next room for a few minutes. The shaving operation over, I was recalled, when I had a long conversation with him about music and the opera in London, and friends of his whom I knew. I had armed myself with the *cavatina* from 'Maometto Secondo,' 'Alle voci della gloria,' in case he wished to hear me. I felt very disappointed, as he did not ask me to sing, yet he offered to give me letters to influential musical friends in Italy ; I did not feel inclined to accept recommendations from a man who did not know what I was capable of except from hearsay.

When he dismissed me, he requested me to call again before I left Paris, which I promised to do, hoping that he would then express a wish to hear what he was recommending. In the meantime I received a letter from a friend of mine who had acted as treasurer to the Pyne and Harrison Company to the effect that Mr. Gye had asked him if he thought I would like to sing at the Italian Opera, as he had a very good chance open, if I cared to avail myself of it. He wished to bring out a new *prima donna*—an Englishwoman who had made a certain reputation in Italy under the name of Fanny Gordosa—early in the season. She was to make her *début* in 'Il Trovatore'; and Graziani, who was to have sustained the part of Di Luna as usual, could not be in London in time. He could not offer me an engagement, nor any pay, except the opportunity of my being heard on the Italian stage, which probably would be to my interest in the future. The other artists were Nantier-Didier, Tamberlik, and Tagliafico. The offer tempted me ; I hoped if I made a success I might attain the object of my ambition, so I consented to play the part. I called again on Rossini, and was again disappointed that he did not ask me to sing. The only interest he displayed was in a *buffo* named Frizzi, who was engaged for Covent Garden. He confessed he had never heard him, nor, I believe, seen him ; but he had been strongly recommended, and Rossini was particularly anxious I should beg Costa to show him all the attention he could. I took leave of the old *maestro* without troubling him for any letters.

My first visit after I returned to London was to Mr. Gye. I agreed to the terms proposed, and he then accompanied me to the stage to inform Costa of my appearance in ' Il Trovatore.' When he left, Costa asked me if I had made an engagement. I said ' No.' ' A mistake,' said he ; ' never do business with the theatre without having all arrangements reduced to writing.' ' But,' said I, ' there is no engagement ;' and I related the terms on which I was going to sing. He merely said, ' Well, I will take care of you ; do your best, and probably something good will come of it.' I spoke to Harris, and he also seemed sanguine about my being engaged.

At the first rehearsal I attended, Tamberlik arrived about twenty minutes late. Costa pulled out his watch and showed it to him ; he made some excuse, having had a heavy performance in ' William Tell ' the night before. ' I excuse you this time,' said Costa ; ' but pray do not let it occur again.'

At the general rehearsal I was so nervous I sang ' Il balen ' nearly half a note sharp throughout. I was perfectly aware of it myself, but could not come down ; everybody thought I was going to make a dreadful failure. When I was dressed for the performance,

Costa came to my room, and, after examining my make-up attentively, requested me to make sundry alterations about my dress and hair. When he was satisfied that my appearance was all correct, he said, ' Now go and do your work, and do not let me hear any more talk about Italian jealousy.' I said I had never mentioned such a thing. He replied, ' It has been repeated to me you have. There are many singers here not Italians—Signor Tagliafico, for instance ; they have never suffered from jealousy.' I still protested my innocence. 'Well, well,' he said, ' I may be misinformed ; but if there should be any jealous feeling towards you, remember that nobody was ever jealous of an ass.'

My reception when I appeared on the stage was such that I was quite overcome. For five minutes I stood bowing whilst the audience and orchestra rose to their feet and cheered me ; the ladies waved their handkerchiefs as they stood up in the boxes and stalls. It was said that such a scene had not been witnessed at the Italian Opera since Grisi made her final bow to the public.

When the applause finished and I had to begin, the first few notes stuck in my throat ; but as I fell into my part, I conquered my agitation, and maintained my ground throughout the opera. I was congratulated by everybody concerned upon my success. It is needless to say I was very pleased ; only one little whisper might have marred my happiness, had not my con- science been perfectly clear on the subject. It was intimated to me that the authorities declared I had packed the house in order to secure the ovation I received. At that time I had no money to spare for such a purpose; I did not purchase a single ticket, nor did I make use of all the manager sent me. I gave a box to my friend who arranged the business between Mr. Gye and me, with strict injunctions not to applaud until the house gave unmistakable signs of approval. I sent Madame Sainton two stalls; and whatever else I received, I deposited in the waste-paper basket. Throughout my career, I have never given a single admission to anyone to applaud me either in theatre or concert-room; I have always depended on the verdict of the public. I sang at two subsequent performances in response to the usual intimation from the theatre; I had a fourth call, but I was engaged to sing in Liverpool the same night, so I was, very unwillingly, obliged to excuse myself. I was the more annoyed, as Rosa Czillag was to have sung in place of Gordosa, who had not been a success. I called on Mr. Gye, by appointment, to see if I could arrange anything definite for the season; he was detained, however, by business of greater importance, and I left the theatre without seeing him. I went directly over to Her Majesty's Theatre to see Mapleson, and ask for a box to witness the first appearance of Madame Guerrabella (Genevieve Ward) in 'I Puritani.' I was denied admission to his room by the Cerberus at the stage-door. I sent in my card, and the messenger returned in a few minutes, and informed me Mr. Mapleson wished to speak to me immediately on important business. He received me in his usual jovial manner—asked me some questions about my engagement at Covent Garden; I told him I was not under any engagement. 'Then you must come to me,' said he.   I demurred, as my secret wish was to be at Covent Garden.   However, Mapleson's cajolery, and my desire to be engaged at the Italian Opera, settled the matter, and I left the theatre with my engagement for that and the following season in my pocket.   The only stipulations I made were that I was not to be called on to play Don Giovanni nor Figaro in the ' Barbiere,' and that I retained the right to sing at private concerts.   I made my first appearance on a Saturday night after I had been singing at the Crystal Palace.   I was very nervous, and sang ' Il balen' atrociously.   I wished I could have dropped through the stage, and hidden myself for very shame ; but the public was merciful, and insisted on my repeating the song.   I pulled myself together, and the second time redeemed my honour.   I felt very disappointed with myself, and feared I had cancelled the success I made at Covent Garden.   The ' Trovatore' became my *bête noire ;* each day it was announced for performance in the evening was, to me, a day of utter misery until I had got through the second act. Strange to say, it was a favourite opera of mine.   I liked the part of Di Luna ; when I played it in English it never cost me a thought.   I presume the two slips I made, at the rehearsal at Covent Garden and the first performance at Her Majesty's, left an impression on my nervous system which I never succeeded in erasing.   During the season, I played De Nevers in 'Gli Ugonotti,' Almaviva in ' Le Nozze di Figaro,' etc.   Almaviva I found the most difficult part I ever attempted, and I never was at all satisfied with my performance of it.

In consequence of the influx of strangers to visit the Exhibition, our season was protracted until the month of September ; for the same reason the English Opera at Covent Garden opened early in the same month, and I was in a dilemma, for I was engaged at both houses. I succeeded in arranging matters amicably by singing at each alternately the few nights they were open together. On Monday I played in 'The Lily of Killarney,' English, at Covent Garden ; on Tuesday in 'Il Trovatore,' Italian, at Her Majesty's ; on Wednesday in 'Dinorah,' English, at Covent Garden. I do not know whether such a combination ever occurred before—it certainly has not since—I played at both Italian Operas and the English Opera in one season.

Until the production of Wallace's 'Love's Triumph,' about the middle of November, the operas of the *répertoire* were successfully played. The new opera was not a success ; the music and libretto were both charming, but the stage of Covent Garden was too large a frame for the picture, and there was a lack of elegance about the whole of the *mise-en-scène* which destroyed the brilliancy of the work. I believe it would have been a great success had it been played with spirit in a theatre such as the Princess's, where the dialogue could have been spoken more rapidly than in the large theatre.

I declined to sing the baritone part ; it was of no importance whatever dramatically or musically ; the only number it contained being a ballad introduced to make weight, *à propos* of nothing particular. I went into the stalls one day to hear a little of the rehearsal, and found Charles Lucas there. I had barely sat down by him than he said, 'Young man, you have made a mistake in refusing the part; the opera will be the greatest success we have had since "The Bohemian Girl."' I replied it would not be a success at all. My reply made him angry, and he asked sharply if I thought his long experience was worth nothing. 'I repeat,' said he, 'it will be an enormous success, and you will be sorry you did not take part in it.' It was not a success, but I was sorry I had refused the part, as Wallace was a good friend of mine, although I could not have done anything with such a part to render him any service.

The last opera of the season, and the last English opera I sang in at Covent Garden, was Balfe's 'Armourer of Nantes.' I had had a disagreement with the management, and in consequence my part in the last act, which was of importance to the development of the plot, was reduced to crossing the stage in a procession. I did not see any fun in waiting in my costume a whole act for this, so I declined to do it; and after some disputing it was arranged I should be represented by a 'double,' the consequence being that the *dénouement* remained a profound mystery.

During the run of the 'Armourer,' the theatre was opened free on the occasion of the marriage of the Prince of Wales. The house was densely crowded, but a more stupid audience I never sang to; there was literally no applause throughout the performance. A short Mask was played the same night, *à propos* of the royal nuptials. I do not recollect the title nor the name of the composer; the libretto was by John Oxenford.

In the first act of the 'Armourer' I had a barcarole to sing in the wing before I made my appearance on the stage; it was written to suit me exactly. Nobody knew better than Balfe how to put music into a singer's throat. In returning to the refrain after the second part of the melody, I made a very long *messa di voce* on the fifth of the key; this was made the subject of a bet among the gentlemen of the orchestra which I was called upon to decide. Some of them concluded that I began the *messa di voce* with my face towards the back of the stage, and then turned round gradually a complete circle, so making the *crescendo* and *diminuendo*. I laughed heartily at the idea, as I adopted no such device, which, indeed, would have had no effect in producing the result desired.

With the 'Armourer of Nantes' I bade farewell to the English Opera for some years. The first two seasons I was with Pyne and Harrison, my engagement did not contain any stipulation regarding the number of nights I was bound to sing, so, if required, and I generally was required, I had to sing every night. At Her Majesty's Theatre, 1860-61, we only played four times a week, the other two nights were devoted to Italian Opera the first half of the season; but on those nights I generally had a concert in London or the provinces, so I might as well, or better, have been playing in an opera. The last season at Covent Garden I would not sign for more than four nights a week; I did not accept engagements out of the theatre, so my work was lighter. Before that it had been tolerably severe. I cannot recapitulate all the operas I took part in, but I will give a sketch of my work during my first four seasons on the operatic stage, as nearly as I can remember.

In 1859-60 I sang in 'Dinorah' (first time on the English stage), 'Victorine' and 'Lurline'—new operas —'The Trovatore,' 'The Rose of Castille,' 'Satanella,' 'The Sonnambula'—new to me ; in 1860-61, 'Robin Hood,' 'The Amber Witch'—new—'Queen Topaz'—first time in England—'The Bohemian Girl' —new to me—'The Trovatore,' etc. ; in 1861-62, 'Ruy Blas,' 'The Puritan's Daughter,' and 'Lily of Killarney'—new—and operas of the *répertoire* which I had already taken part in ; in 1862-63, 'The Armourer of Nantes'—new—and operas of the *répertoire*. The average season must have been at least of five months' duration ; the average number of times I sang in each about 110. I had seldom more than a week's rest from rehearsal. Contrast this with the work young singers are called on to do in the latest edition of English opera ; theirs is a path of roses compared with that we of the old *régime* trod, and our emoluments were on a much more economic scale than are paid now ; though I will venture to remark, as far as my general observation goes, that there are some of the young aspirants of the present day who might have taken a lesson from many of my old comrades. I never had but once a quarrel with one of our company, and that was about some stage business, which was soon made up. With the management we might have been a family of porcupines ; on the slightest provocation quills shot up and caused wounds not readily healed. I wished for nothing more than to do my work in peace to the best of my ability. Earnest at all times, I never thought of the amount imposed on me ; I saw the willing horse invariably carried the heaviest pack, and had the least consideration shown him, but my enthusiasm was proof against the abuse of good-will. The only part I refused was that in 'Love's Triumph,' and had it not been that I was really much in need of rest, I do not think I should have refused it. During these four seasons I can only call to mind three occasions on which I disappointed the public.

We had one or two eccentric characters among the members of the English Opera Company ; George Honey was one. I never could make out why he had anything to do with the opera, or why anyone know-ing anything about the requirements of a singer, even a *buffo*, could have induced him to leave the sphere he was adapted to. He was a clever, eccentric comedian, and in a part like Don Florio in ' The Rose of Cas-tille,' the first part he played under the Pyne and Harrison management, with 'Why did you not say so at first ?' a comic twitch of the head, and an extrava-gant make-up, he made a decided hit. He had a hollow, unmusical voice, and knew very little about the art of singing ; yet he firmly believed his forte lay in serious song. His favourite attempt was ' A father's love ' from ' Lurline.' I never heard it, but I have been told on good authority it was the most comic thing he ever did. I did hear him attempt the long *buffo* scene in Balfe's ' Puritan's Daughter,' and that was one of the most dismal things I ever heard ; and so must it have proved to the audience, as it was entirely omitted after the first or second performance.

On one occasion, when we were playing 'The Rose of Castille' for Louisa Pyne's benefit, Honey, at the rehearsal, took me aside, and begged of me to give him plenty of time to get out the low C in the duet, as it was his great effect, and on former occasions I had done him out of his round of applause. Of course, I promised, and kept my promise; but the low C stuck on passage, and would not come out. I walked up the stage, and waited in expectation; when I turned round I saw my friend red as a peony, almost bursting, but not a sound could he produce. The audience took it as a good joke, and roared with laughter, to Honey's intense disgust. His good sense or good fortune led him back to his own sphere, in which he did excellent service; nobody who saw him as Eccles in 'Caste' will ever forget what an admirable performance it was.

St. Albyn (a second tenor) was another extraordinary character. He never had any voice to speak of, either in power or compass; he was for ever discovering a 'production' by which he could sing (?) the high C from the chest. Like the boa constrictor, in order to seize his prey, St. Albyn, to seize upon the high C, was obliged to have some unyielding object which he could grasp firmly. On the road home after the opera he used to exhibit for any friends who accompanied him, seizing the lamp-post, and uttering the most distressing screams. He gave me a specimen in my dressing-room one evening, and was quite satisfied he was on the highroad to wealth and undying fame. A few nights after he came to me looking very dismal, and informed me he was going to turn baritone. 'Baritone!' said I ; 'what, after the discovery you have made?' 'Ah,' said he, with a sigh, 'there's no help for it.' 'How's that?' I inquired. 'Well, the fact is,' he replied, 'I'm losing my voice.'

A libretto being in request, Palgrave Simpson called to see the manager with a production in his pocket. Said he : 'My dear Harrison, I have the very thing ; a splendid part for you—heroic, passionate—in fact, a part that will fit you like a glove!' The manager's eyes glistened, for he still felt being left out in the cold in 'The Puritan's Daughter.' 'And,' added Simpson, 'the best of it is you are dumb throughout the first two acts—not a line to speak nor a note to sing!'

'Thank you, sir ; I wish you a very good-morning ;' and Simpson, much to his surprise, was bowed out of the managerial presence forthwith.

CHAPTER XIV.

SPITE of the hard work and heart-burnings I experienced, it was with a feeling of deep regret I changed
my stage. I had enjoyed my little triumphs ; I had
won the esteem and friendship of my companions, and
I now found myself among comparative strangers.
Teresa Tietjens, Alboni, and Giuglini I had met at
some of the festivals, and in private concerts, but I
was not on intimate terms with them.   Mlle. Trebelli
I met whilst I was in Paris in 1862 at a party given
by Madame Orfila, to whom I was presented by some
friends of Patey's. At the request of the hostess I
sang a solo piece, after which Mlle. Trebelli, to whom
I was introduced, asked me if I would sing the duet
from ' Il Barbiere ' with her. I replied that it would

give me great pleasure. As we were moving towards the piano, Trebelli's father stepped up and inquired, ' Qu'est ce que tu vas chanter ?' ' Le duo du Barbier.' ' Avec qui ?' ' Avec ce monsieur anglais.' ' Comment ! avec un anglais !' (horrified). ' Mon Dieu !' He must have found reason to change his opinion of English singers, for he complimented me highly, and we became subsequently great friends.

In a short time I found myself as much at home in my new sphere as I had been in the old one. I found many comforts and attentions I had never before experienced. The dressing-room of the English operatic artist (I give my own experience) was uncarpeted, the toilette-table without a cover, the looking-glass, of the commonest description, was just large enough to show the head, and lighted by a jet of gas, protected by a thick wire shade, and a common oil-lamp. When I sang in ' Il Trovatore,' on my first appearance at the Italian Opera, I dressed in the same room I occupied during the English seasons, but what was my surprise at the metamorphosis I found ! Instead of a bare cell, it was converted into a comfortable room with a carpet, a clean table-cover, a cheval glass in addition to my old friend, and the stinking oil-lamp superseded by a couple of wax candles. These latter were the perquisite of the artist occupying the room, who used in most cases to carry them off after the performance, or as much of them as was left, and thus economize the cost of light in private life. It was a custom with the more economical to extinguish the candles, and pack them away as soon as the operation of dressing was over ; or, if the make-up was not elaborate,

they were not lighted at all, and so available as a
marketable commodity.   One, who was a member of
the R. I. O. Company for many years, it was well
known, used to travel with his portmanteau half full
with these spoils of the dressing-room.   I do not suppose Mario, Tamberlik, Faure, etc., travelled about
with a stock of candle-ends ; I know I did not.   I
found, also, a great improvement in the behaviour of
the dressers ; the hail-fellow-well-met, patronizing air
they assumed when I was only an Englishman gave
place to one of deference I was not prepared for when
I became an Italian.   Nor was this confined to
dressers ; outside the theatre I remarked a similar
increase of politeness and attention on the part of
individuals who, in other phases of life, were in the
habit of thanking God they were true John Bulls.
This might be ascribed to a flight of imagination on
my part had I not noticed an equivalent decrease
of attention and interest when I sacrificed health,
strength, and money in endeavouring to secure a home
for opera in the national tongue some twenty years ago.

In the course of my first Italian Opera season I had
two offers of engagements, either of which would probably have changed the whole course of my career.
Madame Carvalho, whom I met frequently at Chorley's and in private parties, asked me, after we had
been singing a duet one evening, to enter into negotiations with her husband with regard to an engagement
for the Théâtre Lyrique in Paris, where they were
about to put ' Don Juan ' on the stage with all the
care and attention for which that house was celebrated.
I declined, on the ground of never having sung in

French, and my imperfect conversational knowledge of the language. She replied that need not present any difficulty ; if I would entertain her proposal, the engagement would be made that I should not be required to sing for three months, during which time there would be ample time to exercise myself in conversation, and pass one or two parts in French with a good master, so as to acquire a proper accent.

Through our chorus-master, Chiaromonte, I had an offer from Calzado for the Italian Opera in Paris ; we did not, however, agree on the subject of terms. Had I had only myself to think of, any difficulty which stood in the way of my accepting either of these engagements might have been overcome ; but I had already a small family, which I could not afford to take about with me, and an establishment of my own which I did not feel inclined to break up, so I took no further steps about either.

At the termination of the English season 1862-63 I again went to Paris, when I paid my first visit to the Théâtre Français ; and I saw Gounod's ' Faust ' for the first time. I was prejudiced against both. I had heard so much about the superiority of French actors, and Chorley had so lauded ' Faust ' to the disparagement of modern Italian opera, that I determined nothing should make me like them. The play at the Français was ' Le fils de Giboyer,' with a cast I have never seen equalled—Got, Delaunay, Bressant, Prévost, Favart, Plessis, etc. The curtain had not long risen before prejudice had given place to admiration ; for the first time I saw what could be achieved by a combination of fine actors working together under a competent head with one common interest—the interest of the drama they were representing. It was a perfect whole ; there were strong situations which stood out, as the scene in which Giboyer discovers himself to his son ; and that of the reception where the daughter of the bourgeois, outraged by the supercilious way in which her lover (her father's secretary) is treated by the guests, offers him a cup of tea—a very simple incident in itself, but a most striking one as played by Favart and Delaunay ; these were only parts of the picture, not merely worked up for the individual display of a particular actor. But my prejudice received the severest rebuke from 'Faust' ; I was completely carried away by the music, and the way the opera was put on the stage. Madame Carvalho was the poetic embodiment of Marguerite ; Monjauze, a singer of whom very few of my readers will remember even the name, I have never seen equalled as 'Faust' ; and Balanqué, with the exception of Junca, who played the part with us at Her Majesty's Theatre in 1864, was the best Mephisto I have seen. The Valentine, whose name I do not remember, was a small man with a small voice, who strutted about like a bantam, and brought to my mind the fable of the frog and the ox. Mapleson had secured 'Faust' for the season of 1863. When he told me and mentioned the intended distribution of the parts, he said nothing about Valentine, so I inquired to whom it was to be confided. He said : 'Oh, anybody ; there is nothing in it.' 'Then,' said I, 'as you have not already disposed of it, give it to me.' 'Nonsense !' he replied ; 'I have something better than that for you ; I am not going to throw you away in such an insignificant part as that.'   In vain I attempted to convince him he was wrong, and that Valentine's death was the finest *ensemble* in the opera.   It was only after much earnest petitioning that he consented to my playing the part.   He only remarked : 'If you are determined I am only too happy, as it will strengthen the cast, and I wish you joy of it.'   His wish was fulfilled ; I had great joy of it !   It turned out so well that Gounod came to my dressing-room immediately after the death-scene to thank me cordially for having undertaken the part and created a new feature in the opera.   My brother baritones were not so cordial in their thanks.   Graziani remonstrated with me for having played it at all, as in consequence it was afterwards always given to the principal baritone, and he could find nothing in it worth doing.   Opinions differ ; it is a short part, but very sympathetic to the audience, and it does not contain one ineffective bar of music.   When 'Faust' was produced in English early in 1864, I suggested that Gounod might write a song for me, taking the melody which occurs in the prelude to the first act as a theme.   At first he demurred, as he considered he had not been well treated with regard to the business arrangements connected with his work ; but he con- sented when he learned it was for me, and in a few days he sent me the P. F. score of 'Even bravest heart may swell,' known in its Italian form as 'Dio possente.'

The season of 1863 opened with the 'Trovatore,' with the same cast as in 1862.   On the 7th May,

Schira's opera 'Niccolò de' Lapi' was produced for the first time, with Tietjens (Selvaggia), Trebelli (Laodomia), Giuglini (Lamberto), and myself (Niccolò) —a very trying part. It was singular that a professor of singing should have had so little perception of the register of a voice. My first number, a romance, 'Qui sulla bianca lapide,' was so high that I was obliged to have it lowered a semitone, and even then it lay at the utmost stretch of my voice, all between B flat and G above the bass stave. In the second act, I had a prayer with chorus which ended on F sharp below the stave. But the last act was the most exigent. Here I had three slow sustained movements to sing one after the other—the first lying on my back asleep in prison; the last, the most fatiguing of all, the prophecy —before Niccolò lays his head on the block, ending with 'L'Italia libera sarà!' It was only played three nights. To satisfy some of the principal singers, there were so many interpolations I think they confused the drama without increasing the musical effect; besides, it was badly put on the stage. We had an Italian stage-manager then, who could not speak two words of English. When anything went wrong, he used to give up the ghost, and march to and fro with his hands under the tails of a long overcoat muttering to himself. My companions were not interested in the work. I had not at that time read D'Azeglio's novel from which the drama was taken; and though I was highly complimented on my performance by those who spoke to me on the subject, I am sure I was not sufficiently imposing to give the proper dignity and weight to such a character as that of Niccolò de' Lapi.

I played Germont the elder in the 'Traviata' on the
first appearance of Mlle. Artôt, a pupil and imitator
of Madame Viardot. As I was leaving the theatre, I
went to her room to wish her 'Good-night,' and found
her lying on the floor in hysterics. She also played
'Maria' in 'La figlia del reggimento,' and 'Adalgisa'
to Tietjens' 'Norma.' She was a good singer, and
possessed undoubted histrionic talent ; but she marred
her performances by exaggeration—she would have
done more had she done less. 'Faust' I have
already mentioned. Tietjens was highly commended
for her 'Marguerite'; Giuglini sang charmingly ;
Trebelli made a great success as Siebel, although I
think it is a mistake to give the part to a contralto ;
Gassier was not a success as Mephisto. A contretemps occurred at the first representation, all the more
serious considering the financial importance of the
success of the opera. When I had finished the scene
of the cross with Mephisto, I walked deliberately up
to my dressing-room. I saw Giuglini in his room
preparing to put on his tights for the change of dress ;
I told him they were waiting on the stage for him—
Marguerite was ready to start for church, but there
was no Faust to meet her. A long wait ensued—ten
minutes or more—which seemed an hour to those who
were on the stage ; fortunately there was a patient
English audience in front, whose anger found vent in
a few hisses bestowed on Giuglini when he at length
reappeared on the scene. 'Faust' was an enormous
success ; we played it frequently throughout the remainder of the season. Early in July 'Oberon' was
reproduced, with Reeves in the character of Sir Huon,

Tietjens as Rezia, Alboni as Fatima, Trebelli as Puck, Bettini as Oberon, Gassier as Babekan, and myself as Scherasmin—a most uninteresting part dramatically, and insignificant musically—his only numbers being the quartet 'Over the dark blue waters,' and the duet 'On the banks of the Garonne.' My chief interest in the opera was Alboni's singing, which was splendid throughout. The song in the third act I can only describe as gorgeous ; and yet I never saw any singer more nervous, though it seemed impossible with such a physique as hers. When I led her on to the stage with my arm round her waist she trembled all over, and the perspiration dropped from her forehead like beads during the entire scene.

I took my holiday at Brunnen, on the Lake of Lucerne, with Patey. We had an adventure which almost ended fatally. We were across the lake at Treib fishing one evening, when I noticed that a storm was brewing. With some difficulty I induced the boatmen (fortunately we had two) to start on our return before it burst. They laughed at my fears ; but by the time we were about half-way across, the waves were so high they could scarcely move the boat. For a few moments even they looked dismayed ; but the danger we were in excited them to strain every nerve, and they managed to pull near in to the shore. It was, however, impossible to effect a landing. I had given up all for lost, when a huge wave lifted the boat round the head of the jetty into smooth water, and we were safe. Shortly after we landed, a cry was raised that there was a barge sinking. She was coming in from Fluelen timber-laden, the three men on board screaming for help. There was no time to be lost ; but nobody seemed inclined to risk going out to their assistance. After a great deal of persuasion, a small crew at last volunteered ; they rescued the men, and fastened a hawser to the prow of the barge, by which she was hauled up to the shore a few feet under water. The steamer could not land her passengers, and passed along on the other side of the lake.

On my return, I made my first appearance at a 'Three Choir Festival' at Worcester. Among other works, I sang in a new oratorio, entitled 'Israel's Return from Babylon,' by Herr Schachner, which did not impress me much. Herr Schachner called on me one morning to run through one or two passages in his work ; I was not in the room, so he amused himself reading through Benedict's 'Richard Cœur de Lion,' which happened to be lying on the piano, as I was studying it for Norwich. 'Ach Gott !' said he, as I returned to my room, 'what is that for music ? It is so weak—so lemonade !' However, at Norwich Festival the week after, it proved stronger than Mr. Schachner anticipated ; it was a great success, and was performed several times after in London and the provinces. After Norwich I joined Mapleson's company for the operatic tour, commencing with a season of three weeks in Dublin. Sims Reeves was engaged to play Edgardo, Sir Huon and Faust. 'Lucia' was the opera on the opening night, with a new addition to our company, Elisa Volpini, a charming Spaniard (who made a real success), Reeves, and myself. I played Enrico for the first time, and for the only time,

in the costume of the Highlander as represented outside a snuff-shop—an absurd fashion adopted in Italy
and most Italian theatres at that time. I afterwards
had a dress of my own made, in accordance with the
locale in which the drama takes place. A photograph
of me in this costume was standing on the chimney-
piece of the house of an intimate friend of mine in
Scotland when his bailiff called upon him one morning
to transact some business. He remarked, 'That is a
very good portrait.' 'Do you recognise the likeness?'
said my friend. 'Oh yes,' he replied; 'it's Oliver
Cromwell!'

The house was packed to suffocation for the first
performance of 'Faust'; expectation had been raised
to such a pitch by the notices of its enormous success
in London, and Tietjens, Trebelli, Reeves and I
formed a very attractive cast. The opera was received with immense applause; on the stage all went
well without a hitch until the church scene. The
gods used to amuse themselves between the acts of
an opera by treating their friends to specimens of
their own vocal talents, and would not allow the opera
to proceed to the interruption of their own displays.
It happened that as all was ready to commence the
third act, a gentleman aloft was regaling the gallery
with a song. The audience began to show signs of
impatience, as they were more interested in the new
opera than in the celestial amateur. Mapleson also
grew impatient, and gave orders to ring up the curtain,
which was no sooner done than a storm burst out in
the gallery, which was only calmed on the curtain
being lowered again; the gentleman then continued

his song.   At the conclusion a voice calmly remarked :
' Now we're ready ; you can go on as soon as you like !'
The   stage-manager   rang   up   and   went   round   to
arrange the procession on the opposite side.   Mephisto
had   to   appear   through   a   trap   which   was   worked
according to signals from the stage—first bell to make
ready, second to send up, third to lower.   Mapleson
came   round   again   very   excited   by   the   disturbance
which had taken place, gave the first pull and retired ;
the stage-manager returned immediately after and gave
what he thought the pull to make ready, instead of
which up came Mephisto, long before he was wanted.
The   next   pull   was   given,   and   down   went   poor
Mephisto just as he was about to open his mouth ;
nor could he induce the carpenters in attendance to
send him back again, so that Marguerite had the
entire scene to herself.

I found the Dublin audience very enthusiastic at all
times ; but occasionally the facetiousness of the gallery
was somewhat troublesome.   My first experience of
it was in the scene of Valentine's death.   After the
duel, Martha, who rushed in at the head of the crowd,
raised my head and held me in her arms during the
first part of the scene.   There was a death-like stillness in the house, which was interrupted by a voice
from the gallery calling out : ' Unbutton his weskit !'
Of course the untimely jest caused a general titter,
and for a few moments took off the attention of the
greater part of the audience ; I felt annoyed, but I
kept my attention fixed on my work, and soon
succeeded in bringing back that of the audience to
myself, and made a great success.

A great many stories have been published *à propos* of the witticisms indulged in by the gods at the Theatre Royal, Dublin; this one I have never seen in print. A celebrated English tenor, by no means a favourite in Dublin, was singing on its first production there in an opera by Balfe, which had been played before her Majesty the Queen, that circumstance being duly announced in playbills and advertisements. In the last act he had a ballad which in London was rapturously encored every evening during the run of the opera. In Dublin it was received in dead silence, and as the singer retired up the stage a voice from the gallery demanded, apparently with great curiosity: 'And was that the way you sung it for the Queen?'

One night when I was playing Plunkett in 'Marta' at the end of the 'Good-night' quartet, according to the business arranged, I took up a candle and proceeded to light the two girls to their room, but I had scarcely put my foot inside the door than a witty individual called out: 'Ah, ah! would ye now?' A quiet joke like that at the end of an act can do no harm; but in the midst of a scene like the death of Valentine, a jest is both ill-natured and vulgar; it robs those who are interested of their enjoyment, it destroys, for a time at least, the illusion, and distracts the performer to the detriment of the scene he is portraying. In the case of the tenor, it was sufficiently humiliating to have to retire without applause; the jest, although perhaps unintentionally so, was simply brutal!

We returned from the provinces to London for

five performances at Her Majesty's Theatre at cheap
prices, 'Faust' being announced for the opening night.
Sims Reeves, who had been in Wales, sent word to
say he had caught a little cold and could not appear.
The house was crammed to suffocation, and there was
nobody in the company who knew the part.   What
was to be done ?   It would have been a fearful loss to
dismiss such a house, and there was not the slightest
hope of them accepting any other opera.   At last
Volpini (husband of the *prima donna* of that name)
was prevailed on to go on, and went through wonder-
fully well, considering that what he knew of the music
he had only picked up by ear.   A little knowledge
happened to be a very useful thing on that occasion.

CHAPTER XV.

ON the 23rd of January, 1864, ' Faust ' was brought out in English at Her Majesty's Theatre, and was played three or four times a week until the 5th of March. I played my original part Valentine, introducing my new song ; Reeves was the Faust ; Marchesi, Mephisto ; Madame Lemmens - Sherrington, Marguerite ; and Madame Florence Lancia, Siebel. Owing to a misunderstanding between Marchesi and the management respecting a renewal of his engagement for two weeks beyond the period originally stipulated, I was called on to play Mephisto at a short notice— too short for me to represent the part as I conceived it. I should have liked to dress it differently, and get rid of that abominable red costume ; but I had no time to arrange anything, barely sufficient to learn my music thoroughly. On the first night I essayed the part I was handicapped by my friend Swift, who was called on suddenly to take Reeves's place. As usual, he did not know his music, and was quite innocent of the stage business. Whenever I had to address him,

I could not find him ; throughout the opera, whenever we had a few bars' rest, he left the scene to take care of itself, and retired to the wings to study what was coming.   I do not know what effect his vagaries had on the audience, but on me they were most distressing.

My eldest daughter, Edith, was taken by her mother to see one of the morning performances—her first visit to a theatre.   She was told of the duel scene, and impressed with the idea that it was only in play, in case it might startle her.   All went well until she saw Reeves and me using our swords, then the little mouth began to pucker up and the lips to tremble, but she kept on repeating to herself, ' It's only in fun,' until at last I received the fatal wound and fell ; then she burst out into a yell, and had to be carried out of the theatre, to which nothing could induce her to return.   She was not satisfied until she saw me safely seated at dinner.

In signing a new agreement with Mapleson for the seasons of 1864 and 1865, I did not notice a paragraph in the contract which precluded me from singing in the United Kingdom otherwise than at Her Majesty's, or other theatre under Mapleson's management, except by his permission.   I was engaged for the operatic tour in the autumn of 1864 and that in the spring of 1865, but I had some months to fill up between the two.   This caused me some anxiety, as I had never thought of singing out of my own country, and consequently had not cultivated the acquaintance of any of the agents who catered for the Continental houses. Through the instrumentality of Volpini, I signed a contract to sing at the Lyceum Theatre, Barcelona, for three months, from about the 1st of December.

In the season of 1864 three operas, new for England, were announced. Of these only one, 'The Merry Wives of Windsor,' with the title of 'Falstaff,' was produced. It was one of the operas in which I enjoyed myself. I had little anxiety, as, with the exception of the duet with Falstaff, there was nothing of any importance to sing, and that was not very exigent. Tietjens and a very good contralto from Vienna, Caroline Bettelheim, played the two merry wives; Gassier and I their respective husbands; Junca was Falstaff; Giuglini, Fenton; Guiseppina Vitali, a fair soprano, Anne Page. Manfredi played Slender (Lyall played it in after-seasons, and admirably), and Mazzetti Dr. Caius, very indifferently. The opera was well put on the stage; the moonlight scene in Windsor Forest at the end was one of Telbin's masterpieces. Tietjens and I used to have great fun in the scene when Ford empties the buck basket, expecting to find Falstaff hidden therein, I turning out the foul linen and she pelting me with it, though occasionally it was a somewhat unsavoury game, for, to carry out the illusion, like the man who painted himself black all over to play Othello, our property man supplied linen which was decidedly foul.

'La forza del destino' was not brought out until some years later, and 'Tannhäuser' not at all during my Italian career. I always regret this, as I had a great desire to play Wolfram. Gounod's 'Mirella,' which had not been promised, was produced on the 5th of July. Tietjens played 'Mirella,' a part which I never thought suited her. I had little to do in it, and that little was cut down after the first night. Owing in a great measure, I believe, to an accident, the whole of the scene between Vincenzo and Ourrias at the beginning of the third act was left out. Ourrias, who has sworn to take Vincenzo's life, strikes down Vincenzo as he leaves the scene. Giuglini would not rehearse the stage business ; the consequence was he did not drop down at the right moment, and my stick, coming in contact with his head, brought him down with a sounding thwack. This opera was also well put on the stage, and well played throughout ; all of us engaged in it exerted ourselves to the utmost to make another success for Gounod. Carvalho and his brother-in-law Miolan came over from Paris on purpose to superintend the last rehearsals.

To assist in making the cast of ' Fidelio ' as complete as possible, I undertook the small part of the Ministro ; I also played Plunkett in ' Martha,' and during the after-season, for the first time, the Duke in ' Lucrezia Borgia.'

The Shakespeare Centenary Festival took place at Stratford-on-Avon in April, at which I sang in a miscellaneous concert and ' The Messiah.' I was much amused when I went to the hall for the latter performance to find men parading outside the doors bearing placards warning the public not to enter and listen to the devil's drums and trumpets. Mellon wrote a song for me to the words ' Take, oh take those lips away,' which I sang at the miscellaneous concert, and also at the supper held at the Freemasons' Tavern on the eve of Shakespeare's birthday, accompanied by Benedict. The assembly had become very much excited in consequence of a scene between

some partisans of G. V. Brooke* (who, unknown to
most of the guests, was present) and the chairman,
Benjamin Webster.   The confusion and clamour
became intolerable.   It was suggested that the only
way of restoring order would be for me to sing ; I
complied, and in an instant silence prevailed.   I
had scarcely finished the last note when the room
became a perfect pandemonium ; the guests mounted
on the tables, cheering and waving their handkerchiefs,
insisting upon an encore.   With this I also complied,
and then, finding the disturbance was about to re-
commence, I made my escape.

I had little time for a holiday, as the season ended
on the 13th of August, and the Hereford Festival
began on the 30th.   I had not very heavy work to
do : the second part of the 'Creation'; the music of
Rossini's 'Stabat Mater,' with English words, which
had nothing to do with the Latin hymn ; a part of
the 'Messiah'; Benedict's 'Richard,' and sundry pieces
at the evening concerts.   The Birmingham Festival
followed on the 5th of September.   Here I had more
to do, namely, Elisha in Costa's 'Naaman,' performed
for the first time ; the whole of the bass solos in the

* Gustavus Vasa Brooke was born in Dublin : he was a student at
Trinity College.   On an occasion when a favourite actor disappointed the
public, he offered his services to play 'Hamlet.'   There was no dress in
the theatre to fit him, and he played the part in a velveteen jacket.   His
success was such that he devoted himself forthwith to the stage.   He
made his first appearance in London, at the Olympic Theatre, in the part
of Othello with great success.   He was a great favourite in the provinces,
especially in Liverpool.   In Australia he was the idol of the public.   He
was on board the *London*, making his second voyage to Australia, when
that steamer took fire.   Nothing would induce him to leave her.   He
remained assisting the other passengers to escape until it was too late to
save himself, and so lost his life.

Messiah ' ; Sullivan's cantata ' Kenilworth,' and songs in the miscellaneous concerts. The part of Elisha was written for Belletti, but as he had left England and retired from professional life, it was Costa's desire I should undertake it. It suited me exactly, and I succeeded in satisfying Costa with my performance. Like Balfe, he knew how to write for singers, an all-important essential in writing a vocal work. Whatever else they may have to find fault with in Costa's work, our young composers would do well to study his treatment of the voice, a subject on which they apparently have never bestowed a thought. At a pianoforte rehearsal at the *maestro's* house, where all the singers taking part in the work were assembled, I had, as usual, an attack of nervousness ; the first words I had to sing were, ' What can I do for thee ?' I had lost my head, and did not sing the right notes, although there is no difficulty about them. Costa turned round laughing, and replied to the question, ' Sing in tune !'

The operatic tour followed immediately, about which I have nothing particular to record, except that Gardoni was our principal tenor, a fine singer, and a much better actor than he generally had credit for. He was a very good Faust and Sir Huon, although the music of the latter, written for Braham, did not suit him. In ' Mirella ' he was excellent, a great improvement in every way on Giuglini. I never could understand why Gardoni should be comparatively forgotten, and Giuglini quoted as one of the great artists who have lived. Gardoni was the superior in every way; his voice was pure, Giuglini's was throaty.   He was a handsome man, and in parts which suited him an excellent actor.   Giuglini was an awkward, ungainly man, and no actor at all ; Gardoni could sing any style of music, *cantabile* or florid ; Giuglini could not execute a rapid passage of four notes.   What I conceive established him as a great favourite was a lackadaisical sentimentality which the public, especially the British public, accepts for poetic sentiment.   Withal, Giuglini was the last of his race ; there has been no tenor on the Italian stage since who has been able to fill the place he left vacant.

I started for Barcelona towards the end of November. At Paris I called on the agent Verger to receive a month's pay in advance, according to my contract, but the money had not arrived.   I amused myself taking my wife, who accompanied me, sight-seeing.   Mapleson was in Paris also at the time, looking after novelties, and we all went one night to the Théâtre Lyrique, where they were playing 'The Magic Flute,' in which Madame Carvalho played Pamina, and Christine Nilsson Astriffiammante.   I was very much delighted with Madame Carvalho ; it was the only time I ever heard Pamina's air really sung.   I do not remember any singer who sang Mozart's music so well as she did ; one of her favourite songs in private concerts was 'Voi che sapete,' which was simply the perfection of singing.   The last time I heard her was in the part of the Countess in ' Le nozze di Figaro ' ; although her voice, never a great one, was much worn and sharp, her singing of the air 'Dove sono' was one of the finest pieces of vocal declamation I ever heard. I was not at all impressed with Nilsson ; she had a charming voice, but her singing was mechanical, and altogether her performance was stiff and cold. Mozart's music is easy to 'get through,' but most difficult to *sing.*   The money was so long on the road that Verger advised me not to wait, but to go on to Barcelona, where it would be 'all right.'   I had not sufficient confidence, and preferred waiting in Paris without being at the expense and trouble of a journey to Spain ; but I gave notice that at the expiration of a given number of days more I would wend my way back to England.   Perhaps this had the effect of wakening them up, for the amount arrived, and I started.   I forgot to add that I saw 'Un ballo in maschera' at the Italian Opera during my stay in Paris, with Madame Charton - Demeur, Fraschini, Delle-Sedie, etc.   Except that Fraschini had a splendid voice, and the men in the stalls generally wore black-dress coats and lavender or other light-coloured pants, and, that the necks of the double basses might not interfere with a view of the stage, the instruments were buried in holes in the floor of the orchestra, so that they might as well have been played in the next street, there was nothing which struck me particularly. We stayed at a hotel kept by a man who had been *concierge* of that I generally put up at, in consequence of a letter he wrote me, promising all sorts of comforts and conveniences at very moderate rates.   The hotel was small, the rooms were small, the number of guests was *very* small, being limited to three—my wife, self, and manservant.   The waiter, a most shaky-looking young man, I found, on inquiring about his health, slept over an open drain.   The only things I found supplied on a liberal scale were dust and the bill. After a great deal of experience of hostelries, I have concluded that the only cheap one is that in which you can procure what you want, whatever you have to pay for it.

The journey from Paris was decidedly tiresome. To relieve the monotony we got on the wrong route. The evening after we left, I began to think we were very late arriving at Perpignan, so after a little hesitation I asked a gentleman what time we ought to reach it. 'Oh,' said he, 'you are not on the way there ; you ought to have changed at Narbonne.' 'Then,' said I, 'where on earth are we going to ?' 'You are on the road to Marseilles, and we shall stop soon at Cette, where you had better get out and take the early morning train back to Perpignan. They will send you back free of expense if you explain that you were not warned about the change at Narbonne.' I thanked my kind fellow-traveller cordially. I did not meet with quite such a friendly reception from the station-master at Cette, though, as my friend predicted ; I did not understand much of what he said, but it sounded very like abuse to my ears. However, station-master number two was more civil, and promised to make all straight for us. There was nothing for it but to find a resting-place for the night, which was soon accomplished. We partook sparingly of a very uninviting meal, and drank the sourest liquid called wine I ever tasted. We hurried off while it was still dark next morning, instead of taking a good long rest, and found, on arriving at Perpignan, that the *diligence* did not start until eight or nine in the evening. The atmosphere was still, to us, summery. We strolled about and enjoyed the sun and blue sky. According to the 'Encyclopædia Britannica' there are some sights to see—a cathedral, etc.; but we did not know of them, so they remained unvisited. From Perpignan we crossed the Pyrenees to Gerona in a *diligence* drawn for most of the journey by the most wretched cattle I ever beheld, and inhabited by industrious fleas. We arri ved at the frontier about five in the morning, and had to wait a couple of hours for the Custom-house officer to examine our baggage. There was a sort of *café* on each side of the narrow street. I tried both, but found it would be impossible to make a meal in either. Each of the rooms I entered had a fire in the middle of the floor, round which squatted three or four old crones looking like the witches watching the caldron in 'Macbeth,' who did not even take the trouble to ask me if I wanted anything. I do not as a rule look for dirt when I am travelling, and often do not see it when it gives great offence to many ; but here no search was necessary—it was evident to the dullest vision.

I had among my luggage three large boxes containing stage necessaries—tights, shirts, collars, wigs, etc. The officer pounced upon one of these to be opened ; he was very much astonished when he found an assortment of firearms, swords, daggers, etc., interspersed with imitation jewellery, decorations, etc. ; he was nevertheless very polite, and when I informed him whither I was bound, and for what purpose, he ordered the box to be closed and not another package to be touched.

Before arriving at Gerona we had to ford two

streams, one of them deep, and with a rapid current. Fortunately we had better horses than during most of the journey. It was afternoon when we arrived at Gerona, very hungry, but we could not find a morsel of food ; the only attempt at eatables was some large almond comfits, which were anything but comforting to an empty stomach. The train seemed to travel as it was convenient to the engine-driver ; we stopped at every station, and many times where there was no sign of one, but we did ultimately arrive at Barcelona. There we had another Custom-house visit ; after the usual preliminaries I was ordered—they were not so polite as at the frontier—to open my wife's portmanteau. The inspector thought he had discovered a prize in a large paper parcel which lay on the top of the contents, and asked me what it was. I told him I did not know, and he had better unfold it and find out. There were so many folds of paper about it, I wondered myself what precious article it could be. At last the unrolling came to an end, and out fell an old pair of stays. I could not help indulging in a quiet snigger as I received instructions to fasten up the portmanteau and clear out.

There was no mistake about being in the land of garlic ; each time the omnibus conductor put his head inside the vehicle I imagined I could see the fumes floating about in the atmosphere, they were so dense. The odour I had already become accustomed to ; it began about a quarter of a mile before arriving at the first Spanish village, gradually increasing until we arrived at Barcelona, where it reached its zenith. In about half an hour after my arriving at the hotel, 'de las cuatro naciones,' I became possessed of, to me, some curious facts. The manager with whom my contract was made did not exist, so far as Barcelona was concerned ; my name was entirely unknown, as it had not appeared in the announcements, and the proprietor of the hotel who gave me the information seemed to me to be wondering what mad freak had brought me so far away from home. However, I sent over a card to the manager informing him of my arrival, and that I was at his disposal whenever he had need of me. To make all complete, the dinner, even after such a long fast, was very bad, and the wine detestable. By appointment I had an interview with the manager next day, and it was arranged I was to make my first appearance with a tenor who had just arrived in a few days in ' Il Trovatore.' I was only acquainted with one member of the company, the orchestral conductor, Bottesini, and he was going away to fulfil another engagement, and would not be conducting when I made my *début*. Before his departure they played an opera of his, ' Marion Delorme,' in which there was some very good music, but I have never heard of it since. We had a rehearsal every day of ' Il Trovatore ' at the piano for about ten days, and one or two with the orchestra, and the general rehearsal the night before the first performance. I found myself in excellent voice when I started, and sang through the first act with great vigour. Everybody seemed perfectly satisfied, and prophesied all kinds of good things ; but suddenly, whilst I was talking after the curtain dropped, my voice left me, and I could scarcely whisper. I had to go through the remainder of the rehearsal in dumb show ; when I returned to the hotel I was perfectly miserable, and really began to think it was a mad freak to come away so far from home. The next day when I awoke I found my voice quite clear and right again ; the loss of it was caused, not by cold, but by nervous excitement, which a good night's rest had carried off. I went more cautiously about my work at the performance, husbanding my resources somewhat in the beginning. The public received me with great favour ; they applauded almost every phrase, and after my song 'Il balen,' I was called down to the footlights several times.

I made my mark with the public, and retained their sympathy throughout my stay. My second opera was 'Rigoletto,' which I had not played before ; that was followed by 'La Traviata,' in which I received a tremendous ovation after 'Di Provenza,' an air which, in my opinion, is often too severely criticised. If it is sung as a barrel-organ would play it, I confess it is monotonous and commonplace ; but if artistically sung and declaimed, it is neither one nor the other, but a charming and effective song.

In 'Rigoletto' the first night I was so terribly in earnest that in the last scene I ripped open the sack without thinking what it might contain, and to my horror beheld an enormous black moustache. I closed it again instantly, but the audience had already seen, and a general titter ensued.

I seemed to have got into a sea of Verdi, for after this they wished me to play 'Macbeth.' I was sorely tempted, I was so anxious to try it ; but I could not see anything approaching a Lady Macbeth in the

MR. SANTLEY IN 'RIGOLETTO.'

To face page 238.

prima donna to whom the part was entrusted, and the *mise-en-scène*, as far as I could make out, was the most inappropriate. It was produced with Colonnese, a *basso cantante*, for whom the part was much too high ; however, he succeeded in going through it all except the romance in the last act, which he suppressed. In Barcelona, it was a recognised rule that an opera should be played entire, unless it was announced that certain pieces would be left out. No notice was taken in the bills of the romance in ' Macbeth,' consequently the audience were all on the *qui vive* to hear it, and when they found it was passed over, and the last scene commenced, some disappointed individual in the gallery called out, ' But where's the romance ?' Others joined in, until at last there arose a fearful hubbub ; the curtain went down, and after a few moments' pause out came the call-boy to explain to the audience that M. Colonnese was not accustomed to sing the romance, and did not know it, therefore could not oblige them. He withdrew, and the storm burst out again more furiously than before ; they were determined to sit there until they heard the romance. Again the call-boy made his appearance ; silence was restored after a time, and he told them that M. Colonnese, although he had never sung the piece, and did not know it without the music, would come forward and sing it if they would allow him to read it from the score. ' Oh yes ;' with or without the score, it did not matter, so that he sang the romance. The curtain rose, and on came Colonnese, looking rather sheepish, with the score of the opera, and went through the piece. At the end he received a tremendous round of applause, and the opera was allowed to proceed in perfect quietness.

I was very glad, when I had seen it, that I had kept to my resolution not to play in it. The *mise-en-scène* and dressing were simply ludicrous. The witches were got up after the fashion of Mother Hubbard, with hats and crutch-sticks, and short petticoats just below the knee, made of plaid stuff of such patterns as were never worn in or out of Scotland. Macduff wore a Highland kilt with a well-starched smooth white collar round his neck, and instead of a claymore he carried a small neat dress-sword hanging at his belt. He had his hair nicely curled, and altogether looked very spruce. Lady Macbeth wore a white flowing robe, with an enormous tartan sash of no particular clan, and only wanted a touch of the brogue to make her complete. I played Enrico in ' Lucia,' the small part of Oberthal in ' Il Profeta,' to oblige the management, and lastly Renato in ' Un ballo in maschera.'

Spite of sundry discomforts, I enjoyed my three months' stay in Barcelona. The bright sky and sun, instead of the fog and darkness in England, were more than sufficient to atone for the indifferent food and accommodation I found. The audience at the opera was very exigent, and at times they used to indulge in rather coarse invective when they were not satisfied ; but personally I found them very interested and attentive, and profuse in applause. The drawback against this was the difficulty I had in conjuring money out of the managerial treasury ; as I went in at one door the manager escaped by another, a game of which I soon grew tired. Even legal threats produced no effect. After some days of fruitless endeavour to catch my man, I pinned him at last in a *cul-de-sac*, and then and there explained my intention—unless the money due to me was forthcoming before twelve the following day, to leave Barcelona by the *diligence* the same evening. As I had become a favourite with the public, he could not afford to lose my services, and before the appointed hour my claim was satisfied. Knowing where the shoe pinched, I had not so much difficulty in obtaining what was justly due to me afterwards.

The Lyceum is a splendid theatre—like the Scala, very good for sound—but the habit of smoking in the corridors and in the ante-chambers of the boxes renders the atmosphere very unpleasant, even to a smoker, to sing in ; the lady singers must find it very trying, unless they are sufficiently strong-minded to indulge in a whiff themselves. At times, when there was a very full house, towards the end of the opera, the back of the pit was scarcely discernible from the stage, in consequence of the dense cloud of smoke which hung over it. The orchestra and chorus were both very fair, and Castagneri, who succeeded Bottesini, was a very able conductor, besides being a very amiable man. For my last performance I played ' Rigoletto,' after which I was called out several times to receive a farewell ovation.

The next day, my birthday, I started on my return journey, with Bottesini's father under my care as far as Paris. I had only two days at home, and then started to join Mapleson's company at Dublin. I arrived on the morning of their first performance. During the forenoon I strolled over to the theatre, and found them rehearsing 'Lucrezia Borgia.' The gentleman who had undertaken the part of the Duke seemed to know very little of it, and I wondered how he was going to get through it. After awhile Tietjens espied me standing in the wings, rushed off the stage, and begged of me to sing in the evening. I pleaded fatigue after my journey from Spain and across to Dublin, and I feared I should not remember the part, as I had only sung it once or twice, and that some time ago. However, she said: 'If you don't sing, the theatre must be closed. You hear that poor man hardly knows a note of his part, and Swift' (my everlasting friend) 'is so hoarse he can scarcely make a sound.' I ultimately gave way, and did sing at night, and such a comical performance I never before or since took part in. Wherever the tenor had anything important to do, we cut the music according as Arditi called to us from the orchestra. Two or three times we were on the point of having a disturbance in the gallery; nothing but the respect the audience entertained for Tietjens and myself could have prevented it. We arrived at the end, and the curtain dropped to a storm of howling and hissing; but we had saved the performance, and went home content.

Towards the end of March I made my first appearance in Italian opera in my native town at the old Theatre Royal. It seemed like a dream to find myself on the stage which I had ten years before contemplated with longing eyes, without a ray of hope that I should ever appear on it. It was a most sympathetic old theatre, easy both to speak and sing in. We played 'Faust,' 'Trovatore,' etc. We finished the spring tour at Manchester. In addition to the operas already in my *répertoire* I played Carlo Quinto in 'Ernani.'

CHAPTER XVI.

IN the season of 1865 two events occurred of importance. Giuglini, who had been ill for some months,
had fallen into so hopeless a condition that his name
was withdrawn from the prospectus—a great disappointment to the subscribers and frequenters of Her
Majesty's Theatre. He was ordered back to his
native place by his medical advisers, where he
lingered until 12th October. He was a great loss,
and as a singer he has never been replaced; he was
the last tenor who appeared in England of the real
Italian school. There have been more powerful lungs,
and more energetic limbs, but not one of the tenors
who succeeded him could compare with him as a
singer; his phrasing was perfect, which everyone who
heard him in 'I Puritani,' 'Faust,' 'Lucrezia Borgia,'
and many other operas, will readily admit.

The other great event was the first appearance of
Ilma di Murska in 'Lucia.' She made a great success artistically and financially; throughout the season
she drew crowded houses whenever she appeared.

She was an excellent artist, and an accomplished and exceedingly well-read woman. She possessed undoubted genius, though of a somewhat erratic order. She possessed something else which was not so pleasant—a big black dog named Pluto, who accompanied her wherever she went. He used to attend rehearsals until I found his odour so offensive that I insisted on his being turned out of the green-room, for which I was severely reprimanded by his mistress. Although her voice would class her as a light soprano, she was, in my opinion, much more at home in the dramatic than the florid opera. For instance, her Senta in the 'Flying Dutchman' was by far the finest impersonation of all the characters I have seen her play. In 'Lucia,' in the 'Sonnambula,' 'Linda,' etc., it was in the dramatic scenes where she made her success. Her Leonora in the 'Trovatore' was admirable; I do not remember any finer. She was most eccentric in her ways, which may be accounted for in some measure by the manners and customs of the people among whom she was born and brought up, which, according to her narration, must have closely bordered on savagery. I was conversing with her on one occasion about the language of her native country, Croatia, when she informed me that the low peasantry were mere cannibals, that when they were blessed with more children than they could conveniently provide for they devoured the infants. I thought she must be jesting, and told her so, but she assured me seriously it was a fact. She was exceedingly superstitious, and at the same time very devout; she always said a short prayer and made the sign of the cross before going on to the stage, and, if she happened to be conversing, would interrupt the conversation in order thus to prepare herself for her work.

She was very sensitive, especially in the matter of age. One evening, when we were playing 'The Magic Flute,' I was waiting in the wings to go on for my second scene, when I heard somebody near at hand sobbing violently. I looked about, but could not discover 'the soul in pain.' The sobs continuing, I stepped around to the next wing, and there discovered Ilma di Murska with a pocket-handkerchief to her eyes, sobbing as though her heart would break. I tried to pacify her, and remonstrated with her on giving way so, having to go on immediately for the great song. For some time I could not induce her to tell me the cause of her grief; at last, after a good deal of persuasion, she sobbed out: 'It is a-all that na-na-nasty X.'s f-f-fault!' 'Why,' said I, 'what has she been doing?' 'Sh-sh-she's been tel-el-elling un-untruths a-bou-bou-bout me!' 'Well, what has she said?' 'Oh! oh! oh! the w-wi-wicked thi-i-ing says I-I-I'm' (with an explosion) 'fo-fo-forty-five!' She had barely time to dry her eyes when she had to go on the stage; her grief, however, did not seem to affect her powers, for, to my astonishment, she sang as well as ever. No other singer whom I have heard, except Jenny Lind, sang the slow movement of 'Non paventar' as well as Di Murska; but she lacked Jenny Lind's firm accent and brilliancy of execution, consequently the quick movement was not on a par with the other, and I must confess I always felt somewhat disappointed with it.

The tenor engaged to take Giuglini's place, Emanuele Carrion, a Spaniard who for many years enjoyed a high reputation in Italy, Russia, Spain, etc., came to England too late to establish himself as a favourite with the public. He was a genuine artist, but his voice had lost its freshness, and age had deprived his presence of what comeliness it had possessed, the consequence being that he made very little impression on the *habitués* of the theatre. M. Joulain, the tenor who had been on the tour with us, played Edgardo in 'Lucia,' and essayed Raoul in the 'Huguenots,' both unsuccessfully.

I played three new important parts during the season—Papageno in 'Il Flauto Magico,' Creonte in Cherubini's 'Medea,' and Pizarro in 'Fidelio.' Cipriani Potter told me many times I was the only Pizarro from whom he heard every note of the *aria* through the instrumentation. I suppose it must have been the quality of my voice, as Staudigl, whom he had heard in the part, must have possessed a more powerful organ. I believe I sang the music of Creonte well enough, but I know that my representation of the Grecian king lacked dignity. I was not satisfied with either my dress or make-up, yet I had nobody but myself to blame; I made a considerable improvement when the opera was revived some years afterwards at Drury Lane. I made a success in the part of Papageno; a celebrated critic told me that I sang the music better than any baritone he had ever heard, and that, although I did not possess the comic powers of Giorgio Ronconi, there was a quiet humour in my acting which gave him great pleasure.

I had nearly fallen a victim to a very unpleasant trick during one performance of this opera. The supper which Tamino commands for the hungry Papageno consisted of pasteboard imitations of good things, but the cup contained real wine, a small draught of which I found refreshing on a hot night in July, amid the dust and heat of the stage. On the occasion in question I was putting the cup to my lips, when I heard somebody call to me from the wings; I felt very angry at the interruption, and was just about to swallow the wine, when I heard an anxious call not to drink. Suspecting something was wrong, I pretended to drink, and deposited the cup on the table. Immediately after the scene I made inquiries about the reason for the caution I received, and was informed that as each night the carpenters, who had no right to it, finished what remained of the wine before the property men, whose perquisite it was, could lay hold of the cup, the latter, to give their despoilers a lesson, had mingled castor-oil with my drink!

At the first performance of 'The Magic Flute,' Madame Sinico and I had just commenced the duet towards the end of the opera, when Ilma di Murska ran across the stage, followed by one or two gentlemen in evening dress; immediately an alarm of fire was raised. My wife and two daughters were in a box on the third tier, which caused me considerable alarm, as I knew there was no possible chance of their escaping. Madame Sinico attempted to leave the stage, but I held her firmly whilst I retired to the wings to make inquiries. The stage-manager hurriedly told me some gauze had caught fire, but the fire had been extinguished, and there was no more danger. When I turned round again, the audience was all in a commotion ; the occupants of the gallery were climbing over each other's heads, and the members of the orchestra were escaping with their instruments. I saw not a moment was to be lost to save many from being trampled to death, so I rushed to the footlights, and called out with more energy than politeness : ' There is no fire ; it is put out! Sit still ; we are going on with the opera !' I then made a sign to Arditi ; we recommenced the duet, and the audience, or what was left of them, seeing that all was right, calmly reseated themselves to enjoy the remainder of the performance.

' Tannhäuser ' was again promised, and again not produced.

In the autumn I made my first appearance at a Gloucester Festival. I sang in the ' Elijah,' the first part of ' St. Paul,' part of the ' Messiah,' and Mendelssohn's ' First Walpurgis Night,' over the rehearsal of which I came to grief with the worthy conductor. He came to me next morning, and our little difference was soon made up. The same evening I sang 'Oh ruddier than the cherry ' at the miscellaneous concert, and when I had finished, the doctor laid down his stick, and, clapping me on the back, said, ' There, I would forgive you anything for that !' It is very singular, I have always thought, that this same doctor had a great liking for me, and yet he was the only musical man with whom I remember having had a quarrel which was never made up. I cannot help expressing my regret, as I feel I was much more to blame than he was.   At one of the performances in the cathedral I sang Gounod's *cantique* 'Nazareth.'   At the end of it, as I was leaving the platform, Howell, the principal double-bass, remarked, on one side, 'What a splendid song, Santley!' the doctor, on the other side, exclaimed, 'What rubbish!'

Of the autumnal operatic tour, I need only note that I essayed the part of Don Giovanni for the first time at Manchester on the 14th of September.   As usual, I had one rehearsal the morning of the day of performance.   Mario, who was always a late riser, did not come in until we were half-way through the rehearsal ; the others, who, except Tietjens, had, like myself, never played in 'Don Giovanni' before, were all present throughout.   Mario, who had played the Don himself, gave me several valuable hints, but of course my performance histrionically fell far short of the ideal dissipated *hidalgo*.   Had I been less diffident, and not feared making mistakes, I should have succeeded better.   Ambrogetti is always quoted as the model Don Giovanni, and by people who could never by any possible chance have seen him.   Strange to say, but a few days ago (this is the 22nd of October, 1891) I read a criticism in an old paper (the *Mirror*, or some such name) on Ambrogetti's Don, in which the writer compared him most unfavourably with the elder Garcia, and found him lacking in all the necessary qualifications for the proper representation of the character.   It is, without doubt, a difficult part to play—a thoroughly unscrupulous blackguard in the garb of a polished gentleman.   I never saw it well played, nor do I think I ever arrived at playing it in such a way as would have satisfied me could I have witnessed my own performance, though in after-years I was many times highly complimented in private on it. How often I wished I had accepted Madame Carvalho's offer, and played it at the Lyrique in Paris; with the advantages which would there have been at my disposal I believe I should have succeeded in laying the ghost of Ambrogetti. I played it throughout the tour, and again in London during the short season in October.

During this short season in London we produced 'Der Freischütz,' in which I played Caspar, a part not musically adapted to my voice, but a part I had always been enamoured of. I succeeded better in this than in Don Giovanni, as all except Tietjens were new to the work, and I had sufficient rehearsals to carry out my ideas. The 'incantation scene' was splendid—another of Telbin's fine efforts. He introduced some very tall skeletons, which made a great effect. I had no idea how they were arranged, until one evening I heard a great laugh as I was intent on casting the bullets. I knew something ludicrous had happened, but I was too intent on my work to examine into the nature of the circumstances; I really enjoyed myself so much in that scene that I was lost to all idea of its being a mere representation. When the cloth fell for the next scene I discovered the cause of the merriment—the drapery had fallen from one of the skeletons and exposed its construction; simple enough — a man holding a mop-handle, on which was fixed a skull. I succeeded in having my way about the working of the incantation, which was performed in dead silence, without the usual accompaniment of clanking chains, etc. I believe the effect must have satisfied the audience, for except on the occasion above referred to, a pin might have been heard to drop in the house during the entire scene.

Soon after this series of performances concluded I started for Milan to fulfil my engagement at the Scala. On my way, I remained a few days in Paris in order to hear 'L'Africaine,' in which I was to play Nelusko, and of course pay a visit to the Théâtre Français, which gave me much greater pleasure. I had letters of introduction to several musical and other influential people in Milan, three of which I delivered, and this I regretted having done, for they were the cause of no little persecution for loans, gifts, etc. One gentleman returned my call the day I had my first quarter's money handed me; the cash was lying on the table when he entered my apartment. It evidently proved too great a temptation to see so many francs lying idle, so after a little conversation he called me out of the room, and told me a long tale of woe which 500 francs would turn to gladness; would I lend him that sum? I could not say I was not in possession of so much, as he had seen the money. After some demur I handed him 500 francs, on the understanding that they were to be refunded before the end of the season. I left Milan without receiving back a penny of the loan, but a friend, who undertook to pursue him, managed to screw 200 francs out of him. But I had no need of letters of introduction to make the acquaintance of similar gentry, all bent on plunder. I had journalists, or people who called themselves such, who wanted subscriptions to papers I had never heard of, and did not wish to see ; one insolent fellow insisted upon being paid a year's subscription to a journal because I had taken in three numbers and kept them. I told him he might take them away if he could find them in the waste-paper basket, where they must have been deposited, as I never opened anything of that kind. He then began to use rude language, which I put an end to by informing him that if he did not quit my room on the instant he would find himself landed in the hall without the trouble of walking down the stairs. He actually then tried humble-pie, but I escorted him to the door, and dismissed him with a caution. Surely artists themselves are to blame that such a nuisance has to be endured.

The opening opera was 'Norma,' with Madame Fricci and a German tenor named Steger, but I did not hear it. This was succeeded by Halévy's 'La Juive,' in which also there is no baritone part. I went in one evening and heard the first act, after which I left, and did not return. The managers began to think it was time to get an opera ready in which Fricci and Steger would not be required, as they might either of them be unable to sing any night, playing five times a week in such heavy operas, consequently I and the other tenor, both of us having a right to choose our opera, were consulted, and to my great annoyance he insisted upon the 'Trovatore.' He being the tenor, there was nothing for it but to submit, which I did, not very graciously, I confess. Besides my own dislike to appearing in it, I heard constant rumours that the subscribers were not at all disposed to accept an opera which had been played to death. However, the managers were satisfied, and we immediately set to work to rehearse. We had a pianoforte rehearsal every day for a fortnight, then three full rehearsals with orchestra and chorus on the stage, and lastly a general rehearsal in costume, at which what they were pleased to call the 'Artistic Commission' presided. We had, besides, a rehearsal for the stage business with the stage-manager, Piave, the author of several of Verdi's librettos, including that of the 'Trovatore.' I was highly amused, for the old gentleman wandered about the dark stage with a coil of wax taper directing us; he had evidently forgotten all about his own work. He told me to come on on the wrong side for my first entrance, and was highly indignant when I suggested he was mistaken, but he soon afterwards begged my pardon when he found his mistake led to a muddle. The *prima donna* was a very good artist, and had been a great favourite at the Scala; the contralto, a Frenchwoman, had never sung in Italy, and, judging from her pronunciation, I should say knew very little about Italian; Bagagiolo was the bass. I thought it would turn out a very fair performance, but the audience had determined otherwise. The tenor they hissed from his first note to his last—very unjustly, I think; the *prima donna* came off almost as badly; the contralto they would not listen to, and even the bell used in the last act in the tower scene received a volley of hisses for tolling out of tune. When I went on in the second act to sing the 'air,' my legs trembled so I could scarcely stand. I received some encouragement in the middle of the song, as they applauded the cadence; but I was obliged to cut my final cadence short, being so nervous that I had not sufficient breath to complete it. To my great surprise and joy, I received immense applause; I was called to the foot-lights four or five times, and there was a general call for an encore, which I was sensible enough to resist. The remainder of the opera gave me no trouble. I received a fair share of applause after each of my phrases in the duet, and I was quite content. I called in to say good-night to the *prima donna* before I went up to my dressing-room, and found the tenor there condoling with her. I felt exceedingly sorry for them, for they had neither of them merited the treatment they received.

The opera, of course, could not be repeated; it was then a question what could be mounted to replace it. Many works were suggested, and at last 'Il Templario,' a weak opera by Nicolai, was chosen. The tenor of the 'Trovatore' was 'protested,'* and left Milan. For the part of Ivanhoe a new one was engaged; a fair singer with a very small voice. To the mezzo-soprano who at Barcelona took the part of Fides in 'Il Profeta' was assigned the *rôle* of Rebecca. A small English lady played Rowena, Bagagiolo Cedric, and I Brian the Templar. The music I found old-fashioned and flimsy; from that point of view the part did not interest me, but I thought I could do something with it dramatically, and so make up for the lack of musical interest. Mazzucato super-intended the rehearsals. He was a very talented man,

---

* 'Protested' means that he received his *congé.*

very courteous, but very stiff and cold in his demeanour, never condescending to use the familiar 'thou' with the artists during rehearsals. I do not know how many rehearsals we had, but I was thoroughly saturated with the music long before we got through those in the green-room. We had several on the stage with full orchestra, and with a multiplicity of directors—Cavallini directing the orchestra with his fiddlestick, and taking the time from Mazzucato, who, seated in front of the stage, beat the time with his hand, whilst the chorus-master stood in front of his regiment also beating time. Altercations between the conductor and the principal instruments were not uncommon. I remember one which amused me very much. Cavallini turned to the principal 'cello and bass, and remarked that a certain B ought to be natural, not flat ; the professors replied he was mistaken, upon which a long argument ensued, ending in the double-bass requesting the conductor to 'shut up,' as he did not know what he was talking about. Rebecca had never sung out at rehearsals, so nobody knew what her capabilities were ; on the stage with the orchestra she was compelled to sing out, and then doubts began to be expressed about the probability of her success. At the general rehearsal the 'Artistic Commission' did not approve, and to save a 'protest' she was requested to resign on the plea of ill-health. I thought we should have had all our trouble for nothing, but the day following a lady was found who undertook to be ready with the part in a few days. Poor girl, she little knew what she was undertaking! The opera was played, and Rebecca was a failure.

The disapprobation of the public was displayed in a
most brutal manner, and again I thought we had
laboured in vain ; but the *prima donna* of the 'Trovatore ' was induced to undertake the part, and with her
we managed six or seven performances, the greater
part being on nights assigned to certain charitable
benefits.

A proposal was then made that the 'Favorita '
should be mounted, for which a new *prima donna*
was to be engaged.   I made some demur, as I never
liked the part of the King, and when I learned who
were to be my companions, I declined.   The part
which I had looked forward to, Nelusko, through
some intrigue, had been assigned to another artist.
Altogether the season had been a wretched one for
me ; singing so seldom, I had no chance of making
way with the public, and now that the part in which I
hoped to gain their sympathy was taken away from
me, I longed to get away.   Luckily, on the night of
the last performance but one of the 'Templario ' the
agent who made my engagement arrived in Milan,
and came to see me in my dressing-room.   I stated
my troubles to him, and asked him to try and break
my engagement, that I might get back to England.
He seemed unwilling to undertake the job, but an
offer of double commission on my salary turned the
scale, and before the termination of the performance
he brought me the welcome news that I was free after
one other performance of the 'Templario.'   The last
performance was given for the benefit of a charitable
institution ; between the second and third acts they
played a ballet which lasted about an hour and a

quarter, and between the third and fourth acts another which lasted three-quarters of an hour. I left Milan the day on which ' L'Africaine ' was produced, and I afterwards learned that all the leading baritone numbers had to be omitted, and I confess I was spiteful enough to be very glad of it. I expected on my return to join Mapleson's operatic tour at Dublin, but our ideas of terms differed so much I would not accept the engagement.

CHAPTER XVII.

MADAME GRISI was announced to appear in a limited
number of performances at Her Majesty's Theatre
during the season of 1866, and as an additional attraction, Mlle. Tietjens was announced to take part in
them, playing Adalgisa in 'Norma,' and Donna Elvira
in 'Don Giovanni,' etc. The only appearance of
Madame Grisi was in 'Lucrezia Borgia.' I had been
singing at the Crystal Palace concert in the afternoon,
and after dining there I went up to the theatre to see
a little of the performance. I felt very sorry for Grisi
that she had been induced to appear again ; it was a
sad sight for anyone who had known her in her prime,
and even long past it. I met her behind the scenes,
and she upbraided me with having forsaken her, as she
particularly wished me to play the Duke. I do not
know why she should have been so desirous of my
assistance, as Gassier played and sang it exceedingly
well ; probably she fancied I would be more careful

about seconding her. Mongini was engaged as first tenor; he certainly had a voice, but it never had any effect on me; he never produced such a startling effect with his high notes as Tamberlik used with the C sharp in the duet in 'Otello'; and, oddly enough, when the high notes were really wanted they did not seem willing to come forth. For instance, in the great scene in 'Lucia,' the high B flat was always half stifled. He was an indifferent singer and actor, but his fine manly presence and robust voice gained him the sympathy of those who know nothing of, and are not interested in, artistic excellence—the bulk of an audience. Mr. Tom Hohler made his first appearance in 'I Puritani,' and sang a few times during the remainder of the season.

Another tenor, a M. Arvin, Italianized into Arvini, came out in 'Il Trovatore,' and went in again immediately. 'La Donna del Lago' (Rossini) and 'La Vestale' (Spontini) were both promised, but not given. 'Ifigenia in Tauride' was promised and performed with Tietjens as Ifigenia, Gardoni as Pilade, myself as Oreste, and Gassier as Thoas. I mentioned that I had already sung in some performances of this opera at Charles Hallé's concerts in Manchester. A great deal of enthusiasm, which, however, did not last very long, had been got up about Gluck at the time Hallé performed it in Manchester, in 1860 and 1861, in consequence of which the Earl of Dudley, then Lord Ward, I believe, arranged to have two performances at his residence in Park Lane, for which Tietjens, Reeves, Belletti and I were engaged. The accompaniments were played on the pianoforte by

Ganz, and by a quintet of strings, with Carrodus as leader. At the rehearsals Lord Ward requested Belletti to present me to him. He said he had not yet had the pleasure of hearing me, although he had heard a great deal about me, as he always looked to the artists of the Italian Opera for his musical entertainments. On the evening of the performance I had to sing at Hanover Square Rooms first. I arrived about ten o'clock, but the performance was delayed awaiting the arrival of some royal or otherwise important guest. We commenced the opera at twenty minutes past midnight; I was already beginning to feel exhausted, having dined at 3.30; however, I was in good form, and got through the most arduous scene, on which I was inwardly congratulating myself, when his lordship stepped up and begged of me (to my horror) to repeat it. I tried to excuse myself, but in the end I was obliged to give in. As soon as I could, I got away without visiting the supper-room, and I could not find a morsel to eat when I arrived at home. I was in a measure repaid, for a few days after, when Hallé called upon me to pay me for my services, he brought a message from Lord Ward to the effect that, as I had done more work than any other of the artists, he did not see why I should not receive at least the same compensation (my terms were fifteen guineas, the others' twenty-five), and he begged of me to accept the additional ten guineas, with his earnest thanks for my admirable performance.

The opera was fairly well performed at Her Majesty's; at any rate, we all did our best, but it did not prove attractive, and was only played three nights. There are fine bits in it, but to me Gluck's music is tedious; and, judging from experience, the public is much of my opinion. An exception may be made in favour of 'Orfeo,' which, with a highly-talented artist in the principal character, proved successful lately at Covent Garden. Hallé revived 'Ifigenia' a few years ago at his Manchester concerts, but the performance fell perfectly flat.

'Dinorah' was produced for Ilma di Murska, with Gardoni as Corentino and I as Hoel; it was a great success, and we played it several nights to crowded houses. It is a part which dramatically suited Murska perfectly, and musically, except for the 'Shadow song,' where her execution was very ragged, although the public appeared quite satisfied. I was within an ace of killing her during one of the performances. She insisted upon crossing the bridge and doing the fall, when it breaks, herself, instead of having a double, as I had always seen it done before, and in consequence I was obliged to jump in to save her myself. There were some mattresses on the stage to prevent breaking bones. On the evening in question she had not fallen in the usual place; had I made my ordinary jump, she would have come to an untimely end to a dead certainty; but fortunately I saw her danger, and made, I believe, the biggest jump (except once when I was pursued by a horse) that I ever made in my life, and cleared her. She was fearfully alarmed, and it took me some little time to recover the shock.

On the first night or two I had enough to attend to, without paying much attention to my fellow-artists, except in so far as the work required; but when I had time to observe minor particulars, I noticed some change in Di Murska's attire in the last act. She fell into the water with a plain band round her waist, and her hair adorned solely by its natural gloss ; when I carried her on the stage, after rescuing her from a watery grave, I found her waist was encircled by a gold or gilt zone, and her hair was bright with gold powder. I was so amused and astonished that I forgot all about the romance until the ophicleide (I could never understand why Meyerbeer gave those few notes to that instrument) wakened me from my reverie. I was very fond of the part of Hoel, but I always wished the few pieces stuck in at the commencement of the third act had been left out ; they retard the *dénouement*, when, after the bustle of the storm scene, the audience are all anxious to know the fate of the lovers—and it left time for my voice and enthusiasm to cool. I strove hard to have them eliminated, but manager and conductor were afraid the public would not have enough for their money, so there was nothing for it but patience. The goat was always a great nuisance ; it never would do what was required of it, and was always getting in the way. According to the attendant at Covent Garden, when I was playing Hoel in 1859, the poor animal was the means of saving me from a serious accident. At the beginning of the second act I used to cross the bridge and wait at the other end until I made my second entrance. The goat and attendant also took up their quarters at the end of the rostrum, and I generally filled up the time with a little conversation with the latter. One night he told me that, had it not been for his crossing the bridge as he did each night by way of a little drill for the goat, I would certainly have broken my neck, as he found the bolt which kept up the bridge had been inadvertently left out, and he and the goat had very nearly been precipitated on to the stage.   I rewarded him for having prevented a serious accident, after which it was extraordinary the number of perils I escaped, saved, according to his account, through his instrumentality !

'Ernani,' which had not been played for many years, was revived, with Tietjens, Tasca, Gassier, and myself.   Carlo Quinto is a part I always enjoyed ; it is full of singing.   However, it presents one difficulty, which I have seldom heard overcome.   The air 'Lo vedremo o veglio audace,' a very rugged declamatory address to old Silva, is succeeded by a *cabaletta*, all grace and tenderness, addressed to Elvira.   As a rule this air is bellowed, and consequently the voice cannot sustain the soft delicate melody which comes almost immediately after it.   It is a question of accent : if properly declaimed, the air requires no extraordinary expenditure of force, which may then be preserved for the more trying, because much more sustained, *cabaletta*, and the singer (provided the part suits his voice) who depends on art rather than on physical strength will suffer no distress in the execution of this —one of the most trying scenes I know in Italian opera.

Mozart's 'Il Seraglio' was produced, with Tietjens, Sinico, Dr. Gunz, Foli, and Rokitansky in the principal parts ; it was played three or four times at most.   I did not see it, and cannot say anything about the performance.

After the holidays came Worcester Festival, of which there is nothing to say, followed at the end of October by Norwich Festival, the only new feature of any importance in which was Benedict's cantata ' St. Cecilia,' libretto by H. F. Chorley. Costa's ' Naaman ' was given, conducted by the composer, the Prince and Princess of Wales being present at the performance. The rest of the autumn and winter was filled up with the operatic and concert tours, and various concerts between the two, ' Monday Pops,' Sacred Harmonic, etc., and a couple of weeks at Her Majesty's Theatre in November, during which I played Leporello in ' Don Giovanni,' according to accounts, with great success. I liked playing the part very much, though the music is much too low for me in the concerted parts.

The particulars of the season of both Italian operas were always announced with a great flourish of trumpets, but the season of 1867 at Her Majesty's was heralded by a perfect symphony in several movements for those instruments. The first movement gave a summary of all the wonders which had been produced from the foundation of the Italian Opera, and the wonderful people who had executed them, terminating with a confident assertion by Mr. Mapleson ' that in no other house have new works and revivals been produced in such rapid succession, or with such complete efficiency, as at Her Majesty's Theatre '; and a kind of *coda*, intimating the principal works to be produced. The second movement consisted of puffs of the principal artists, the third of the casts of the different operas, and the fourth was a medley of stage *personnel*, *répertoire*, and rates of subscription. As usual, a great many promises were not performed, *e.g.*, 'Guglielmo Tell,' 'La Vestale,' and 'La Donna del Lago'; 'Mirella,' with Christine Nilsson, also fell under this category ; but 'La Forza del Destino' (promised so many times) and 'I Lombardi' were produced, and 'Falstaff' revived.

The great theme of the second movement of the brazen symphony was the engagement of Mlle. Christine Nilsson. 'It is with the *highest* satisfaction ' Mr. Mapleson announces he has secured the services of Mlle. Christine Nilsson, etc. ' This young Swedish singer, upon whom it has been said by connoisseurs the mantle of Jenny Lind has fallen, will come,' etc. She wore a mantle handsomely trimmed and lined, but it was not Jenny Lind's! She made her first appearance on the 8th of June in the 'Traviata,' Mongini playing Alfredo, and I old Germont. She was charming to behold, and sang charmingly, and made an immense success.

' I Lombardi ' was performed on the 30th of April, the second night of the season ; it is one of Verdi's earlier operas. It abounds in melody, but the noisy scoring imparts a vulgar tone to many numbers which would otherwise stand out in bold and rugged relief. ' I Lombardi ' is certainly not a favourite opera of mine, nor did I find Pagano a very interesting part generally ; but there is one recitative and air, ' Ma quando un'suon terribile,' which is worthy of any singer's attention. It made such an effect on the audience that on the first night I received a great round of applause after a fine phrase which occurs in the middle of it, and a regular ovation at the end.

' Falstaff' was revived in May, the title *rôle* being played by Rokitansky, who was not an improvement on Junca, spite of possessing a much more sonorous organ. Slender was played by Charles Lyall—his first season at the Italian Opera—an immense improvement on his predecessor. It was a piece of genuine comedy ; Gassier always called him the English Saintefoy. For the benefit of those who may not have heard Saintefoy, or do not remember him, I may as well mention that he was comic tenor at the Opéra Comique for many years, one of his last creations being the part of Corentin in ' Dinorah.'

On Saturday, the 22nd of June, ' La Forza del Destino ' was produced. We had a great deal of rehearsing, but unfortunately we had lost our clever old stage-manager ' Billy ' West, and his successor had never had any experience, consequently we all went our own way, the result being, to say the least of it, unsatisfactory. After the general rehearsal it was found impossible to set the second scene (Scene 5 of the libretto) of the second act unless the cloth of the back of Scene 1 was removed a couple of wings nearer the footlights, so that at the first performance we all had to scramble for room. In addition to this, on the very day of performance I received notice that the words of the grace before the supper must be altered or omitted by order of the licenser of plays ; yet, spite of these *contretemps*, which were of themselves sufficient to upset those concerned without the anxiety of a first night, we got through creditably enough. After many and many such experiences of the getting up and rehearsing of operas in which I have been engaged, my only wonder is that we got through some of them at all ; and I can only conclude that we must be an extraordinary race of people to perform such miracles —producing attractive performances by means of such wretched rehearsals.

There is some beautiful music in ' La Forza,' but, judging from the only performance I ever saw at the Teatro Dal Verme, in Milan, some years ago, with a very good cast and very well put on the stage, I should say on the whole it is tiresome.   I was in Paris for a few days before the opening of our season.   At Arditi's request I called on Verdi to ask him if he would point out to me any particular effects he wished brought out in my part.   He received me very coldly, and said as he had gone through the opera with Arditi, he did not see any reason why he should go through it with me.   I was a little astonished at his brusque manner, and excused myself the best way I could, and was retiring, when he called me back and told me if I liked to call again on another day, appointing it himself and the hour, he would consider about what he could do.   I returned on the day, when he informed me he was very busy at the opera with the revival of ' Les Vêpres Siciliennes,' and had no piano in his rooms, so he could not assist me in any way.   I told him not to disturb himself, and that I was quite satisfied with having had the honour of making his acquaintance, on which he bowed me out. I confess I was a little hurt, as I presented myself and made my request very modestly.   I determined, how- ever, to do my best with my part, and I worked more than ordinarily at it, and I think my labour was repaid,

as I made a great success in it. I was very much
amused with Mongini, with whom I had to sing three
duets. The first one, when I assisted him into the
tent after he was wounded, was very soft, and at
rehearsal one day he impressed strongly on me that it
should be sung as *piano* as possible, as he was supposed to be dying from loss of blood. At the next
rehearsal I began my part in a whisper, but he
evidently forgot about the loss of blood and did not
husband his voice; I could not hear myself, so was
obliged to use more power too, which did not result in
a model *piano*. However, he expressed himself perfectly satisfied, so I made no remark.

He used to grow very excited over his work, so
much so that towards the end of an opera in which he
took great interest he seemed scarcely able to control
himself.

He had been a dragoon and used to the broad-
sword, and when excited laid about him most
vigorously. I am no swordsman; I never studied
anything except the small sword for a short time, more
to acquire greater freedom in my joints than for actual
sword practice. I was consequently no match for
such an adversary, and I confess he made me feel
somewhat nervous in the duel at the end of 'La
Forza.' He did pink me one night. I thought he
had cut off the end of my first finger, the blow so
benumbed it. When I dropped dead, my right hand
being out of sight of the audience, I felt with my
thumb and found the blood trickling freely. I had to
lie on the stage about ten minutes before the curtain
fell, and a very long ten minutes they appeared. I

was very much relieved when I found my finger, except for a tolerably large cut, all safe.

We played it only a few times, and I do not think it has ever been revived since.

'Don Giovanni' was played with Nilsson as Donna Elvira. It was intended that I should play Don Giovanni; but Gassier, who was asked to play Leporello, refused. He was a very good comrade, and I could quite understand his objection to giving up a part he had always played during his engagement at Her Majesty's to a comparatively new-comer; so, to avoid annoyance to him and trouble to the manager, having played the part already, and successfully, I undertook the part of Leporello. Tietjens, of course, played Donna Anna; Sinico was the Zerlina, Gardoni Ottavio, and Rokitansky Il Commendatore. I think it must have been a very good performance; it certainly was attractive, as it drew several full houses.

'Dinorah,' with the same cast as the year before, was performed, as also were 'Fidelio'; 'Oberon,' with Mongini as Sir Huon; 'Medea,' given once for Mongini's benefit, he playing Jason; 'Freischütz,' in which Mongini played Rodolfo; and 'Les Huguenots,' in which he played Raoul. There were several new ladies announced to appear in the list of engagements. I forget whether any of them did appear; if they did, they disappeared, as nothing more was ever heard of them, and I have not the slightest recollection of what they did or did not do. The season must have been good. Nilsson was a great success—in fact, took the opera-going public by storm, crowded houses whenever she sang being the result ; but it was not so wonderful as the brazen symphony would have led the public to expect.

After a few weeks' rest came the Hereford Festival, this year before Birmingham, as they found the greater attraction of Birmingham detrimental to the interests of the smaller festival. I had little to do, as Weiss sang 'Elijah,' and most of the sacred music. The great event to me was singing with Jenny Lind, for the first time, in her husband's oratorio 'Ruth.' I was greatly elated at having to take part in a work, and sing an important duet, with an artist who had been always one of my deities. It is not my business to criticise any work in which I take part ; only one thing I will take the liberty of saying, as it applies not alone to the composer of ' Ruth,' but to all the composers of modern oratorios except Costa. The work showed an intimate knowledge of the powers of every instrument except the human voice, which, I contend, ought to have the first consideration with the composer of a vocal work. The principal feature of ' Ruth ' was the air in which Ruth says : ' Thy people shall be my people, and thy God my God.' Though thoroughly unvocal, Jenny Lind declaimed it in such a way that I trembled with excitement. This was not the only feat she performed. She sang ' I know that my Redeemer liveth ' as she only ever did sing it, in my opinion ; but it was in a much smaller effort that she made a lasting impression on me. The tenor was not on the orchestra at the commencement of the second part. Townshend Smith turned to me, and asked me if I would sing the tenor recitative ' Unto

which of the angels said He at any time, Thou art My
Son; this day have I begotten Thee?' I replied: 'I
cannot; it is too high.' 'Oh,' said he, 'it only goes
up to G!' 'Yes,' said I, 'but how? Ask Madame
Goldschmidt.' He did, and she immediately arose
and sang it. I was so struck with the way in which
she rendered those words I scarcely breathed. It
was a lesson to me, and at the same time a reprimand,
which I never forgot. It was one of the great lessons
I have had in my life, by which I may confidently say
I profited. It was a reprimand, inasmuch as I had
never given my mind to the deep study which the
words of the oratorio necessitated on the part of a
singer who is desirous of impressing the audience
with their true meaning.

Birmingham came immediately after. Weiss sang
both in 'Elijah' and 'St. Paul,' so my share in the
oratorio was pretty light. I sang the three songs in
the 'Messiah'; 'But who may abide,' according to
the custom prevailing there, being sung by the
contralto. They say it was written for alto—possibly !*
I know in my young days, when I used to be hauled
off, pretty much against my will, to the performances
of the 'Old Festival Choral Society' in Liverpool (I
suppose I was about nine or ten when I first went),
'But who may abide' was always sung by a bass;
moreover, I never heard an alto attempt to sing it, and
I certainly have never heard a contralto who could
sing it with any effect. I sang in Sterndale Bennett's

* Since the above was written, I learn that the point has been cleared
up by the recently discovered annotated programme book of the original
performance of the 'Messiah.' On that occasion it was sung by the
bass.

oratorio, in which I had only a slight morsel—which
he wrote on his journey from London to Birmingham
on the Sunday evening preceding the festival—and in
Gounod's Mass. Benedict's 'St. Cecilia' and J. F.
Barnett's 'Ancient Mariner' were included in the
evening programmes ; I took part in both. I had
some friends to sup with me one evening after the
performance — Sterndale Bennett, Benedict, J. W.
Davison, C. L. Gruneisen, Charles Lucas, etc. The
conversation somehow worked round to an ancient
quarrel between Costa and Bennett, when, to my
great surprise, Charles Lucas proposed that I should
act as mediator in endeavouring to restore friendship
between them. I have often wished since I had had
the courage to undertake it, as a man like Lucas was
not likely to propose such a thing without well
weighing his proposal. I excused myself entirely on
the ground that such an attempt on the part of a man
so much younger than those with whom he was
requested to treat would no doubt savour strongly
of impertinence.

The operatic tour commenced soon after. I see
we played the 'Huguenots,' with Alessandro Bettini as
Raoul. The notice says, ' " Les Huguenots " seems
to have created an extraordinary effect.' I should
think it did ! I remember a tale about a tomtit on a
pear-tree, which might have been applied to this
performance. At the rehearsal I heard the orchestra
trying something which seemed to a certain extent
familiar to my ears, but I could not put a name to it.
I asked Arditi if it was some overture they were going
to play before the opera. 'What overture?' said he.

'That you have just been rehearsing.' 'Oh, don't bother me' (very angrily); 'it's the introduction to the opera.' 'I certainly did not recognise it,' said I. 'No, nor Meyerbeer himself, with half an orchestra—and such a half!' Oh, we did have joyous times at the opera in the Emerald Isle, and made many extraordinary effects — a great many quite unintentionally !

Some effects, and very inartistic ones, however, were made intentionally—for instance, on the last night of our Dublin season the *prima donna*, after the great air in 'Oberon,' went forward to the footlights, an upright piano was wheeled on to the stage, at which a gentleman in evening dress took his place, and accompanied the lady in 'The Last Rose of Summer.' I know such things are asked for by audiences. I have been requested in Dublin to sing 'The Stirrup Cup' as an encore in 'Il Flauto Magico,' and I have been asked to substitute the same song for the air in 'Il Trovatore' in America. I cannot help saying I think it is not only bad taste, but bad judgment, to give way to such requests.

We returned to town for the customary short season, and opened on the 2nd of November with 'Faust,' in which Clara Louise Kellogg, of whom much had been said during her career in America, made her first appearance on this side of the Atlantic. She also played during the same season in 'La Traviata,' 'Marta,' and 'Linda di Chamounix' (in which I played Antonio for the first time). She had genius, yet though she was successful in almost all the parts she attempted, she did not attain the position her talents merited, but through no fault of her own.

On Thursday, the 5th of December, we played 'Don Giovanni,' in which Kellogg played Zerlina ; the next day I went to Brighton, to fulfil an engagement at a small festival. I sang 'Elijah' on the Friday morning, and in a miscellaneous concert in the evening I sang 'Oh, ruddier than the cherry.' On Saturday morning I was having breakfast, when Lewis Thomas was announced. I thought it was an early hour to receive a visit, and when I saw his doleful countenance I thought he was unwell and could not sing, and had come to ask me to do his share of the work in addition to my own ; I felt uneasy for the moment, as the thought passed through my mind, for I had to get back to town to play Pizarro in 'Fidelio' at night. After keeping me in suspense for a few moments, he informed me that Her Majesty's Theatre had been burnt to the ground. It was a shock, for I had become much attached to the old place ; I felt a little uneasy, too, about my theatrical wardrobe, worth about £500, which I anticipated had been destroyed in the fire, and was not insured. However, that did not trouble me so much as the loss of the splendid theatre, the number of people who would be thrown out of employment, and the almost certainty that an auditorium possessing such perfect acoustic properties would never be erected again. On my return to town I hastened round to look on the remains of my old home, where I had enjoyed many modest triumphs, and in which I sang the last notes heard within its walls by the public. My wardrobe had been saved through the presence of mind of one of the firemen belonging to the theatre, named Easten, who cut off the bottom of the staircase leading to my dressing-room just as the fire was laying hold of the wood-work.

CHAPTER XVIII.

AT the beginning of the year 1868 various concerts —Monday Popular, Sacred Harmonic, Martin's Choir, etc.—kept me occupied until Mapleson's tour began (I have no record of the date, but I presume early in February), and continued until shortly before the opera season at Drury Lane Theatre. About the end of January was announced the death of Mr. J. C. Tully, a very clever musician. He was best known as an arranger of music for burlesques, pantomimes, and melodramas, for which he had a singular aptitude. He, however, did much service as a conductor of English opera, and directed the performance of 'The Amber Witch' at Drury Lane in 1861. He was, likewise, composer of a very successful opera on the subject of 'Black-eyed Susan,' which enjoyed a long run at Drury Lane Theatre. In 1857, or about that time, he had an English opera company of his own at Sadlers' Wells. I have heard a good story in connection with the venture, which may perhaps

17

amuse my readers. He engaged as principal tenor an American gentleman who, having made a small reputation as a concert singer, imagined he had become an artist of importance ; the terms were left open, at his suggestion, until he had shown what his capabilities were. The public did not appear so satisfied with them as he himself, and occasionally gave vent to their disapprobation. On Saturday Mr. Tenor presented himself at the treasury, when Tully asked him what he thought the salary ought to be ; there was a great deal of explanation about enormous success and public favour, etc., so, to cut the matter short, Tully requested that, without further parley, he would name a sum. The tenor replied, with great confidence, that he thought he was worth £20 per week, or nothing. 'Then,' said Tully, 'suppose we say the latter.' Tully was a genial man, and a great favourite with all who knew him well ; he was also a 'gourmet,' and had a splendid caterer in his wife. He confided to me, when we were discussing gastronomy, that anybody who had not partaken of Mrs. T.'s lobster salad had no idea what lobster salad meant.

The opera season, which commenced on the 28th of March, was much more modestly announced than the preceding one. The only new addition to the list of singers was Fraschini, the tenor. He had sung in England in 1847, at Her Majesty's Theatre, but he had then to compete with other tenors who were already great favourites, and he failed to establish a position. He had a magnificent voice, of which he made more lavish use than the delicate subscribers to the Italian opera cared for ; he phrased well, and certain passages I have never heard any other tenor make so much effect with ; for instance, that in the duet of the last act of ' Marta ' with the soprano, ' Era la stella dell' amor.'   He was uninteresting on the stage, which may account for his not meeting with the success his talents and gifts as a singer merited. Auber's ' Gustave ' and Wagner's ' Lohengrin ' were promised, but not performed.   Of the latter we had three or four rehearsals, but for some cause, to me unknown, it was abandoned.   I was not sorry, for I did not conceive any great affection for the part of Federico.   ' La Gazza Ladra,' also promised, was pro- duced, with Kellogg as Ninetta, Trebelli as Pippo, Foli as Il Podestà, Bettini as Giannetto, Lyall as the Jew pedlar—in which he made a great success—and myself as Fernando.   It was one of the few operas in which I had an opportunity of displaying my powers as a florid singer, and judging from accounts my efforts were successful.   My master always said it was the style I should most excel in ; it was the one he was most desirous I should cultivate, as there were few male singers, even at that time, who could execute the music Rossini wrote.   Whether the composers did not care to write in that style, or could not find singers to execute it, I do not know, but since Rossini no composer except Mercadante has entrusted male singers with florid music.   It is a style now considered old-fashioned and out of date, which no doubt is true as regards public performance ; but it is a pity the practice of it by students is fast becoming obsolete.

The constant study of what is very often miscalled declamatory music by those who have made but a cursory study of joining notes together in groups of two, three, four, six, etc., has a bad effect on the tone produced ; it becomes hard and uneven.   Thus the *cantabile* style, which really means the singing a succession of notes without cessation of sound, and which is the foundation of all good singing, is never acquired.   Why do pianists study five-finger exercises ? Is it merely to acquire facility of execution ?   Certainly not ; it is, for the greater part, to give equality of tone to each note, and to join the notes that there shall not be any sensible cessation of sound, without running one into another, as they are struck in succession.   So with singing ; the practice of groups of notes is to give equality of tone to each note in the voice.   This study is really the study of 'production,' about which so much nonsense is talked at the present day by many who profess to teach singing, but who know nothing about it themselves.

I will not say any more on this subject at present, as I intend to speak fully upon it at some future time.

Early in the season I played in 'Rigoletto' with Kellogg (Gilda) and Fraschini (the Duke). Of course, reference was made to Giorgio Ronconi. I do not object, but I think I was much more aware than those who criticised me of how far behind my great model I was.   However, credit was given me for progress in the histrionic part of my work, so I am comforted. Kellogg sang and played the part of Gilda to perfection ; she was always thoroughly in earnest. Her earnestness excited my emulation, and materially assisted in my making a success. 'Les Huguenots' was played with a tenor called at Her Majesty's Theatre Signor Ferensi, a Hungarian, whose real name was Ferensky. I do not remember anything about him, except that, after coming out, he soon went in, and I never heard any more of him.

Nilsson essayed the part of Cherubino in 'Le Nozze di Figaro.' It was pleasant to hear the music in the proper keys, but the impersonation was not a success. She wore a nondescript dress which spoiled her figure; instead of a sprightly page, she looked exactly what she was, a woman dressed in male attire, and very unhappy without the petticoats. Kellogg did not arouse great enthusiasm with her Maria in 'La Figlia del Reggimento.' I think the drum spoiled it. She had been practising the roll for some time, and mastered it as far as private performance went, but when it came to the point in public where she had to exhibit her dexterity, the drum was not forthcoming, and the public were highly amused at her dashing off the stage, and interpolating a scene not in the libretto : 'Where's my drum? where's my drum?' A trifle such as this is sufficient to upset an entire impersonation, or, at any rate, a great portion of it. The drumming did not go off so well as it might have done, and the agitation it caused the drummer was very noticeable in the address to the regiment, 'Convien partir.' She made a great mistake, too, for which, however, she had ample precedent, of substituting a flimsy waltz for the original finale of the opera. I have wondered many a time why Leonora in the 'Trovatore' was not resuscitated to execute a waltz and make all things end happily.

To Nilsson was assigned the part of Margarita in 'Faust.' After Madame Carvalho she was, in my opinion, the nearest approach to the ideal Margarita. On the 15th of July I took part in a monstrosity at the Crystal Palace for the benefit of Mr. Mapleson, consisting of a concert in the afternoon and a performance of ' Le Nozze di Figaro ' in the evening. The *Musical World* says : ' The glimpses of the brilliantly-lighted stage from the semi-gloom of distant points were singularly striking and effective !'   I could not judge of that, but the effect of the semi-gloom of distant points from the stage produced a gloom throughout my whole system, which spite of every effort on my part I could not shake off.   I went through my part mechanically ; it was one of the most dismal exhibitions, as far as I myself was concerned, that I ever took part in ; it was like one of the disturbed dreams I am accustomed to when my mind is troubled or overworked.   I invariably dream I am back again in the old office where I served my time, with my books all in confusion, or that I have to sing an opera which I have quite forgotten or never known.   I am aware it is accounted a silly thing to relate one's dreams, but I will venture to give an example of my troubled ones.   In one I had to sing an opera composed by Signor Pezze, the violoncellist, of which there were three representations.   I had never seen a note or word of it, but I dressed and went through the first performance without a mistake ; at the second I had some difficulty about my dress, and I was constantly going down wrong turnings in the music.   At the third I could not find several parts of my costume, and at last was obliged to rush on the stage without hat, jacket, or boots, and when I found myself before the footlights I could not remember a word or note of my part. In another curious dream, I was playing in 'Don Giovanni' with my usual companions at Her Majesty's. At the end of the first act I thought I would like a blow of fresh air, as the theatre was very close and hot, so I laid aside my costume, put on my walking-dress, and set out for a stroll. After some time I found myself at one of the landing-places on the Lake of Como ; the moon was shining brightly, so I thought a short sail would be pleasant. Accordingly I hired a boat and rowed about for a considerable time, until I thought perhaps I might be wanted to finish the opera. I hastened back and was met at the door by Madame Trebelli (Zerlina), who told me the stage was waiting. I got on my costume in that short space of time in which one accomplishes all kinds of wonders in dreams, went on, and to my astonishment found myself in a real cemetery. All was dark ; I could only distinguish the white tombstones ; there was no orchestra and no public, and whilst I was debating what I had better do, everything faded away and left me to finish my sleep in peace.

The Handel Festival took place in June. I sang the solos in the 'Messiah,' and on the selection day two airs, 'O voi dell' Erebo,' from 'La Resurrezione,' and 'Oh, ruddier than the cherry,' from 'Acis and Galatea.' The former was little known ; it was shown to me by Manuel Garcia when I was having lessons from him, and for some reason it was published with a recitative taken from another part of the work, while that which precedes it, and naturally leads into it, was left out. I restored the original recitative. I think it is one of Handel's finest songs, but very difficult. I sang it first in 1858 at a concert given by Molique, but never succeeded in satisfying myself about the execution of it until the last Handel Festival in 1891. On the Friday I joined Foli in the duet 'The Lord is a man of war.' During the week Dr. Wesley called upon me to make arrangements about the Gloucester Festival. He brought an air from a work of his father, or uncle, which he asked me to sing at one of the performances in the cathedral, saying that it was far finer than that stupid song of Handel's he had heard me sing at the Crystal Palace (referring to 'O voi dell' Erebo'). We were not of the same opinion, but I said little, though I thought much about the difference of tastes. I have already mentioned the little brush I had with him at the festival of 1865. At Hereford, subsequently, we sang his fine anthem, 'The Wilderness.' When I came down from the orchestra I met the Doctor, who had just descended from the organ-loft, and complimented him on his work, asking him why he did not write an oratorio. He held his pocket-handkerchief over his mouth as though to prevent a breath escaping (a nervous trick habitual to him), and after chuckling for a few moments, in a half-whisper he confided to me that his great desire was to write an opera —with fairies in it! Done, of Worcester, told me a very good story of him, and very characteristic of the man. The Sunday preceding a Worcester Festival the two were invited to dine with one of the patrons who lived about a couple of miles from Done's house, where Dr. Wesley was put up for the festival week. At dinner there was a fine haunch of venison which everybody seemed to enjoy very much. Returning home on foot, Wesley walked in the middle of the road and did not utter a single word until Done had put the key into the lock of the house-door, when, touching him on the arm to call his attention, he said, with a very grave face, ' Did they give you any of the fat ?' At the festival in 1865 I forgot to mention one of the Doctor's little vagaries, which I think was rather amusing. I was waiting with Louisa Pyne to go on to the orchestra to commence the ' Elijah,' when Dr. Wesley stepped up, saying he would give us a signal to follow. We waited some minutes, when, to my astonishment, I heard the orchestra attack the opening bars of the first recitative. Blagrove suggested it would be as well to wait until the singers appeared, so a pause ensued. Miss Pyne and I immediately proceeded to take our places, but before I could reach mine, the conductor started again, and I began the recitative as I walked across the platform.

The opera tour followed. Among our company we had Carl Formes, whose voice and hair created such emulation in my bosom when I first attacked the bass clef. He was another eccentric man, who drew the long bow further than any other individual I have ever known ; but his wonderful adventures, much after the style of Baron Munchausen, were related in perfect good faith. He was a remarkably good shot. Madame Rudersdorff told me that he used, when they were on tour together, as a specimen of his skill, to hit a penny, which she held betwixt her finger and thumb at the full length of a large room, with a pistol shot. He told me a story of how he once went for a holiday to the Rocky Mountains. He was out in quest of bears—a sort of game worthy of his prowess —and had wandered a long time without meeting any, when at last, turning a corner in the mountain-path he was pursuing, he heard a noise, and, looking up, descried a grizzly bear advancing towards him. He had scarcely time to put his rifle in position, when the beast was close in front ; he fired both barrels and missed. He then attacked the bear with his hunting-knife, and succeeded in killing him. While he was in the act of skinning him, a strange sound attracted his attention, and to his horror he descried another grizzly coming down ; this time he went more calmly to work, and brought his quarry down with his rifle. I suppose he skinned this fellow also, but how he carried the skins away, or what became of them, I do not remember. He also related how, through his tact and foresight, the victory was gained at Bull's Run during the American War, and how in a storm on the Atlantic he saved the ship in which he was sailing —one of the German Lloyd Line—by supplying the place of the quartermaster, who was thrown down and severely hurt by a sudden turn of the wheel. But he could act as well as talk ; he played Rocco in ' Fidelio,' Marcel in the ' Huguenots,' in a style that no man in my time has approached, and except Giorgio Ronconi his Leporello was the finest I remember, especially in the last scene. He was inferior to Ronconi in the comic scenes. I had not known him long before I discovered that, with all his terrible talk and bluster, he was as gentle as a lamb. We became very intimate friends, and continued so until he died two years ago. On one occasion, when he was 'up a tree,' he borrowed a small sum from me—about the year 1869 or 1870, I should think; I thought he had forgotten all about it—I had myself—but during his last visit to London, in 1888, he mentioned it, and said that as soon as he was in a position to do so he would repay me. I told him not to trouble himself, as I had forgotten all about it; but he kept his word, and I received P.O. orders for the sum—with interest—at Brindisi, on my way to Australia in 1889, whither his letter was forwarded to me. I wish some others would imitate his example, albeit without the interest!

Our London autumn season was carried on at Covent Garden, where we had an addition to our company in Miss Minnie Hauck. She made her first appearance in 'La Sonnambula'; it was a very crude and imperfect performance, both lyrically and histrionically. Mongini played Elvino; he was about as unlike the ideal Elvino as anything could possibly be, but his voice pulled him through. I find that Mr. Santley was indisposed, and Signor Tagliafico took his place. Mr. Santley never felt very disposed when he had to appear as the Count in the 'Sonnambula.' It must have been in the course of this tour that I first played Tom Tug in the 'Waterman.' I was intimate with Mrs. Glover, the late lessee of the Theatre Royal, Glasgow, and most of her family. She wrote asking me as a favour to sing a song on the occasion of her eldest daughter's benefit at the Theatre Royal, Leeds. I always had a decided objection to appearing in evening dress before the footlights between the acts of a drama, so I declined singing a song; but I told Mrs. Glover, if I could obtain permission from Mapleson to go to Leeds, and her daughter were willing to play a short musical piece, I would do that with pleasure. My offer was joyfully accepted. I got my friend Lyall to help me to work up the dialogue, as I knew I could have but one rehearsal, and that probably a scratch one. Fortunately the manager was strict about business, and I found all concerned in the drama were perfect in their parts. I was highly amused at his anxiety about my reception. He insisted that, instead of being discovered seated at the table with old Bundle, I should enter after the curtain rose, something being interpolated to increase the expectations of the audience. I objected to the Crummlesonian dodge, and was discovered when the curtain rose, but received as enthusiastic a reception as man could desire. The piece went very well; the house was crammed from floor to ceiling, and the manager said they had never seen such a house before.

In the following spring, at a time when there was little doing, I had an offer made me by the manager of the other theatre in Leeds—a son-in-law of Mrs. Glover—to play 'Tom Tug' twice in that town—once in Sheffield and once in Bradford. I accepted, as the terms (sharing) seemed highly satisfactory, and, judging from the success of my former performance, I looked forward to making a substantial sum. I began at Bradford, but there was a poor house; except Miss Glover, none of the actors knew their parts. Mr. Bundle did not know even the first line, and I had to prompt him all through the first scene. I felt somewhat depressed. The second performance was in Leeds—the house, to my astonishment, very poor ; but Sheffield was a trifle better. The last night was the second performance in Leeds ; at the hour when those who intend being present at a performance are about leaving their homes, there came on a storm ; the rain fell in sheets of water, not a soul could stir out, and umbrellas were quite useless. I arrived at the theatre, and found my dressing-room floor covered with water—I had to stand on a plank to dress myself. When I was nearly ready, the call-boy came in to ask me if I was going to play. 'Certainly!' I said. 'Why not ? What have I come for ?' 'Well, sir,' said he, 'there's hardly anybody in the house.' 'Is there anyone at all ?' I asked. 'Yes, but very few.' 'No matter,' I said ; 'if there's only one, I'll do the best I can in return for his good-nature in turning out on such a night as this.' When the curtain rose, I could not distinguish a single being in the house. There were a few determined admirers, though, for the receipts were twelve shillings and sixpence. I think I may boast of having played to the smallest, or one of the smallest, houses ever known. The whole venture netted a sum of eleven pounds for my share, one of which I gave to the attendants at the theatre ; the rest I handed to Miss Glover, as she had lost her purse, with ten pounds in it, in one of the hotels. I had my week's trouble for nothing, minus my travelling and hotel expenses.

CHAPTER XIX.

THE season of 1869 is a memorable one in the annals
of Italian opera. About the beginning of the year an
announcement appeared in the *Queen*, written, I presume, by C. L. Gruneisen, to this effect : ‘We have
reason to believe that the two Italian Opera House
potentates, Mr. Gye and Mr. Mapleson, have signed
and sealed for the long-rumoured fusion of the two
establishments which they have directed. The details
of the convention have not yet transpired, but the main
clause is that there will be only one Italian Opera
House for the year 1869, and that is to be at Covent
Garden Theatre. Her Majesty’s Theatre will remain
closed for that season, at all events, as Mr. Mapleson
has one year unexpired of his lease under Lord
Dudley. His lordship having declined to renew it
for a longer period, Mr. Mapleson naturally could not
make the outlay for the *mise-en-scène* of one year only.
It is given out that the two *troupes* will be wedded, so as
to form one very powerful company, which will include

Adelina Patti and Mlles. Nilsson, Tietjens and Trebelli-Bettini, Mario and Mongini, Graziani and Santley, etc. Whether there are to be two directors or only one is not officially stated as yet, but report affirms that Mr. Gye will vacate to leave Mr. Mapleson in office. It is also added that, if Costa and Arditi will consent to work together, they are to be alternate conductors. Of the fact of the "fusion" there can be no doubt ; about its successful working opinions will differ. Those who believe in the union of the Guelphs and Ghibellines, the Montagues and the Capulets, or of any two Corsican families who have pronounced for the *vendetta*, can attach faith to an artistic *accolade*. The directors may manage to agree, but how will the *prima donnas*, the tender tenors, and the profound *bassi ?*'

It is worthy of note that the blustering baritones are not mentioned amongst those of the company likely to be victims of the green-eyed monster.

The combination was effected, and out of the long list of artists, only one of importance, Pauline Lucca, did not appear. I was much disappointed that Costa would not consent to the arrangement to have two conductors, and consequently seceded. I hoped to have served under his command again at the opera. There were probably heart-burnings and rivalries amongst some members of the company, but as I did not interfere with other people's business, I could only conjecture from certain indications and occasional repressed hints. Most of the operas promised were performed, also one of which the prospectus said, ' Negotiations are in progress for the performance for

the first time in England of Ambroise Thomas's celebrated opera " Hamlet," the character of Ophelia by
Mlle. Christine Nilsson.'

The season opened with ' Norma,' Tietjens, Sinico,
Mongini, and Foli ; followed by ' Rigoletto,' with Van-
zini (Mrs. Van Zandt, mother of the Mlle. Van Zandt
who came out at the Opéra Comique), Scalchi, Mongini, Foli, and myself.

' Fidelio,' ' Linda di Chamounix,' and the evergreen
'Trovatore,' came in their turn.   Ilma di Murska
played Linda, but I never liked her in it.   She introduced at the end a wretched air with variations by
Proch, which acted like a cold linseed-poultice on the
last finale, and bored everybody both in the house and
on the stage.   Her execution of the *cavatina* was
very limp, and though a few extra high notes brought
the house down, she was entirely out of her element in
the opera.   We had an importation in the shape of a
buffo named Bottero, of whom great things were
written in Italian musical journals (no great recommendation for anyone who knew how they were com-
piled), and of whom I heard from one who ought to
have known better that he was a combination of Luigi
Lablache and Giorgio Ronconi under one skin !   He
made his first appearance in a trivial work, ' Don
Bucefalo,' by Cagnoni, a fifth-rate Italian composer.
The   audience   evidently   did   not   agree   with   my
informant, as the theatre was half emptied of its
occupants before the second act had nearly approached
its termination.   The piece was repeated once, and
withdrawn.   Signor Bottero subsequently essayed the
part of the Podestà in ' La Gazza Ladra,' with Adelina

Patti, Trebelli, Bettini, and myself. I never saw Lablache on the stage, but I have seen Giorgio Ronconi play this part, and certainly did not discover a ghost of him in Signor Bottero. He soon returned to his native heath.

The great sensation of the season was undoubtedly the production of 'Hamlet,' with Nilsson in the character of Ophelia. With the exception of the 'Brindisi,' I liked the part of Hamlet very much, and took great pains to study not only the opera, but the drama. The costume adopted I did not like, nor could I procure a wig of the colour I wished, so I was not at all satisfied with my make-up. Notwithstanding, I had the satisfaction of being complimented on all sides. I met Thomas at breakfast the morning after the first performance, who thanked me very cordially for the pains I had taken with the part, and expressed himself perfectly satisfied with both my singing and acting, adding that the play scene had never been acted so well before. At the breakfast I was seated between two members of the press, musical critics both. My right-hand neighbour, in the course of conversation, remarked 'that I was a very lucky man.' I wished to know why. He replied, 'Why? Imagine you, a young man and an Englishman, being entrusted with the part of Hamlet at the Royal Italian Opera!' What could I answer? I said, 'I do not quite see what luck has to do with it; do you suppose the managers or the composer would have entrusted me with it if they had not considered I had sufficient ability to perform it?' Whilst still at the table my left-hand neighbour happened to make a remark about my playing the last scene of 'I due Foscari' on the occasion of Nilsson's benefit at Drury Lane the previous season. I explained to him that Mapleson asked me to sing one extra night that week, as he wished to make the benefits of the three *prima donnas* as strong as possible. After a moment's thought I agreed, on consideration that I might play the final scene of 'I due Foscari.' Finding that the parts were in the theatre and the chorus knew the music, it was settled I should do it. 'It was a fancy I had nursed for a long time,' I continued, 'although I only knew the opera from reading it, as I had never seen it performed.' 'Do you mean to say,' said my neighbour, 'you never saw Giorgio Ronconi play the Doge?' 'No,' I replied, 'nor anyone else.' 'I am sorry I did not know that before,' he remarked, 'or I would have said a great deal more about it ; I thought you had seen Ronconi in it more than once, and were giving us an imitation of his performance.' I felt much flattered, but I heartily wished he had known the facts before. I may as well add that the morning after the benefit I received a most charming letter from the Earl of Dudley, in which he said that he had entered the theatre as the scene from 'I due Foscari' was going on, and not distinguishing who was playing the Doge, inquired, and found to his astonishment it was Santley. He expressed himself highly pleased with my performance, and added he hoped Mr. Mapleson would see his way to bring out the opera the following season, that I might have the opportunity of playing the part in its integrity.

At the beginning of the season 1869 I was somewhat indisposed ; I had been working too hard all the winter, and during our operatic season in Scotland after Christmas we had encountered some severe weather. I caught a cold which I could not shake off during the prevalence of east wind in the spring. However, I had to get into harness as soon as the opera season opened. By way of a rest, early in the month of May I accompanied Arditi to Paris to hear ' Hamlet,' and get an idea of the *mise-en-scène*. The performance was very fine. The success was attributed almost entirely to Nilsson's performance of Ophelia, with which I. did not agree. Faure was an excellent Hamlet, and I am certain without the co-operation of such a great artiste, the representation, spite of Nilsson's splendid singing in the mad scene, would have been exceedingly dull. I was very much fidgeted by the way in which the conductor used his fiddlestick ; he flourished it to such an extent that at times he drew my attention entirely away from the stage. I was very much amused when Arditi turned to me during the interval between the second and third acts, and exclaimed, ' If that conductor continues to make those flourishes with his stick I shall be obliged to leave the theatre ; I cannot pay the slightest attention to the singers !' We attended a performance of Wagner's ' Rienzi ' during our stay. It was splendidly put on the stage, and in every way an excellent performance. Monjauze, the tenor I have already spoken of in connection with ' Faust ' the first time I heard it, played Rienzi finely. But the theatre was hot and stuffy, and I did not feel very well, so after the third act I left the theatre and went for a drive by moonlight in the Champs Elysées, which I enjoyed much better than the opera.

On our return we had hard work rehearsing every day, and I had three or four performances each week ; during that in which 'Hamlet' was produced on the Saturday, I had two other performances. On the Wednesday we had a full rehearsal of the new opera from eleven until nearly four ; I then had to rush off to Kuhe's concert, where I sang two pieces ; and in the evening I had to play Tom Tug in the 'Waterman' at the Adelphi Theatre for the benefit of the Misses Harris, daughters of Augustus Harris, the stage-manager. I felt anything but fit after my morning's work, but a bottle of dry champagne with my dinner, a good cigar, and forty winks, restored me, and when I was dressed to go on I felt as fresh as a lark.

I had the great pleasure of playing Hoel in 'Dinorah' with Adelina Patti, an opera in which she shone to greater advantage than in any other in which I have seen her. We rehearsed the stage business well ; she was the only *prima donna* I have known who did not resent interference with the business she was accustomed to. I suggested that a little more or much more passion would be a great improvement when she recovered her senses in the last act and recognised her lover, and that she should throw herself without fear into my arms. She acted on my suggestion, and the result was such a storm of applause that we had to wait some moments before we could proceed with the opera.

Patti was very anxious to have 'L'Étoile du Nord' reproduced, as Catarina was one of her favourite parts.

She wished me to play Peter, which I would have done with all my heart ; but after the hard work I had done, and in view of the fact that it was late in the season, I was obliged to decline ; I really could not have studied a new part, and one so exigent, at that time.

Towards the close of the season I played ' Rigoletto ' for the only time with Adelina Patti, on the occasion of her benefit, Tamberlik playing the Duke.

The only important performance for me beside the opera during the season was a Rossini Festival at the Crystal Palace, held in the Transept, with a chorus and orchestra numbering about 3,000. The programme consisted of the ' Stabat Mater ' and a selection from Rossini's works, among them the Blessing of the Banners from ' The Siege of Corinth,' in which I sang the solo part. I may as well mention the fact, as I am certain nobody would otherwise be aware of it, as I myself could not hear my voice. Costa, who had been seriously ill for a little time and confined to his room, left his sick-bed to do homage to the master he loved. Though he was not in a fit state to be at work, he conducted throughout with unflagging spirit, and never more emphatically proved himself ' conductor of conductors.'

Rossini's ' Messe Solennelle ' was performed for the first time in England about the middle of May—I cannot find the exact date. Tietjens, Scalchi, Mongini and I sang the solo parts. With the exception of the ' Kyrie ' I do not care for the work, and it made very little effect. It was performed at the Worcester Festival the same year, and occasionally after, but was

soon all but lost sight of.   At this festival Sullivan's
'Prodigal Son,' one of his best serious works, was performed for the first time ; Sullivan himself conducted.
Nobody who heard it can surely ever forget how magnificently Sims Reeves sang the scene, 'I will arise
and go to my father '—a sort of thing one hears once
in a lifetime.

Returning from this festival, I and some of my comrades had a narrow escape.   The train started from
Worcester about three-quarters of an hour late, in consequence of the railway officials having neglected to
provide sufficient accommodation for the unusually
large number of people returning to London.   On the
road we lost more time ; and as we were nearing London we were almost an hour and a half behind time.
The engine-driver had just slackened speed to enter
Westbourne Park Station when he became aware of a
train, heedless of signals, coming on to cross our line.
He put on full speed, hoping to clear the other train,
but to no purpose ; it came on and struck ours just in
the middle, smashing a luggage-van immediately in
front of the coach I and my companions occupied,
which was thrown off the line and ran for a short distance bouncing over the sleepers.   Looking out, the
first thing I saw was a shower of musical instrument
cases, among them a double bass.   The doors were
jammed with the concussion, so we scrambled out of
the windows.   The coaches in front were lying upside
down.   I asked an official who came by how the accident had happened, but the only reply I received was,
'Have you got your ticket ?'   I went on to the station,
where I heard the guard was seriously hurt, and

having his wounds dressed in the waiting-room. I popped my head in at the door and asked the surgeon who was attending on him if he was badly hurt. The doctor turned round, and after a glance called, ' Is that you, man ? Are ye hurt ?' I recognised in him a calico - printer I had known in Glasgow. 'No.' said I, 'thank God !' ' Then go to your carriage, and I will come to you presently.' In a few minutes he came up and begged of me to keep myself within doors for a couple of weeks and he would get me £1,000 damages. I replied that I was thankful to be unhurt, and preferred going to Norwich, where I was due the next week, and earn my money doing my duty.

At Norwich we performed a selection from an oratorio called ' Hezekiah,' by Hugo Pierson—very dry stuff indeed—of which I never heard any more ; also Rossini's ' Messe Solennelle,' which did not rouse any enthusiasm.

We played ' Hamlet ' on the operatic tour which succeeded, in Manchester and Liverpool, and also in London, during the short season, with Ilma di Murska as Ophelia. She did not sing the music as well as Nilsson ; otherwise there was little difference between the two representations. I had my own dress (a fac-simile of Fechter's) and make-up, which not only improved my appearance, but, feeling I looked more like Hamlet, I am sure I played better. One great improvement was the substitution of Carl Formes as the Ghost for the *buffo* who essayed it on the first production of the opera.

The year 1870 was the last year of my connection

with the Italian opera in England—it marks an epoch in my life which I have ever since looked back on with regret. My ambition and delight were the stage; the concert-room, save under exceptional circumstances, had little attraction for me. I believe I would have preferred being an actor of moderate fame to being the most renowned singer on earth. I worked during the four seasons of English opera and nine years of Italian opera with an object in view, and if I did not become a consummate actor I earned fame even in that capacity. Often I think now, when I have an hour and a half to wait between two songs, having no relation to each other, in a miscellaneous concert, how much more satisfying it was to have to embody a part, and to have my attention riveted throughout the evening on the delineation of a character I was representing.

The beginning of the year seemed to be prophetic; I made my first appearance at the London ballad concerts, and also sang at a series called the Exeter Hall Saturday Evening Concerts, under the management of Mr. George Wood. A concert tour was arranged in my name by this gentleman from the end of January for about six weeks, and my companions were Madame Sinico, Miss Helen D'Alton, Wilhelmj, and Arabella Goddard, with Sidney Naylor as accompanist. I know nothing of the business part, but I believe the tour was fairly successful. I had two genial companions in Wilhelmj and Naylor, and the time passed more pleasantly than I anticipated. Concert touring I always found exceedingly disagreeable after the novelty of the first few days had passed. A journey every day, Sunday included very often; the same dinner day after day (on one tour nine times out of ten it consisted of bad soup, fish, a saddle of mutton indifferently roasted, and a pair of boiled fowls buried in a mass of bookbinder's paste); the same programme to go through every evening, and a different bed to sleep in each night. The monotony is appalling, yet I have known artists who say they enjoy such a life. I do not; I abhor it, and always did. The only relief from the daily routine was when little scenes of jealousy arose about encores, or some such subject, and they were not a pleasant change. On one of the first evenings we had a scene with Wilhelmj and Madame Goddard; they played one of Beethoven's sonatas, which, being long, Wilhelmj suggested might be cut, as it was usually. Madame Goddard would not consent to cutting anything of Beethoven, but insisted on playing the last movement at a speed which did not at all accord with Wilhelmj's notion. At the end of the sonata he came down off the orchestra in despair, and cried like a child. To end the dispute the cuts were made and the movement played at a proper speed.

Towards the end of the tour we went to Ireland. Madame Goddard objected to crossing the channel, so Ernst Pauer was engaged to take her place. In Dublin and Belfast everybody was perfectly satisfied, but in Cork, where I fancy they had omitted to make a proper announcement of the change, there was quite a hubbub when, instead of an elegant female form, a tall, gaunt-looking male appeared and sat down at the piano. The disturbance continued for some time, but was stopped at last, if I remember rightly, by our genial manager, Edward Murray, stepping forward to explain why the change was necessary. During the interval between the two parts of the concert Miss Helen D'Alton was presented with a handsome testimonial in the shape of a necklace, brooch, and earrings, as a token of the esteem and admiration in which she was held by her fellow citizens. She was a native of Cork, which city her father had served as Mayor. The testimonial was presented by the then Mayor, who was requested by the gallery boys to 'spake up.' I replied for Miss D'Alton ; my speech having been provided for me, I had merely to read it, which I did without any shyness or nervousness, and evidently to the satisfaction of the audience, as they gave me a tremendous round of applause at the end, with an accompaniment of ' Bravo, Santley !'

From Ireland we crossed over to Scotland to commence an operatic tour. Among the *soprani* we had Mlle. Monbelli and Mlle. Reboux, both French, the former an elegant and accomplished lady and a charming singer, possessing good qualities as an actress, although lacking experience sufficient to develop her intentions. Except Madame Viardot I never heard anyone who sang Spanish songs so well. Of Mlle. Reboux, who sang the small part of Vincenette in 'Mireille' at Her Majesty's Theatre in 1864, I recollect little, except that I did not find her a great acquisition. We had also a new contralto, Mlle. Morensi, a handsome American, who played Zerlina to my Don Giovanni. She was so tall I felt like a pigmy and suggested in our scenes together Leporello might attend with a step-ladder to enable me to put myself on a level with her.

After Scotland we played in Liverpool at the old Amphitheatre, one of the best theatres for sound I have sung in ; its perfect acoustic properties must have been quite accidental. I believe it was run up in about six weeks in order to hold a great political meeting. In my youthful days it was the home of John Vandenhoff, Gustavus Brooke, Barry Sullivan, and other celebrated actors under the management of W. R. Copeland. I have already mentioned it was *my* first theatre, where I was taken to see Ducrow's circus. It was here that Walter Lacy made his first appearance riding on an elephant's trunk in ' Blue Beard.' An accident occurred to Vandenhoff at one of his benefits when he was playing Brutus in ' Julius Cæsar,' similar to the one I have related as happening to me during a performance of the ' Bohemian Girl.' As he commenced the speech, ' Romans, countrymen and lovers,' a goat which used to be kept in the stable belonging to the theatre marched gravely on to the stage and planted itself between his legs, facing the audience, and there remained, apparently wrapt in admiration, until the speech was finished, when it took itself off as gravely as it entered.

CHAPTER XX.

THE Royal Italian Opera, Covent Garden, opened on March 29, still under the joint management of Messrs. Gye and Mapleson. With the exception of Tietjens all Mr. Mapleson's old company were engaged by Mr. George Wood, who undertook the management of an Italian Opera at Drury Lane. The announcement of both operas appeared in the same number of the *Musical World.* In addition to the company we had on the tour, the engagements were announced of Madame Volpini (from the Imperial Opera, St. Petersburg), already a favourite in London in 1864 ; Mlle. Savertal (from the Opera, Pisa), who did not appear ; and Mlle. Pauline Lewitsky, a Russian, who did appear, a graceful girl and pretty singer, and nothing more. The novelties produced were Ambroise Thomas's ' Mignon,' in which I hoped to have played Lothario, as Thomas expressed himself so satisfied with me in ' Hamlet'; but for some reason Faure was engaged at the last moment, and the part was given to him. I did not admire Nilsson as Mignon. She sang exceedingly well, and acted a great deal and looked much more like a boy, when dressed in male attire, than she did when she tried Cherubino. Some of her scenes were very charming, but the *feu sacré* necessary to represent Mignon was wanting. It was a great mistake to give the part of Federico to a woman ; it upset the concerted music, and did not add to the interest of the performance.

The ' Flying Dutchman,' the first opera of Wagner produced in England, was not brought out until ten days before the close of the season. I thought it was going to be shelved, and I was anxious to play Vanderdecken, as I felt sure it was a part which would suit me well. I found Ilma di Murska, who was to be the Senta, was partly the cause of the delay, so I asked her plainly where her objection lay, and after a little beating about the bush she said because it was all Flying Dutchman, while Senta was nobody. I told her she was wrong, that Senta was of quite as much importance as the Dutchman, for without Senta certainly he would be nobody. She afterwards altered her mind when she came to look into the part, and we worked together very earnestly at all the stage business. The audience from their applause showed they enjoyed the performance. Wagner, however, failed to attract the public. We only played it two or three nights, and to very poor houses. I had another adventure with an animal, this time a cat, on the first night. I had finished my opening scene, and was leaning on a piece of rock waiting for Daland to make his entry, when I heard a sound of 'Ts! Ts!' behind me.   I looked out of the corner of my eye, and espied a cat stealthily crossing the stage.   Instead of leaving her to go on her way, one of the men in the boat was trying to send her back.   Being very tame and knowing all the people belonging to the theatre, she stopped to see who was calling her.   I was in dread, for I knew that if the public saw her, she would attract all their attention and the rest of the act would go for nothing.   It does not matter how interesting a scene on the stage may be, a song or solo in a concert, a speech or a sermon ; a cat or a dog, or even a mouse, appearing unexpectedly will carry away the attention of the entire audience.   To my great joy the cat did not recognise a friend in the boatman, so went quietly off.   I spoke about the carelessness of allowing a cat to wander about the stage during a performance ; but I was told she was only looking for her customary supply of milk—and the first act of the opera might have been ruined in consequence.   Ilma di Murska was better suited with the part of Senta than with any part I saw her play.   She looked it to perfection : the weird, earnest, yet dreamy, expression on her face denoted a spirit ready to make the sacrifice that was to be demanded of her—to give her life to save the soul of the unhappy man, whose curse it was to wander until he should find a being capable of such a sacrifice.   She acknowledged the mistake she had at first made, and played with an energy and spirit I had never before seen her display.

'L'Oca del Cairo' (Mozart) and 'Abou Hassan' (Weber), two comic operas, each in one act, were produced together. They are both pretty, but were not seen to advantage in so large a theatre, and made very little effect. For the second time in my operatic experience I was announced to play Macbeth in Verdi's opera, this time with Mlle. Savertal, but, as I before said, Mlle. Savertal did not arrive, and nothing was heard of the opera. Cherubini's ' Les Deux Journées ' was also promised, with the dialogue set to accompanied recitative by Signor Arditi. I was very glad it was not performed ; it is not, properly speaking, an opera, but a drama with incidental music ; and I am certain, however compressed the dialogue might be—as it is the principal part of the work—and however well set, the result would have been a very heavy, tiresome performance. Rossini's ' Tancredi ' was promised, but not performed.

At the termination of the season I was asked to accept an engagement for the following year at the Italian Opera, under the joint management of Messrs. Gye and Mapleson. The loss on the season at Drury Lane had been such that Mr. George Wood gave up the idea of carrying on his management, but I did not like changing about from one company to another, and overtures had been made to me to appear in English opera at the Gaiety Theatre, which, on my consenting, would be changed into a lyric theatre entirely. I fancied the reputation and position I had gained at the Italian Opera would be sufficient to make my name a solid attraction, and in combination with as good a company as could be got together, an attractive opera, good orchestra and chorus, and proper stage management, I should have an opportunity to establish a permanent home for opera in England.   My wife and most of my friends endeavoured to dissuade me from quitting the Italian Opera ; but obstinacy and, I must candidly confess, a certain amount of vanity prevailed, and I entered into an engagement to appear at the Gaiety Theatre in the month of September following.   The band of the theatre was not sufficient for the requirements of an opera ; there were not sufficient strings, and the wind, especially the 'wood,' was incomplete.   I had a promise that all this should be remedied.   The chorus consisted chiefly of young fresh voices, and I was satisfied that with the attention Meyer Lutz, the conductor, would bestow on it, there would be little left to desire.   The *mise-en-scène* and dressing I had no doubt about.   But the greatest difficulty of all had to be overcome : what opera were we to produce ?   Suggestion after suggestion was made, each of which for one reason or other was abandoned.   At last I recollected what Balfe had told me some years before, if ever I could find an opportunity to play 'Zampa' not to miss it, as the part would suit me perfectly, and the music also, with very little transposition.   It was written for Chollet, a tenor, or, I fancy, a sort of baritone with a powerful falsetto, as no pure tenor could have reached the low notes written in the part.

For my holiday I went to Jersey with my friend Lyall.   I took with me the score of 'Zampa,' and was convinced if well put on the stage it would prove attractive.   When I returned there were only three weeks left before the production of the opera ; I had not seen a word of the translation, and at last, when I did, I found the words had been translated without any regard to the musical accent, and that it would be impossible to make use of them, so I set to work and retranslated the whole of my part and the scenes in which I was concerned. The dialogue I did not like, and I re-adapted that also. The rehearsals began and went on vigorously, for, with one exception, I found my companions as zealous and earnest as myself; we rehearsed the greater part of the day, and at night, after studying my part, I went on with the translation of what we had still to rehearse—a serious task for me, as I am very slow at such work. When we came to the orchestral rehearsal, I found that the promises made me had not been kept; the band, with the exception of a change of 'cello and one or two additional violins, was the same as before. I expostulated in vain. It was too late to retract, or I would have left the theatre. Lutz had done his best (and that is saying a great deal) to remedy the deficiencies in the wind department; he was very vigilant, and made everything go, as far as the means at his command would permit, to my satisfaction. The opera was successful, thanks to the efforts of all concerned. I felt especially grateful to Madame Lancia, who undertook the part of Camilla, one of the most ungrateful parts for a *prima donna* I know, and played it with as much earnestness and ability as though it had been one of the most sympathetic. We played 'Zampa' for nine weeks in succession. The manager was anxious to make a change, as there were no rehearsals going on, a thing he did not seem to understand. I asked what he had an idea of doing. 'Don Giovanni.'

'Oh, indeed!' I said; 'and who are your singers?'
Amongst the ladies he mentioned two who were little
better, if any, than music-hall singers. I wanted to
know then who was to play Don Giovanni. 'Why,
you, of course.' 'No,' I said, 'I do not. If you want
me to play Don Giovanni, you must engage three
lady singers of whom I approve, and you must have
a better orchestra, and you must have the opera properly translated, as I decline adopting any translation
I have yet seen.' He talked about managerial
authority, etc. I replied, being master of the situation, that I intended to maintain my position. After
some discussion, it was ultimately agreed we were to
produce 'Fra Diavolo,' in which I was to play the
hero. It was brought out a week or two before
Christmas. I endeavoured to make the part quite the
opposite to Zampa. Zampa, according to the story,
was a gentleman of a roving, unsettled, wild disposition,
whilst Fra Diavolo was nothing more nor less than
a common vulgar thief, whose Brummagem airs of
gentility were the very thing to captivate a silly,
empty-pated, vain lady like Lady Allcash. I have
no idea what success, if any, I made in the part; I
never read a line about it, and two opinions I had
from friends were so contrary that from them I could
not judge. One, a Dublin friend, recommended me
never to attempt Fra Diavolo again. Another, a
German, told me he had seen every notable Fra
Diavolo in his time, and he had never seen anyone who represented the character as well as I
did. Those, if any live, who saw it can judge for
themselves; those who did not must regret or rejoice

MR. SANTLEY IN 'FRA DIAVOLO.'

To face page 290.

as they think proper. The theatre was closed on Christmas Eve—a Saturday. The five nights preceding of the same week, in addition to Fra Diavolo, I played Tom Tug in 'The Waterman' as an after-piece, and right glad I was when Christmas Eve arrived, and I was free.

Between the end of the Italian opera season and my holiday there were the Hereford Festival, of which nothing particular need be said, and the Birmingham Festival in the succeeding week. Of the new music I took part in was a cantata by Dr. Ferdinand Hiller, 'Nala and Damayanti,' to my taste a very heavy work ; it was of the numerous compositions of the same class which I had all the trouble of learning and rehearsing for a single performance. I never heard of it again. I also took the part of St. Peter in Benedict's oratorio, about which there was a great deal of unamiable correspondence published in the *Musical World*. It was a very unequal work, not to be compared with his last opera, ' The Lily of Killarney.' The libretto was poor, and a great portion of the music written in a hurry, the result being an uninteresting composition. With the exception of an air, 'Oh that my head were water!' I did not feel interested in my part. The scene of the 'denial,' which might be made an effective scene, I was quite disappointed with, it was so insignificant. The oratorio was performed a few times during the succeeding winter season, but has rarely been heard of since.

I cannot help noticing the number of deaths which occurred this year of celebrated people connected with music and the drama. Leigh Murray, the best *jeune premier* of his time, in January ; George Hogarth, Charles Dickens's father-in-law, many years musical critic of the *Daily News*, in February ; Mary Keeley (Mrs. Albert Smith), in April ; Charles Green, the aeronaut, in the same month ; Charles Dickens, on the 9th of June ; John Cooper, said to be the last actor of the Kemble school, and R. K. Bowley, a leading man in the Sacred Harmonic Society, and for some years preceding his death manager of the Crystal Palace, in August ; M. W. Balfe on October the 21st ; and Adolfo Ferrari, a well-known professor of singing, on the 27th of December.

I was much grieved at the death of Charles Dickens, for our intimacy had ripened, and I was on the eve of enjoying his hospitality as a domestic friend at Gad's Hill. From our first meeting I fancied he had a liking for me ; he always had a kind, encouraging word to say to me. Our friendship reached the point of intimacy through the misfortunes of a mutual friend —Charles Fechter, the celebrated actor, who after several brilliant seasons suffered the reverses consequent upon making artistic merit the sole means of attracting the public. Without speaking of him as an actor, no man in my time has ever clothed the pieces he produced with such artistic effect as he did. Each piece was a perfect picture, of which he himself formed the bright centre, shedding such light upon his fellow workers that they developed powers which before they had never been deemed capable of. I will only instance one play, ' Hamlet,' as he produced it at the Lyceum. It was a masterpiece of acting and stage management. He made a large sum of money by his earlier productions at that theatre, which he spent on remodelling and rebuilding the stage; but the public require something they have a capacity to appreciate, which is not artistic excellence, and little by little they abandoned Fechter, until he found himself in difficulties. He made a very fine engagement for the United States, but he could not leave England without settling certain imperative claims. Then it was that, being aware of my intimacy with Fechter, Dickens asked me to join him in supplying Fechter with the means of satisfying those claims. We each advanced him five hundred pounds, which was repaid in a short time after he had entered on his engagement in the States. I met Dickens one morning in Manchester, as he was leaving the Free Trade Hall, where he had been arranging the platform for his reading; we had a little commonplace chat and parted. About two years after I was at a musical party at his house, opposite the Marble Arch; I arrived very early, and found him and G. Dolby only. I had grown much thinner since the last time we met, and he inquired if I was preparing to come out as Romeo, and, ' By-the-bye,' said he, 'what has become of that heavy chain you wore last time I saw you? Oh, I know, Dolby; now he has grown so thin he's afraid of the weight overbalancing him !'

I cannot recollect the precise date, but it was during the season at the Gaiety, at Boucicault's request, I accompanied him and Benedict to the Albert Hall, which was then nearly completed, as he was desirous of testing its acoustic properties. I sang a couple of pieces whilst he roamed about from one part of the building to another, to test it from various points. Benedict afterwards played a couple of pieces on the piano, when I joined Boucicault in the auditorium, and we both came to the conclusion that it was not a good room for sound. The opening, at which her Majesty was present, took place in April, 1871, when our judgment was verified. I was engaged for the Gaiety, to open as soon as the Christmas burlesque was withdrawn ; the new work chosen was Lortzing's ' Czar und Zimmerman,' christened in English ' Peter the Shipwright ' ; as it was deemed wiser to keep this back until Easter, we played ' Fra Diavolo ' for three weeks, rehearsing the new opera during the day. Madame Lancia could not return, as she had a prior engagement for a tour in the provinces, so Madame Blanche Cole was engaged to replace her. She lacked the warmth and earnestness of her predecessor ; but with a fresh voice, well cultivated, and the graceful naïve manner in which she played Zerlina in ' Fra Diavolo,' and Maria in ' Peter the Shipwright,' she proved an attractive acquisition to our company. Lortzing's opera ran for some weeks. I began to feel the strain of singing every night the same piece, and, to make matters worse, I took cold, which, having to continue singing, I could not throw off. I was glad, however, of a real excuse for bringing the season to a close, for I was thoroughly disappointed ; as far as I could see, my attempt at assisting to make a home for opera in my native tongue was totally unsuccessful. I sacrificed money, as during the same period I could have earned double the sum I was paid at the theatre by singing at concerts. I sacrificed health to a certain extent ; the atmosphere of a dressing-room under the stage, without ventilation, and the dreary monotony of going on the treadmill every night, disposed or indisposed, told on me. I was glad at Christmas, when I was released from my toil; but *now* I rejoiced, as I had no intention of returning to it any more.

I tried hard to induce the management to produce Auber's 'Le Cheval de Bronze.' There are many of the operas belonging to the 'opéra comique' *répertoire* which I feel sure would even now attract the British public provided they were translated decently and elegantly put on the stage. Nor would it be necessary to have a band of ninety performers, as the music depends on the singers, who would consequently have to be heard. At that time there would have been little difficulty in establishing a lyric theatre attractive to the public and remunerative to the management. The opportunity was lost, and has never been recovered. English people do not care for 'grand opera' in their own language, although a round sum of money was made by Balfe's *grand* opera 'The Rose of Castille,' and others so designated. They like what the French call, and for which we have no equivalent name, 'opéra comique,' in which a great portion of the drama is in spoken dialogue. It is said that speaking dialogue fatigues the singing voice; I must say I have never found it the case. Hoel in 'Dinorah,' my first part, is long, both in music and dialogue, and after two weeks' hard work at rehearsals and studying at home, I played it for five weeks every night, at the expiration of which, for a rest, I played Di Luna in 'Il Trovatore' on the succeeding Monday night, and my voice was as fresh, or fresher, than when I began the season. Of course in these days, when young people have not learned to use their voices properly, any excuse is better than none for not being able to get through more than three or four nights a week, and for not studying elocution sufficiently to be able to recite decently.

I resolved I would throw away neither money nor health longer on what was surely a chimera, and decided to devote the rest of my career to the concert platform ; but what I proposed was otherwise disposed, for I had yet to undergo a theatrical ordeal far more trying than any I had hitherto passed through.

It grieved me deeply to abandon all my cherished hopes and the object of my whole life's ambition—the stage. I had one small solace, the oratorio, for in those days there was a society where oratorios were performed in a way worthy of the great composers who wrote them. It was but a small solace, though—an oratorio now and then as a set-off against a crowd of miscellaneous concerts, where the ' Erl King,' or some other fine song, would be ushered in by some imbecile trash about two old fogies warming their toes and indulging in sentimental balderdash, or about children dropping asleep over their evening porridge and being put to bed, with the great probability, unexpressed in the ditty, that they would be victims to indigestion and consequent nightmare. And worse than all, to know that ninety-nine hundredths of those composing the audience would christen such stuff poetry, and the melancholy meandering of the exponent singing. And it is to be classed along with incompetence, such as the like exponents display, that one makes a life-study of the art of expressing poetry in song.

CHAPTER XXI.

I WAS very glad when the opportunity occurred by which I could get away from my old associations for a time. I was offered an engagement to go with a concert party to the United States on very fair terms. The party was to consist of Miss Edith Wynne, Mr. and Mrs. Patey, Mr. W. H. Cummings, and myself, with Mr. Lindsay Sloper as accompanist and sole pianist. It was my old love of the sea which presented the greatest inducement to my leaving England. I had long had a wish to cross the ocean, and here my wish was to be gratified—my singing in America was in comparison a matter of indifference. I certainly looked forward to a friendly greeting, as I had met with many pleasant Americans, professional and otherwise, who all promised me a gratifying reception if I should ever visit the States.

Our agent started to prepare the way some weeks ahead of us. Before leaving I proposed to give a farewell concert at Liverpool the night before we sailed. The secretary of the Philharmonic Society threw cold water on the suggestion ; he was sure it would be a failure. The consequence was, luckily for me, that the society would not share with me, but demanded thirty guineas for the hire of their hall. I made the arrangements, engaged my fellow-travellers, and put forth a popular attractive programme. A few days before the day of the concert I wrote to the secretary to ask him to reserve a box for my family. His reply was that he would be able to reserve any number, as there was plenty of room left. I felt somewhat surprised that the townsmen who professed to take such pride in me should not honour me with a crowd when I was about to say farewell for an indefinite period. I was much more pleasantly surprised, when I arrived at the hall for the concert, to find they had responded so heartily that the hall was crowded in every part, very little else, except the box I had had reserved, being given away. The concert, as I have said, was a popular one, the prices not on a high scale, but the result was very satisfactory, being net £275. The next time I gave a concert at the same hall, which was during a tour I made after my return from America, they would not let me the room at any price except a share of the proceeds.

To describe a voyage to America, made in 1871, would be simply ludicrous now. It was, to a certain extent, an undertaking even then ; now it is little more than a run down to Greenwich by boat to eat whitebait, except that occasionally the water is rougher. I liked it so much, I should have preferred carrying out my engagement on board ship. I am what is called a good sailor, which means I am a stranger to sea-sickness, which all real sailors are not. I knew one who, after each watch, threw himself on the floor of his cabin and lay there like a log, sick as a dog. Still the sea air affected me seriously; I was nearly always hungry; meal-times seemed as though they would never come round, although there was not much space between them—breakfast at nine, lunch at twelve, dinner at four, tea at half-past six, and supper at nine. I was not an exception in this; I was amused and astonished at the prowess some of my fellow-travellers displayed, notably a very pretty little American lady, my *vis-à-vis* at table. I expected that a cup of tea and a little toast would be about as much as she would undertake for breakfast, but I saw her the first morning eat a good solid rump-steak, followed by a dish of ham and eggs, topped up with sundry little frivolities, such as jam, muffins, etc. At the dinner, when all sat down, we were uncomfortably crowded, and I was glad when a little rough weather thinned the benches. Mr. and Mrs. Patey retired altogether for about three days; Cummings, who complained of headache, at last went in search of them; they had been very bad, and he found Patey restoring his wasted form with devilled ham and bottled porter—a novel remedy for sea-sickness. I had not been used to the company of cockroaches in bed, but after a night or two on board I became accustomed to them, and left them to amuse themselves after their own fashion. The captain—Theodore Cook—was a very quiet, gentlemanly man; many of the passengers complained of his want of civility when they addressed him; for my part, I often wished I had the faculty of keeping my own counsel as he had, as it would have been better for me. If people would only reflect on the responsibility a captain of a large ship, with a valuable cargo and a large number of passengers on board, has to bear, they would not be so apt to find fault with his apparent taciturnity. I found him an exceedingly pleasant man, but I never addressed him when I saw he was occupied; I left him to address me, and we got on very well together.

The voyage seemed very short, and I felt quite sad at leaving the ship; however, there was a new place to see, new people to know, so my spirits gradually rose. Near the quay we mounted on a machine which seemed a cross between a break for exercising horses and a circus-van, and away we sped, over hill and over dale (literally, for the pavement of New York was then, and is still, a series of ridges and valleys), to our hotel. I found my dormitory high up in the air; hot and cold water laid on, though the hot never came when it was bidden. One great comfort there was, a comfort which with very little exception I have found wherever I have been in the United States and Canada, a really comfortable bed. As a particular favour we had our meals in private; they were very well served, with plenty and great variety. I cannot say much in praise of the wine-cellar; its contents, as far as I became acquainted with them, were of a very in-different order. In the exuberance of my spirits once, after a morning concert, I ordered a bottle of what was described as port, vintage 1834, but it turned out to be cherry brandy. Soon after our arrival I was invited along with the other male members of our company to a guest-night at the Lotus Club, where we met with a most cordial reception. A stout elderly member accosted me during the evening, asking me if I remembered meeting him in London—at Alboni's house, or apartments somewhere in Regent's Park. I replied I did not. 'Perhaps,' said he, 'you will be able to recollect the occasion when I remind you we dined there, and before dinner you sang the duet from " Semiramide " with Alboni; it was in the year 1857.' I replied he must be mistaken, as I never dined with Alboni. I never sang the duet from ' Semiramide ' with her, and in the year 1857 I was living in Milan. He insisted he was right, and that I had forgotten all about it, so I left him to enjoy the fruits of his imagination. I had often heard of the celebrated American oyster which half a dozen people had tried to swallow without success, and was anxious to learn if the story were founded on fact. Cummings conducted me to a cellar in Broadway, where, upon his order, a waiter produced two plates, on which were half a dozen objects, about the size and shape of the sole of an ordinary lady's shoe, on each of which lay what appeared to me to be a very bilious tongue, accompanied by smaller plates containing shredded white cabbage raw. I did not admire the look of the repast, but I never discard food on account of looks. I took up an oyster, and tried to get it into my mouth, but it was of no use; I tried to ram it in with the butt-end of the fork, but all to no purpose, and I had to drop it ; and, to the great indignation of the waiter, paid and left the oysters for him to dispose of as he might like best. I presume those oysters are eaten, but I cannot imagine by whom ; I have rarely seen a mouth capable of the necessary expansion. I soon found out that there were plenty of delicious oysters in the States within the compass of ordinary jaws.

According to my usual plan, I wandered all over the city from the Battery to Central Park, and from one river across to the other, and soon became acquainted with all the ins and outs thereof. I saw plenty to admire, except it was all so new, and only one thing displeased me really—the incessant noise. We have noise, plenty and to spare, in the city of London, or in any of our great towns in Great Britain, but nothing to compare with the din in New York. These little things I mention first, being my first impressions of the place, but I had not lost sight of the important object of my visit. My strolling propensities having been remarked, one paper published a statement to the effect that Mr. Santley took a great deal of exercise, and that he walked from the Battery to Central Park every morning before breakfast. Another got hold of a remark I made in jest at table, and informed its readers that 'Santley says squash pie is the best thing to sing on he knows !' I was asked once if I would like to live in New York. I incautiously (referring to the intolerable din) replied I would prefer a lodging in the Strand, London, with an income of £100 per annum, to the best house in Fifth Avenue with £10,000 a year ; this was also published, so I thought it was high time to study to keep my own counsel. I had an early interview with our manager on the prospects of the campaign, and I was bound to confess to myself they looked like failure. He was sanguine ; there were all sorts of reasons why business should not be so good at first. For my part, I was satisfied it would not improve ; if people want to hear or see anything, they turn out, spite of weather or bad times ; an epidemic is about the only thing I know of which will prevent the public from seeking amusement. We were supposed to give *Ballad Concerts*, but though the American public liked ballads, they were not accustomed to concerts made up of that commodity. Perhaps had the trumpets been blown, and the various and varied beauties of our programme been explained in glowing colours, we might have made a sensation. Individually, we were all received with enthusiasm ; it was only rarely we had not to sing a double programme. Our audiences were extremely enthusiastic, but not sufficiently numerous to cover the great expense of such a company. At Boston we met with the same amount of enthusiasm, which we were led to suppose would not be the case, owing to the rivalry between that city and New York ; our audiences were also more numerous. For the oratorios—' Elijah,' ' St. Paul,' ' The Messiah,' ' Judas Maccabæus,' etc.—we had splendid houses, and I was exceedingly pleased to note that the attention of the audience was not fixed, as it invariably is in England, on those few pieces which have become stock encores, no matter how they are sung or murdered. Especially in ' Elijah ' I felt the audience following the prophet throughout as the principal object of their attention.

The first night we sang in New York the great fire broke out in Chicago, which reduced a great part of that city to ashes. It was intended that after New York, Boston, and the neighbouring towns of importance, we should turn westward to Chicago, Pittsburg, St. Louis, etc., etc., but our manager for some unaccountable reason changed our route. He contended that Chicago, the principal musical centre westward, being in such a plight, it would be useless to give a concert there, and without the seal of Chicago it would be worse than useless to attempt anything in the other Western cities. I opposed him to the best of my ability. I had never been over the ground, certainly, but his notion was absurd on the face of it, that because Chicago was suffering from a calamity no other city of the West would welcome us. I went so far as to make him an offer. I would go the tour of the principal Western cities (to be named), and if any loss occurred, I would forego my salary for the time and pay my own expenses. He refused my offer, and took up a tour which had been dropped by Ole Bull, the violinist, in consequence of his serious illness; instead of appearing in places of importance we were thus for three weeks dragging about in small towns where music such as we performed was no attraction. Amongst the rest we went to Canandaigua. I do not know what it is now, but at that time it barely contained 4,000 inhabitants. We arrived at dusk one evening after a long day's travelling, very tired and very hungry. We were shown our rooms; then I asked if we could have some supper, as we had not had a decent meal the whole day. 'Guess you can't have supper.' 'Good gracious! you can give us something to eat, surely?' 'Waal, I guess lunch'll be

ready at nine ; there's ham and eggs and a good piece
of cold beef.'   'Call it what you like, lunch or supper,
only I never before heard of lunch at nine p.m., but
let us satisfy our craving stomachs,' said I.   'Waal, at
nine o'clock it'll be on the table.'   As we had still
about three-quarters of an hour to wait, Cummings
and I turned out for a stroll.   I was struck with the
stillness, and suggested that there were either very
few inhabitants, or they had been visited by a plague
and the major part of them were defunct ; 'besides,'
I added, 'I don't see where the town lies.'   'Oh !'
said Cummings, 'it lies off to the right here.'   We
came to a cross street ; I looked to the right, but could
not discern anything except a few houses scattered at
distant intervals, distinguishable by the lights in the
windows.   I said, 'There's no town there ; nothing
but fields.'   'Oh !' said he, 'I was mistaken ; I remember now, it lies on the other side.'   We turned to
go back to the hotel, and took the other side of the
way.   I peered up each street, but there was no
vestige of town to be discovered.   Not likely, as
Canandaigua consisted of one street.   But it was not
the worst place by any means that we visited ; even
there we had upwards of five hundred dollars in the
room—an exceedingly good return for such a small
place.   We visited coal cities, oil cities, and timber
cities ; but none of them seemed to care for concerts.

Before this wretched tour we had been to Philadelphia, Baltimore, and Washington.   Of all the cities
I visited during my stay in the States, Baltimore
was to me the most sympathetic ; I can hardly tell
why, but it struck me as soon as I landed there.   We

had a very indifferent house, but the small number present were most enthusiastic. The morning after the concert, our manager sent to me to go to his room, as there was an influential gentleman there desirous of making my personal acquaintance. I descended and was presented. We had a pleasant conversation respecting my impressions of and my reception in America, which introduced the subject of our concert the night before. He expressed great regret we had not been favoured with a larger audience; 'but,' said he, 'our people have not sufficient appreciation of art to be attracted by singing such as yours. Now, if by some means you could arrange a story of how you were found in a cradle of bulrushes by the President's daughter away up the river as she went out bathing, like Moses was by Pharaoh's daughter, all Baltimore would turn out to see you.' I was often requested to sing 'Hail, Columbia'; I said I had no objection, provided they would permit me to sing 'Hearts of Oak' after it. *A propos* of 'Hearts of Oak,' I did sing the song once in New York at a party given by a gentleman in his apartment at Delmonico's. We had enjoyed a very jolly evening. Towards midnight two new guests arrived rather the worse for wear. They had been at a dinner at the Brooklyn Club, to which the officers of a Russian man-of-war lying in the harbour had been invited, with the express intention of making them all drunk and seeing them under the table; but the hosts had not calculated on the resisting power of a Russian head, and the tables were turned; the guests remained perfectly sober, whilst the hosts were all more or less intoxicated. The two new arrivals were pretty far gone. The younger of the two pounced upon me as soon as he saw me in the room ; he knew me, as he had attended all of our concerts ; he pestered my life out, and I could not get rid of his blandishments until I had danced a waltz with him. I had peace for a while, but at length, having disposed of egg-nog and sundry other beverages, the tormenting spirit again moved him, and he insisted on my singing a song ; this I flatly refused, until our host, to put him to silence, begged me to comply with any little thing that would give me no trouble, apologizing at the same time for the rude behaviour of my tormentor. ' Very well,' said I, ' I will sing a song ; it shall be " Hearts of Oak," and the windows must be thrown open that the passers-by may have a treat too.' I went through the performance to the satisfaction of my host and his guests, and especially of my inebriated friend, who swore me eternal friendship.

Soon after Christmas we paid a visit to Buffalo, where we gave two concerts, fairly well attended. A fire broke out on the second night ; the weather was so cold that the water froze on the firemen's jackets, close as they were to the fire. We crossed over to Toronto, in Canada, and remained on our way a day at Niagara, to see the Falls. Contrary to what I had been told, the first glimpse I had of them made a great impression on me. I think it must have been seeing them first in the depth of winter. I have since seen them in the height of summer, but there is no comparison ; the scenery surrounding them is of a poor description, to which the snow and ice lend a false picturesqueness. The thermometer was down I know not where, but I did not suffer from the cold, the air being so dry and brisk ; the only inconvenience that I had to bear, and that was a slight one, was carrying an icicle on the tip of each moustache all day. At Toronto we had a packed room, and a most enthusiastic public. Our programme had been arranged to suit, as well as we could, the American taste ; it contained sundry Italian and French pieces. A gentleman waited on me just before we dined to ask if it might not be possible to change it, as the public were anxious to hear as many of our English songs as possible. I promised we would do so, but at that hour it would not be possible to print a new programme. The audience appeared to grow frantic, and the applause was deafening. We had to repeat each piece or sing something else in place of it, and when we concluded with 'God save the Queen,' they almost tore the place down. On our return journey by Rochester and Syracuse to Boston, we were detained somewhat by a heavy snowstorm ; but by dint of using the locomotive as a battering-ram we did not stick fast. When we arrived at Boston the snow was so deep we had to drive to the Parker House in sledges. Two hours after, when we had dined and turned out to cross over to the Museum, the snow had almost disappeared, and the streets were nearly knee-deep in slush and water, so quick are the changes from extreme cold to a mild temperature.

Our concert tour ended at Boston, in the month of February. Miss Wynne, Mr. Cummings and Mr. and Mrs. Patey returned almost immediately to England. I remained in Boston for about a fortnight after my friends had left. I was present one evening at a dinner given by the Harvard Musical Society, when my health was proposed in most poetic terms by James T. Fields, and responded to most enthusiastically by the assembled guests. I heard some excellent speeches, and was particularly pleased to notice that none of the speakers fell back on that senseless mock modesty so common in England, which takes the form of stating that any other person in the room, or anyhow a great number of them, would be much more fit to propose or second the toast in hand. I have regretted since that I did not accept an invitation from James T. Fields to an 'evening at home' to hear Emerson read his last book ; I felt fatigued and dispirited after so much uncomfortable travelling, and the disappointment of our efforts not being attended with financial success. I had no share in that part, as I was paid a stipulated sum, but perhaps I felt more for my employers than I should have done for myself had the loss been my own.

During this stay in Boston I met with the only instance of inhospitality which occurred to me in the United States. I should not probably remember it, but I received on all sides such hearty hospitality that this instance shows out like a dark shadow in a sunny landscape. It is comical, or I would not relate it. A certain theatrical manager, who with his wife used to favour us with his company at supper at the Parker House after our concerts, was constantly imploring us to go and have dinner with him, without naming the glad day. At last he settled on Christmas Day. We had to sing the 'Messiah' in the evening at seven o'clock, so dinner was fixed for three sharp. I would not go, as I never go visiting when I have work to do in public. All the others except Sloper accepted. They went and waited, but there were no signs of dinner; about five tea was handed round and muffins, I believe—capital preparations for singing. The end was they had to sing the ' Messiah ' on empty stomachs. After they had departed for England, Sloper and I were bound to atone for our absence from the festive board on Christmas Day; we arranged to sup with them one Sunday, as being the one day on which the manager could enjoy an evening with his friends. We dined pretty early, and arrived at our host's house towards seven; we regaled ourselves with our own cigars for an hour or more, when our host suggested perhaps we were growing thirsty. I acknowledged the soft impeachment, and confessed I should like a drink. I was then offered a pitcher of iced water (it was still winter), which I unceremoniously declined. After a great deal of searching, a square Hollands bottle was fished out, with just enough to supply Sloper and me with a glass apiece. Another hour of smoke exhausted my patience, and I made a movement to retire. Then came the tug-of-war; I should not leave the house until I had supped; the more I insisted upon going the more they insisted on my staying. I suspected it was all put on, so I thought I would enjoy a joke at their expense, and I suddenly changed my mind and said I would stay; I winked at Sloper, and he, too, suddenly determined he would let our hosts have their own way. Then dismay seized them; they were taken in their own net, and there was no withdrawing. They scuffled in and out of the room, bringing in table-cloth, knives and forks, etc., to arrange the table. I remonstrated, and said they need not hurry, but let the servant do all. 'Servant!' said the hostess, 'why, she's in bed long ago.' I chuckled and commenced to enjoy the fun in good earnest. A cold roast fowl nicely browned appeared, together with a tart and sundry other fixings; also a bottle of claret, which was carefully deposited on the sideboard. We sat down; our victim, with a flourish of his knife, and trying to put on a jovial air, began, 'Now, Charlie, will you take a bit of chicken?' 'Rather,' said I. 'What part?' said he. 'A wing,' said I, 'and a nice thick cut of the breast.' Sloper followed suit, and we very ungallantly left the legs for our hosts. 'And what would you like to drink, my boy?' Said I, 'I see a bottle of claret there, that'll do.' I never remember such an obstinate cork as the one which stuck in the neck of that bottle. To end the story, we demolished the greater part of the chicken, finished the bottle of claret between us (I mean Sloper and I, for our friends stuck to iced water), made a large hole in the tart, and when we had, as far as lay in our power, completed the desolation of the larder, we stuck cigars in our mouths, thanked our hosts for a delightful entertainment, and bidding them a hearty farewell, returned to the Parker House, chuckling over the gruesome countenances we had left behind. We were never invited again!

CHAPTER XXII.

I HAD made an engagement with Mr. Carl Rosa to
join his company, which was to open in March, at
the Academy, in New York, with his wife Madame
Parepa, Adelaide Phillips, and Wachtel, the German
tenor, for Italian opera. As I did not feel inclined to
remain all the intervening time idle, I made a stipulation that I should be engaged for his English opera
tour, and joined them at New York, where I played
' Zampa ' and ' Fra Diavolo.' ' Zampa ' was a great
success, here and in each town we played it ; it always
brought a crowded house, and my favourite, Baltimore,
made up for her neglect during the concert tour, and
packed the house three nights in a week to see me
play ' Zampa.' At Philadelphia I played Valentine in
' Faust,' for Mrs. Jenny Van Zandt's benefit, and it
was a bumper. We were to play ' Zampa ' in Newark,
New Jersey, one night during our stay in New York ;
being a short journey, I went across after dinner. I
was busy making up in my dressing-room, when the
call-boy came to ask if I had a score of the opera with
me. I had not ; neither had anyone else. On inquiry

why a score was in such request, I learned that everything necessary had been sent on, except the band
parts. There were those of other operas, ' Trovatore,'
' Bohemian Girl,' and I don't know what else, but
' Zampa ' had been carefully excluded. The worst
part of the difficulty was, the same thing had occurred
at the last visit of Rosa's company to Newark. The
announcement that we should be obliged to substitute
something else for ' Zampa ' was received with a storm
of disapprobation, which did not entirely subside
throughout the evening. I sang my scene from the
second act of ' Il Trovatore ' in Italian, including
' Il balen,' the chorus joining in in English ; also ' The
heart bowed down,' and some other piece which I
do not recollect. If I remember rightly I did not
change my dress, but played Di Luna, Arnheim, and
whatever the other was, disguised as Zampa.

The Italian season in New York began about the
middle of March, and ended on the 30th of April. We
played ' Il Trovatore,' ' Rigoletto,' ' Lucrezia Borgia,'
' Martha,' ' Gli Ugonotti,' ' Don Giovanni,' and
' Guglielmo Tell.' In ' Gli Ugonotti ' I was once
more associated with my old comrade, Carl Formes,
whose Marcel even then was better than any I ever
heard. His voice was too much worn to last out the
whole opera, but his representation of the rough old
soldier was as perfect as ever. He only played at one
performance ; a chorus singer (! !) was substituted for
him after, who had a voice which he could not use,
so the opera was literally played without Marcel—a
building without a foundation ! However, he was
cheap, so it did not matter about the fabric tottering.

I had the pleasure of singing in the same season with my other old friend, Giorgio Ronconi, for the only time, in 'Don Giovanni,' in which he played Leporello. The house was crammed, but my attention was all centred in Ronconi; I did not care a button what the audience thought, all my endeavour was to satisfy him. 'William Tell' I had never played before, and I had only a short time to learn it in, and very few rehearsals; the tenor declined to attend the orchestral rehearsal, to my annoyance, as he was a wretched bad actor, and I did not know what he might be capable of doing or leaving undone; and accordingly, at the performance, he led me a pretty dance; I found him anywhere but where he ought to have been. A very clever girl played Jemmy, but she was very prim. In my scene with her at the rehearsal I begged her to go through the action as I wished it done at the performance; and finding her a trifle formal, to tease her, I introduced more embracing than was absolutely necessary. At the end she remarked she liked the part very much, but it seemed to her there was a superabundance of hugging in it. I advanced the claim of a loving father, sending his beloved child on such a perilous errand, with such fervour that she offered no further objection and resigned herself to her fate. I was not a little disturbed in the meeting of the cantons, when one strolled on singing in German and another in Italian; it was realistic, but it served to confuse me, as I had not had time to learn the part as thoroughly as I would have wished. I had always heard wonderful accounts of the 'high C' which our Arnold gave in the last air. I listened for it, for I confess to a weakness for high C's when they are given out as Tamberlik used, but no high C came. and at the subsequent performance, or performances, the air was omitted.

In some of the operas I had a charming companion in Adelaide Phillips, an exceedingly good singer (although then her voice was on the wane) and an excellent actress. Madame Parepa played in all the operas ; in ' Il Trovatore,' ' Rigoletto,' and ' William Tell,' she appeared to great advantage, but in the more tragic operas she was less successful, her histrionic abilities being of a very moderate calibre. I did not enjoy the season at all ; the weather was bitterly cold, the theatre comfortless ; the company contained few congenial spirits, and the crowded houses which flocked to every performance appeared to me to be attracted more by the advertisement of the 'Great Star Combination ' than by the artistic merit of the company. The receipts were enormous—of course, I have only the crowds I saw and the report of the manager to judge by—and on the last night they reached the sum of 11,000 dollars. That may or may not be, but the house was so crammed the people stood in the parterre packed like sardines, and the stage was so crowded with those who could not find room in the auditorium that we had scarcely room to pass on or off the stage. Spite of the failure of the concert tour and certain drawbacks connected with my operatic engagement, I had a ' real good time ' in the States, and felt some regret at leaving their hospitable shores. At the same time, I was longing to get back to England and enjoy a little peace and quietness

after the hurry and scurry of American life. I left
on the 1st of May, the day after our last performance,
by the *Cuba*, Captain Moodie, a real jovial sailor, and
a gentleman. On board we had Christine Nilsson
and one member of her company, Charles Lyall ;
Carl Rosa and his wife, and sundry members of our
company. A crowd of friends came on board to bid
us farewell, most of whom accompanied us in two rival
steam tugs, one on either quarter, each provided with
a brass band, whose horrible din served to drown the
parting grief of the more tender-hearted. Giorgio
Ronconi was among the number ; it was the last time
we met, for although he lived until the beginning of
the year 1890, he never came again to England, and
our paths in life lay wide apart. He went for a tour
to South America, and afterwards settled in Madrid
as a teacher of singing. We had a very pleasant
voyage. Most of us males used to meet together in
the officers' mess-room each evening, where we supped,
smoked, drank grog, and told tales and sang songs.
The greater part of the saloon passengers used to
crowd round outside and cheer lustily when we gave
them something which excited their admiration. As
we were approaching Queenstown, I saw a sight to me
exquisitely beautiful, one that perhaps I may never
see again. We passed an outward-bound steamer of
the same line as ours (the Cunard) as the sun was
about setting in a perfectly cloudless sky. Just as
three-fourths of its disc were visible above the horizon,
the ship we had seen pass appeared broad-side as
though painted on it, every line clearly defined. We
arrived at Liverpool on the 11th of May, and as we

went up the Mersey, I could not help contrasting the splendid docks and quays with the wretched wharves which disfigured, and still disfigure, the shores of the Hudson at New York.

The season in New York was the last of my connection with Italian opera. I really intended it should be the end of my connection with any opera. The stage had proved my great *illusion perdue ;* my own enthusiasm and love for it had not abated, but I could not fight almost single-handed against the lack of earnestness, except for pecuniary gain, which I encountered, turn which way I might, and I resolved to quit it.

I have often been asked, when I have been speaking of those artists I look upon as the high peaks which overtop a mountain range, if I did not think the enthusiasm and unfledged impressions of youth had not influenced my opinions. I do not think so, because in later years an intimate connection with them both as friend and comrade (except in two instances, those of Staudigl and Luigi Lablache) only served to confirm my youthful impressions. My peaks are Viardot Garcia, Jenny Lind, Miolan-Carvalho, Alboni, Mario, Giorgio Ronconi, Luigi Lablache, Sims Reeves, and Staudigl. I have sung with all except Lablache and Staudigl ; with the first three ladies only in concerts, with Alboni, Mario, Reeves, and Ronconi, both in the concert room and theatre. Of these the Everest and Aconcagua were Ronconi and Viardot, vocally and histrionically ; neither of them possessing charm of voice or personal appearance, both the charm of genius, which overtops all other. Mario was handsome, and the best proportioned man I ever knew; he was a genius, but more limited than the other two; Viardot and Ronconi were thoroughly at home both in tragedy and comedy —Donna Anna or Papagena, Iago or Papageno— always great. Mario was great in 'Les Huguenots,' 'Le Prophète,' 'I Puritani,' 'Un ballo in maschera,' and in numerous operas; but he was a failure in 'Othello,' and 'Don Giovanni,' and I, personally, never thought his Faust a good performance for him. He was dreadfully lazy, and a very slow study. Viardot used to say of him that he began to have some notion what his part in an opera was about, when everybody else concerned was soaked with theirs. I had the pleasure and advantage of his intimate acquaintance for some years before he retired from the stage. When we were together on operatic tours, we generally lived together in the same hotel, and always occupied the same dressing-room in the theatre, where he smoked incessantly, leaving his cigar in his dresser's hands as he went on the stage, and taking it up immediately as he came off.

I tried all in my power to induce him to rise at a decent hour—it was generally mid-day or later before he left his bedroom—but I only succeeded on one occasion. I had been relating to him the beauty of the scenery about Bolton Abbey and of the ruins of the Abbey itself; he was much interested, and expressed a desire to visit them; but then came the question of starting in time. We were in Hull, and had to return to Leeds to take a train to Skipton, from which we were to take a carriage to the Abbey. The train started about half-past eight a.m. What was to be done? Calling was useless, so it was arranged I should pull him out of bed. When I found him peacefully slumbering, remorse seized me for a moment, and I felt inclined to leave him to his repose and make the expedition alone; then I thought perhaps he might feel disappointed if I left him, so I pulled down the bed-clothes and literally hauled him out. I must admit, he was much more good-natured than I should have been myself. I went into the station, took the tickets, and stood watching the clock until the finger pointed to two minutes before starting time. I told the guard of my anxiety about my friend, and as he knew me he promised to delay the train two minutes. I had given up all hope, when I descried Mario, hat in hand, rushing frantically towards the ticket-office. I rushed after him, seized him by the collar, and did not let go until I landed him safely in a carriage. In a few moments he was fast asleep, so I left him in peace until we arrived at Leeds; we went across to the other train, and just as that was about to depart I missed him. Half asleep when he left the train from Hull, he had left his hat behind him, so again I had to ask the indulgence of the guard. We ultimately arrived all safe and sound at the Abbey, and when we returned to Leeds in the evening he told me he had never enjoyed a day so much in his life. 'But I should not have gone,' said he, 'if you had not pulled me out of bed.'

When we were not engaged in the evening we used to settle ourselves after dinner for a good smoke and chat; the former we plied so vigorously that we were literally among the clouds. One evening our topic of

conversation fell on the wonderful conquests some of
our comrades, according to their own accounts, were
constantly making.   He told me that with one exception, all the conquests he had ever been cognisant of
had been old women ; as he said, it was somewhat
strange, he having always been a very attractive
man.   One instance he related to me.   Whilst he was
still studying preparatory to his *début* at the Paris
Opera, he had received several notes from an unknown correspondent of the fair sex ; at last, with a
billet doux, came a truffled turkey from Chabot's.   This
seemed more to the purpose ; so Mario invited some
friends to dispose of it at supper.   A few days after
another note arrived, inviting him to a rendezvous in
some church, at eight a.m., on a certain day.   Mario
did not relish rising so early, but as he was curious to
see what his correspondent was like, he stretched a
point, or several, I should rather say, and repaired to the
church at the appointed time.   He could not discern
anybody answering to the description of a passionate
admirer, and was on the point of leaving, Mass being
over, when in the porch he was accosted by an elderly
female, who, after inquiring his name, begged him to
wait a moment, as her mistress desired a few moments'
conversation with him.   He politely remained ; at
length the lady appeared, a charmer of upwards of
seventy years of age ; he could not help laughing at
himself, spite of the adventure having deprived him
of three or four hours' sleep ; but the turkey troubled
his conscience.   He had no money to spare at that
time, and restitution must be made, so he exacted a
contribution from some of those who had assisted at

the banquet, and a truffled turkey was returned to the lady with compliments.

Two anecdotes which he related to me, being decidedly characteristic, will, I think, be interesting to my readers, and cannot offend any of his relations still living. He was driving up from Fulham to the theatre one evening, when a costermonger got in the way of his carriage with his cart and donkey, which were upset and the vegetables strewed all about. An altercation ensued between the coachman and the costermonger; Mario put his head out of the window and, giving his name and address, said he would be responsible for any damage. On arriving at the theatre, he told Lumley what had happened, and asked him to settle the matter for ten pounds. Lumley insisted it was too much, and refused to give the coster more than five pounds. Some angry correspondence followed, which ended in the coster bringing an action against Mario for damages. At the trial a number of witnesses, who were not present at the catastrophe, swore to the coachman being in fault; Mario lost the case, and was mulcted in a heavy sum for damages and costs. He left immediately after for the Continent, and did not return to London for some time, when, amongst other documents which had not been forwarded, he found a bill of £250 for costs and damages, with the addition of £200 for contempt of court, he having neglected to settle the amount on the proper day.

When he lived at Clapham, he had a friend who took charge of the house during his absence. The friend noticed that the gardener, without permission, disposed of the fruit and vegetables grown on the premises. Being determined to act as a faithful steward, he remonstrated with the gardener, though to no purpose, for the fruit and vegetables were still unlawfully disposed of. On Mario's return, his friend made such a fuss that, to satisfy him, he gave him permission to bring the man up to justice. He was summoned before the police-court; Mario had to turn out at some (to him) very early hour; the case came on, when it was found that the gardener was a left-handed relation of Mario's landlord, and after a consultation between the lawyers it was agreed to stop the action. Mario thought there would be no further trouble and he would get off with a small account from his solicitor. His surprise was great when he found that after his early rising, and, as he thought, pardoning a malefactor, he had to pay costs on both sides, which amounted to about £400.

Of Madames Miolan-Carvalho and Alboni I have already spoken. They were as different personally and artistically as two human beings could possibly be; yet they had one trait in common: at rehearsal I remarked that both of them employed their unoccupied time in knitting stockings.

A great artist who had a line of his own I cannot refrain from mentioning; he was one of my earliest adorations—I heard him first when I was about thirteen or fourteen years of age — John Parry! He was unique! inimitable! I had the great pleasure of knowing him personally and numbering him among my friends for some years before he died, and I had once the felicity of appearing at a performance with him.

We both went on in ' The School for Scandal,' at
Buckstone's benefit, at Drury Lane some years ago ; I
sang the song ' Here's to the maiden,' which he accompanied on an old piano. I dressed in the same
room with Charles Mathews and Parry ; I laughed
so much at Parry's flashes of wit that I had to beg
of him for mercy's sake to be quiet, or I should not
have a scrap of voice left to sing the song.

CHAPTER XXIII.

In concluding this portion of my memoirs, there are
many points connected with my art which the public
might expect me to discuss, but the fact of my being
still in the active pursuit of my profession prevents
me. There is one, however, which I should like to
offer to the notice of those who are interested—the
enormous increase in the number of students of music,
and the limited opportunities for making their talents
available when their studies are completed ; and I
would propose two questions for their consideration :
How many of these students possess the necessary
natural qualifications to justify them in adopting music
as a profession ? And what opportunities have those
who make music a profession of exercising it ?

It may be said that most of them study with the
sole object of becoming better acquainted with music,
in order to enjoy its performance more thoroughly. I
do not believe it, and I feel no diffidence about saying
so, when I see the abundance of half-amateur element
which has crept into the profession in the course of
the last few years. Ambition to shine in public as

performers, in the majority of cases, overrules their ostensible intention ; and defended from criticism under the cloak of the amateur, they appear in public performances where they do not advance the cause of art, and where they often deprive young deserving professionals of engagements on which they are dependent for their livelihood.

In the year 1860 the Royal Academy of Music was the only institution of the kind in London, if not in England.   Since then have been established the Royal College of Music, Trinity College, and the Guildhall School of Music, besides a host of other academies, schools, or conservatories in the suburbs of London and in the provinces.   In 1860 there were seventy students in the Royal Academy of Music. At the present time, taking all the academies together, I think I am within the mark when I estimate the number of musical students in Great Britain at 10,000, and there is very little increase in the opportunities for making their talents available when their studies are completed.

In a prospectus issued by the promoters of the Royal College of Music, one of the reasons assigned for its institution was the probability of its leading to the establishment of a national opera.   The college has been in existence ten years, and the probability remains just as improbable as ever!   A few years ago, the then Lord Mayor convened a meeting at the Mansion House to discuss the question of establishing a national opera.   Two men, Sims Reeves and myself, with our experience, could have been of great service in such a discussion ; we were neither of us invited to attend the meeting. I never heard anything about the proceedings, but I believe they ended in—smoke!

If people will insist upon spending money in the study of an art for which they do not possess the necessary qualifications, and find schools ready to receive them, nobody has a right to interfere either with the students or with the schools ; but if the nation desires to have a conservatory, where those possessing natural artistic qualifications can be educated, the nation must be prepared to endow an institution with sufficient means to maintain and educate the students free of cost, and to pay efficient masters such emolument as will enable them to devote their chief attention to those students. Only those students must be admitted who, after a rigorous examination, are found to possess the necessary qualifications. Moreover, every student must submit to further examinations at the expiration of six months, and again after twelve months' study, in order to verify the result of the first examination, and determine whether the progress made be sufficient to justify the student being permitted to continue his or her studies.

Again, the nation must provide a home for those she has educated ; there must be a national theatre in each of the principal cities in Great Britain, where opera, oratorio, or concerts can be given.

This may all read like a wild dream ; it is nothing of the kind, and can be done if there is the will. The money wasted on teaching Board and other school children nothing, would amply suffice to accomplish all I have suggested.

In Germany and France it is done, and in one country, if not in both, the artists, after a term of service, are entitled to a pension on retiring from the theatre to which they have been attached, the enjoyment of which does not preclude them from exercising their art in their own country or elsewhere as long as they feel inclined, or their powers permit them.

If these things can be achieved in other countries, surely in rich England they are possible.

In conclusion, I beg to say I am not actuated by any personal considerations. I speak on behalf of my young professional sisters and brothers, for whom, under the existing conditions of musical education and performances, I see little else than disappointment.

THE END.

BILLING AND SONS, PRINTERS, GUILDFORD.